SHERRILYN
KENYON
DEATH DOESN'T
BARGAIN

piatkus

PIATKUS

First published in the US in 2018 by Tor Books, New York
First published in Great Britain in 2018 by Piatkus
This paperback edition published in 2019 by Piatkus

1 3 5 7 9 10 8 6 4 2

A CIP catalogue record for this book
is available from the British Library.

ISBN 978-0-349-41222-1

Printed and bound by CPI Group (UK) Ltd, Croydon, CR0 4YY

Papers used by Piatkus are from well-managed forests
and other responsible sources.

Piatkus
An imprint of
Little, Brown Book Group
Carmelite House
50 Victoria Embankment
London EC4Y 0DZ

An Hachette UK Company
www.hachette.co.uk

www.littlebrown.co.uk

For Shannon. Sleep in peace my precious Simi.
You are so missed every day.
To John Stone for being awesome!
And for my incredible Tor Team! Claire, Linda,
Tom, Alexis, Kristin, Seth, et al! You all are the
best! Thank you so much for everything you do!
Words cannot express how much I adore you!
As always for Robert for all the hard work! And
for Team Kenyon at home! Laura, Paco, Kerrie,
Carl, and crew, and especially my hubby and boys,
and my Kims!
Last, but never least, my Menyons and you, the
reader, this book's for you!

DEATH DOESN'T BARGAIN

PROLOGUE

"When I said I'd give you any hell-locked soul to claim for the *Sea Witch*'s crew, I'm thinking I should have seriously set some limitations. Sanity being a more obvious one . . . and one that should have gone without saying."

That comment was met with a stoic glare from the demon who showed about as much emotion as Devyl Bane did remorse for all the lives he'd ruthlessly taken while he'd worn the flesh of a human man. "I've agreed to take on all the souls of the damned you suggested without complaint or hesitation, Leucious. Now, I want the Myrcian for me crew. Release him from this infernal realm or I'm staying right where I am and you can face Vine and her army without me. Let's see how far you get on resealing those gates and holding back the damned then, eh?"

Irritated and furious almost beyond rational thought over Devyl's insistence on using a name he hated and had abandoned using centuries ago, Thorn dragged his forefinger along his bottom lip while he struggled with the sudden urge to gut the difficult warrior before him. Not that it would matter.

Wouldn't kill him.

Just piss him off and cause him to return the gesture.

Dón-Dueli of the Dumnonii had ever been the single most aggravating warlord to wield a sword against him.

Sadly, he'd also been the most successful, which was why Thorn was here to make this regrettable bargain.

He needed the dark, deadly bastard. And the Devyl's Bane, as he called himself these days, knew it. Hence that evil, satisfied red gleam in his demonic eyes as he dared him into this with a smirking sneer. He had Thorn by the figurative bullocks.

As much as it pained him to admit it, he couldn't defeat Vine and her army without Devyl's help. For that matter, Devyl was the sole reason that particular breed of demon bitchtress had ever been trapped behind the gates to begin with—and that incredible feat the bastard had managed *after* his death. Which said it all about how crafty and resourceful a beast Bane was.

Still . . .

Thorn turned his attention to the pit where Kalder Dupree was engaged in an impressive brawl against the worst of Mephistopheles's pets. Using barbed and fiery whips, they were beating the Myrcian warrior down with a sick glee, and still Kalder fought them with everything he had. He met every bloody lash and blow with a defiant curse as he psychotically begged them for more and goaded them to hit him ever harder.

Kalder even questioned their parentage, as if any demon here had a clue as to who or what had fathered them on their whore of a mother.

There was a macabre beauty to Kalder's stubborn rebellion.

A warrior's code that few could really understand unless they were one of them. That innate need to give as good as he got. A refusal to surrender, no matter the odds or pain. Indeed, the harder the blow, the more determined the resolve.

With my shield or upon it.

It was a warrior's code Thorn knew well. One he lived by himself, as he'd been raised up on it by his own merciless relatives.

No damned demon kills me and lives.

If he had to come back from hell itself for vengeance and satisfaction, he would have their throats as payment. Better to die on his feet with blood on his fists than on his knees with piss in his drawers. And he would go out choking on the flesh of his enemies, not on his own bile.

Aye, he understood both of these demon-spawned men implicitly. They were like-minded beasts, even if they had once fought on opposite sides of a most bitter war for the world. Ironic that now they were allies.

How the world changes. . . .

Resigning himself to this inevitable nightmare he was sure to regret, he met Bane's dark glower. "Is he to be your first mate, then?"

Devyl laughed out loud—a rare sound for him. Then he cut it short as he realized that Thorn had been serious. "I'm insane and rather suicidal most days, not stupid. *Big* difference, that."

"Perhaps. But ofttimes 'tis a fine line that divides the three."

"I disagree. Takes a great deal of intelligence to run insanity and pull back from death before he takes you. You've got to know right where that line is at all times. Only the most observant and wisest amongst us can toe it in good measure, and dance its tune without losing the beat, or your head. Nay, they are not lovers, or even close cousins. Rather, they are strangers and should ever remain so if you value your limbs at all."

And Du was always good at keeping himself intact—as well as his men and army. Of all the warlords, gods, and demons Thorn had battled over the centuries, none had been more skillful or cunning than the beast at his side. Had Du's wife not cut his throat, and slit his gullet, he'd have taken the world and they'd all have been paying homage to this bastard's sword.

Which was exactly what had brought them here today.

Aye, he needed Devyl's extreme form of fighting. To face madness, it took madness.

Evil to combat evil.

And no one understood Vine's insanity or war plans better than Devyl did. If the world was to be saved this go-round, their only hope lay in the hands of this demon and his band of . . .

Thorn cringed at the thought of the Deadmen Bane had assembled to fight for the world and save it.

May the gods help us all.

This had disaster written all over it and he was about to sign them all up for a front-row seat at the Apocalypse.

Relegated to his part in this disaster, Thorn gave him a curt nod. "Let me see for the bargain."

Devyl turned his attention back to the fight as Thorn left his side to negotiate for Kalder's soul. The Myrcian was badly dehydrated—no doubt part of his torture. As a mermaid, Kalder needed water much more than a regular human or any other species did. And it appeared as if he'd been without any for weeks now. Point of fact, his skin was peeling back from his very bones. Something that had to be excruciating.

Yet it slowed him down not at all.

Nothing ever had, and that was one of the things Devyl respected most about the much younger warrior. He was a creature to be reckoned with and feared.

"Captain?"

He glanced over his shoulder at the tiny, powerful West African shaman they'd picked up earlier. Her dark skin was flawless and made her amber eyes practically glow. Though she was currently dressed in rags, she carried herself with the presence of a noble queen and he gave her the due of one.

Belle Morte.

She was a creature of many secrets, but he saw her heart as clearly as he saw the Myrcian's. She was a woman to be reckoned with and admired.

If not always trusted.

"What is it, Lady Belle?"

She jerked her chin toward Kalder. "Why that one?"

"You're questioning me?"

She rubbed her hands over her arms. The gesture rattled the multitude of silver bangles that lined both her wrists. "He's a deep darkness in his heart. Not like the others you've chosen thus far."

Nay, he was nothing like the others. Kalder had always been unique unto himself. And that was why Devyl wanted him as part of their crew.

"So you think I should leave him to rot and bleed here, then?"

Belle bit her lip and scowled. "Most would say you should have left *me*, Captain. That I not be worth a chance for salvation, given what all I've done."

"Are you one of them?"

She glanced around the fiery pits where so many were being ruthlessly tortured to consider her answer carefully before she stared at the new mark Thorn had placed on their wrists when he'd pulled each of them from similar hellholes and made their sacred pact—a bargain sealed in blood and marked with their "Deadman's" brand—a ribbon with a skull in its center. That unique brand designated them as part of Thorn's Hellchaser army, and temporarily kept their rotted souls in the mortal realm so that they could fight for a chance to save their own condemned souls from the damnation they'd earned while human.

This was the only chance most of them would ever have to spare themselves infernal torture and damnation.

Belle shook her head. "I'm too grateful for your mercy in giving me a second chance when no one else would. I would never betray you."

And that was why he'd agreed with Thorn to spare her soul. She saw more than the others. Deeper. Nothing and no one could hide from her sage seer's sight. "Anyone else is fair game, then?"

One corner of her mouth lifted ever so subtly, letting him know that he'd been correct in surmising her character. "Nothing escapes your notice, does it?"

He glanced back at the Myrcian as he laid low one of the fiercest of the demons. With a hell-born growl of glee, Kalder ripped out the heart of the beast in such a manner that it caused three of them to shrink back in sudden fear of him. No easy feat, that, to cow the fearless and set them on their heels. And it said it all about Kalder's skills and why Devyl wanted him for this mission.

To fight the damned and hold them back from the world of man, you needed someone who didn't flinch at their approach. Someone who had nothing to lose.

More than that, Devyl had once known the man's father. A fierce, nasty bastard.

Unstoppable. Untamable.

Filled with such rage that he'd destroyed an entire population and cost thousands their lives. He wondered if Kalder's mother had ever shared *that* story with her son. For that was the thing of the Myrcians.

You never really knew where you stood with them.

They would lure you in, make you comfortable, and then serve you up your own intestines.

While smiling in your face.

He respected that about them. And it was what had caused Kalder to be damned here. The mother who'd raised and nurtured him had murdered him when he'd gone to her for comfort after the death of his younger brother.

Aye, they were all a treacherous, bloodthirsty lot. It ran deep in their bloodlines and was part of their genetic stock. You could bank your very death upon it.

And Devyl would have it no other way.

1

North Bimini, 1717

"Welcome to Hell, Mr. Death."

"Deeth!" William corrected habitually, knowing his dark and deadly captain couldn't care less how to properly pronounce his name. Cantankerous tosslington did it apurpose, as he lived to rankle everyone around him, especially his crew.

Proof to that point came as an amused, sharp glint in the depths of Bane's demonically red eyes.

Even so, and ever reckless in the face of imminent threat, Will cocked a brow at the aptly named Devyl

Bane and his screwy sense of humor as they approached a dingy yellow building in the middle of a rain-soaked street in the Bahamas. Only as they neared civilians whom they were supposed to hide their preternatural existence from did Devyl dampen the hue of his eyes from red to black.

"Interesting way to open up a conversation there, Captain. Feel like you ought to have some sort of evil laugh to punctuate it. You know? Just for affectation."

With a wicked grin to make Old Scratch proud, Bane clapped him on his shoulder. "Not really." He jerked his bearded chin toward the devil-emblazoned tavern sign over their heads. "Name of the place. *Hell's Underbelly*. I's merely welcoming you to it, since we should be at home here. Though this one seems a mite tame when compared to the one Thorn dredged us from."

It did, indeed. In spite of the rough drunkard who was thrown through the doors by two burly blokes to land sprawling at their feet.

Devyl didn't break his stride as he casually stepped over the battered man's prone body and entered the dark tavern.

Unsure of how he felt about the captain's disregard of the drunkard's plight, William skirted around the side of the unfortunate man and followed the captain in, where he was met by the sound of shrill revelry and foul curses.

Then he rethought his earlier assumption about the place, since it smelled about the same as the sulphuric pits they'd once called home.

Rotten, unwashed humans . . .

Rotten, farting demons . . .

Both disgusting in equal measure.

Only difference was killing demons, unlike humans, didn't get you damned to hell, it got you liberated out of it. Hence why they were here.

Save some humans. Kill some demons.

Same mission. Different day.

Or was it different mission, same day? Here lately, it was getting harder to tell those two apart.

Maybe they were in hell again, after all . . .

It'd be just the kind of sinister trap Lucifer might concoct as punishment for them. Old Scratch was a treacherous blighter that way.

Suddenly, Will's gut was tight enough to form a lump of coal at the thought.

"What'd you do to poor Will now, Captain? He looks like you just gave him watch duty over Mr. Meer's nastiest boots."

Will stepped back as Cameron Jack joined their meager company. Dressed as a lad in a red linen coat and tan breeches, the lady held a quiet, respectful grace. Her dark chestnut hair was pulled back into a circumspect queue and hidden beneath a sharp black tricorne that accentuated her pretty, angular features. How he'd ever mistaken her for a man, he couldn't fathom nowadays.

Yet the first time they'd met, he'd definitely been fooled by her boyish garb and sharp, crisp mannerisms.

Only Devyl had known that night in the back room of a Port Royal tavern. He'd blame it on the dim lighting, but then no one got anything past their captain.

"What kept you?"

Cameron passed a small parcel to him. "Lady Belle told me to give this to you. She said the one to be bartered with will require it."

There was no missing the guilt in her eyes as she spoke those words, and none could blame her there. Their missing crewmember, Kalder Dupree, was only trapped in hell now because he'd swapped places to free her and her brother.

Since then, they'd all been desperate to get him out. Having been abandoned and betrayed by their families and the world, none of them were willing to do it to each other.

The Deadmen were their own family now. Not crew or shipmates.

Family. One and all. Brothers. Sisters. And crazy uncles they had to keep from drinking too much on holidays and special occasions. With a tighter bond than any born of the same womb could ever achieve.

And their rebirths had been no less painful.

Devyl took her parcel and tucked it into a leather pouch that dangled from his belt. "Let's see this met. It's time we brought our brother home."

"Agreed."

William didn't speak. There was nothing to say, as he concurred with that. Yet there was a feeling in the air and in his gut that he couldn't quite shake. A sense of mistrustful unease. As if someone had walked upon his grave again.

You're being paranoid.

Perhaps. But that was a normal state for the likes of them. And given what unholy threats they faced on a routine basis, none could find fault there. Hard to relax your guard when there were devils and demons abounding. All out to steal or devour your soul and end your life.

"Head! Get some good head here! Big head. Little head. Matters naught! I've something for every budget, mates! Just tell me what's your pleasure!"

Stunned completely, William drew up short. It took him a second to realize the man yelling had a basket of shrunken heads he was peddling to the occupants, who were basically ignoring his grisly wares.

Arching his brow as the grimy man brushed rudely against them without a polite acknowledgment, Devyl swept his hand over the shrunken, leathery offerings. The instant he did so, their shriveled mouths opened.

As did their eyes.

With an echoing shriek, the man dropped the basket of heads, which began singing hymns a cappella like a bunch of Sunday Protestants, and ran for the door.

William snorted. "You're an evil bugger, Captain."

"Merely putting the fear of God into him, Mr. Death. Besides, it's what he gets for soliciting head in a public place. I'm just trying to keep the pub decent for hardworking sailors."

As if! William laughed while Cameron let out a squeak of horror at his indelicate language.

"Well, well," a deep, sultry voice said beside them. "I can see the rumors that your newly married state has mellowed you have been greatly exaggerated. You're still the same rotten beast, *mon cher*, you've always been."

All the humor died on Bane's face. A tic started in his jaw. "Menyara. You old sea hag. What are *you* doing here?"

Will blinked, then blinked again and rubbed his eyes that had to be deceiving him.

Unless Bane was drunk, and the man had never been such that

Will had ever witnessed, there was nothing old or ugly about the tiny little island woman in front of them. Indeed, her caramel skin was flawless. Her braided hair intertwined with expensive beads and colorful ribbons. And though she barely reached mid-chest on him, her voluptuous body said she was certainly no girl, yet by no means was she matronly.

Fortunately, she took Bane's insult in stride. "Is that any way to greet an old friend, *cher*?"

"Friends? You stabbed me. Thrice."

Unabashed, she smiled as she brushed her hand over his arm in a tender gesture of affection. "Well, what did you expect? Your army was destroying mine. I had to do something to distract you before you killed every last one of my soldiers."

With a rude dismissive noise, he stepped back to make room for Cameron. "And that's why you sent an innocent young girl to me? Punishment or revenge?"

"Neither. I knew you would protect her."

"Hell of a gamble, given my proclivity for feasting on the hearts of innocents."

Menyara inclined her head to him. "Not when I knew how much you loved your sister. And I was right. You protected our Miss Cameron. As I knew you would. Thank you for not disappointing me."

Bane made a gruff "heh" sound in the back of his throat. "You still haven't answered me question. Why are you here?"

"To warn you."

He passed an annoyed *do-you-see-what-I-mean* glare at William. "About?" he prompted when she failed to continue her sentence.

And even then Menyara waited before she answered. "Kadar knows the truth about your missing mermaid . . . and so does Shyamala."

The blood drained from his face at those ominous words. "Do they have him?"

"Not yet. But they're trying to find him, same as you."

"Who's Kadar and Shyamala?" William asked, baffled by the unfamiliar names. And he wasn't the only one. Cameron didn't appear any more familiar with them than he was.

Devyl ground his teeth. "Only the deepest, darkest evil you can imagine. They were the snake in the Garden of Eden, Mr. Death. The shiver that goes down your spine whenever you think you're being watched in the night. They are the whisper that tempts good men to the animal side of corruption. That lapse of conscience that drives humanity to do its worst."

"Oh, fun! Sounds like our kind of people."

But the grim expression on Devyl's face said that he didn't appreciate Will's sarcasm.

"Actually, they were once Du's people. He fought long and hard for their cause and killed many in their name."

That took the humor right out of William's spirit. "Beg pardon?"

Menyara nodded. "Your good captain once led his army for them."

"And what did it get me? A knife in me gullet and bled out at the feet of the bitch who betrayed me to serve them, until I killed her and locked her in a special hell for it."

The same hell that was now breaking open and that they had hopefully sent Vine back to when they'd killed her for trying to murder Bane's new wife, Mara.

The Carian Gate.

His eyes flared as he stepped back. "Come, Lady Cameron and Mr. Death, let's see about our mission."

As he started away, Menyara stopped him. "Before you leave, there's something else I must tell you."

Devyl placed his hand high on his black baldric of three flint-locks. "And that is?"

Menyara turned toward William with a beautiful, dazzling smile. Beguiling and sweet. Without a word, she approached him slowly and reached for his belt.

Stunned, he didn't move. Not until she reached for his daggers. In one fluid motion, she grabbed them, kicked him back, and spun toward Devyl.

As she closed the distance between them, her entire being changed from the petite Menyara into a tall, graceful, red-headed beauty.

William gasped as he realized that this was Devyl's ex-wife they'd destroyed.

Or at least, they thought they had.

How was this possible? Even though the Carian Gate had broken open, how could she have returned to life?

Yet there was no denying that this was the very sorceress they'd fought, and she was back from her grave to take vengeance on them all for killing her.

Hissing, she rushed at Devyl. "You didn't end me, you worthless bastard! But I will see you back to hell for what you've done! And I plan to send that sniveling little Myrcian bitch there with you!"

2

Cameron Jack cursed as Captain Bane was forced to reveal his powers before the humans in the pub. Something strictly forbidden to them by Thorn. The Hellchasers and Deadmen were to never let a mortal know they'd been brought back to life under any circumstances. Nor were they to put their preternatural abilities on display for the public.

Never mind the laws that governed her own breed of Necrodemians, or Hell-Hunters as they were more commonly known. The Sarim Council that she and her brother answered to had an even stricter code of conduct they were required to follow.

The worst rule being that Hell-Hunters couldn't fight dirty.

For any reason.

Or endanger a human life, or reveal their powers to mundanes.

Yet had the captain failed to reveal his powers, Vine would have consumed them with her unholy fire that she launched behind the daggers.

But by unleashing his fire, the captain deflected hers with his own. The humans ran, screaming, for cover.

Wiser ones, for the door.

Sad to say, Cameron wasn't so smart. She chose to stay and fight, as was her nature. But then that was all she'd ever known. Fighting ran thick within her Celtic blood. And twice as deep in her Necrodemian bloodline. So she unsheathed her sword and made ready to cover the good captain's back with William as more of Vine's allies moved in for them.

"Well," William said to her. "Makes me so glad I volunteered for this, eh? Could have stayed onboard the ship with Bart, Kat, and Simon and the rest. But, nay. Had to stick me foot in the fodder. 'Got your back, Captain,' had to say. Aye, a fool I be for sure, and then some. Next time I speak up, Miss Jack, feel free to run me through and save these devils the trouble of it."

Laughing at his surly tone that belied the fact he was loyal to the bone and meant none of it, she parried against the first demon to reach her and twisted away from the beast. "If there is a next time, Mr. Death. Not so sure we'll make it out." She barely caught the next demon as he tried to sink his fangs into her shoulder. Luckily, she beheaded the beast before he drew her blood and turned her into who knew what.

Then, kicking up the abandoned heads the peddler had left behind, she let them sink their fangs into the wanker, who screeched mightily from the pain of their bites.

"Anyone have a good idea on how to survive this?" she asked while Captain Bane continued to fight with his ex-wife. And if they'd fought like that while married, it was easy to see how their marriage had ended in murder.

Multiple times.

William knocked his opponent into the fire. The demon shrieked then burst into flames. Cinders rained down all over them and threatened to set fire to the pub. "I vote we join a new crew. Preferably a human one that hell itself isn't trying to kill at every turn. That should increase our chances of survival exponentially."

She snorted, knowing he was japing. "Aye, but it won't redeem your soul, now, will it?"

And unlike her and the captain, Will wasn't free to leave the *Sea Witch*'s crew. The Deadman's mark on his wrist bound him tight to their enchanted band and prevented him from seeking new company until he'd regained his freedom from Thorn's bargain. Not that it mattered.

When it came to the Deadmen who sailed onboard the *Sea Witch,* they weren't about to abandon each other, no matter what. Through thick and thin, and demons galore, they were one united insane family.

At least that was her thought until the demon in front of her burst apart with a stench so foul it caused her to choke and gasp.

Ugh! Never had she smelled anything more putrid, and given some of the hovels where she and her brother had taken refuge after their parents had orphaned them, that said a lot.

"You were saying, Miss Jack?" Will taunted her as he rested his sword on his shoulder. Pressing his hand to his nose, he made a face she was sure mirrored her own distaste of the stench. "I'm really not seeing much difference between here and hell lately."

Honestly? Neither was she.

And it was indeed getting harder and harder to tell the demons from the humans at times, too. Which made her wonder at their mission. Why were they bothering to save a world that seemed hell-bent on remaking itself into the very visage of what they were trying to save it from?

Don't forget, you're not fighting for the world right now. . . .

True. Right now, she was fighting for the man who'd traded his life for hers. And that one decent, selfless act needed to be repaid in kindness, not treachery.

Kalder deserved to be rescued and not abandoned. She would not do to him what everyone else had done.

I will keep me word to you, Kalder. We will find you.

If she had to break hell itself open and battle Lucifer to bring Kalder home, she would.

And so Cameron renewed her fight against their enemies so that they could quickly behead the last three demons before they claimed another innocent human life or soul.

Or even one of their not-so-innocent ones.

Leaving only Vine to be dealt with.

Her breathing ragged, the Titian-haired demon curled her lips at them. Vine was a great beauty, Cameron would give her that. It was easy to see why the captain had been duped into marrying her.

Easier still to see how he'd been blinded enough to drop his guard long enough in their marriage that she'd been able to kill him.

But Devyl Bane was no longer under her spell, and no longer was he fooled by her charms or enchantments.

"You always favored your little water pet. And Kalder will pay dearly for your defiance here tonight, Duel. Take your comfort in that. And I'll make sure he knows who caused it for him when I feed him to the Dark Powers myself." Then she vanished with one last shrieking cry.

Captain Bane cursed as she withdrew. "Come back and face me, you worthless bitchington!"

It was too late. She was gone.

"Shall I go after her, Captain?"

He passed a droll stare at William and answered in a tone that dripped with utter sarcasm. "By all means, Mr. Death. I commend you to the task. On your way, lad. There's the door. Off with you now. No need in dawdling."

"Oh, I didn't mean *alone*. Not quite *that* stupid, sir."

Sheathing his sword, he glared at William. "You're a cheeky bastard here lately, Mr. Death. If I didn't know better, I'd think our Cimmerian enemies had already laid fang to you and converted you to their army."

Cameron ignored them while she studied the blood on the floor the demons had left behind. It was a strange brew indeed. Instead of staining the wood as most blood would, this was pooling quite a bit differently. As if it were a living creature trying to move on its own.

Indeed, it seemed to defy gravity and slither like a bug. "Say, Captain? Have you ever seen the likes of this?"

He moved to stand near her so that he could examine it.

At first she thought she was imagining things. Given some of the knocks to her noggin she'd taken during their fight, it wouldn't be unlikely that her vision would have been compromised.

Or her wits.

But as he stooped down to better study the goo, she knew this wasn't the case.

The scowl on his handsome face told her that she'd seen exactly what she thought she had.

That was bad enough. Worse came when the good captain lifted a bit of the blood to his lips to taste it. Ew!

Cameron cringed in distaste and had to fight back the urge to go a-heaving.

"Should we ask?" William shivered visibly. "Or leave you alone for your feast, Captain?"

The captain gave him an even more peeved glare. Rising to his feet, he licked his fingers clean. "This is a foul night, serving the foulest brew to be measured." His features paled as he met their gazes one by one. "We needs get back to the ship and warn the others. They'll be coming for Mara and the rest of the crew."

"They?" Cameron asked.

"The plat-eyes we have yet to find. And the souls of those Vine is torturing."

Her heart sank at his words. The plat-eyes were vicious shape-shifters who took over the bodies of their victims and used them to attack others. Absolute soulless killing machines, they wouldn't stop their insatiable mutilations until the bodies of their original victims were located and given a proper burial. They feasted on blood and souls.

And just as the captain feared for his newly wedded wife, Mara, Cameron feared for their missing mate. "What of Mr. Dupree?"

"No fear there, Miss Jack. We'll get him back, I promise you. Just as I promised him."

Her throat tightening even more than her stomach, she nodded. And she prayed he was right. That Kalder didn't spend a single minute longer in hell than what was absolutely necessary.

Because it's all me fault that he's there.

The worst part was that she knew exactly what they were doing to Kalder.

She involuntarily flinched at the memory of their cruelty, and their laughter while they'd done it. The demonic bastards had pitted her against her brother, the entire time she'd been among them. They had reveled in their unholy torture. Had done unspeakable things that had kept her from having a decent sleep since her return to the land of the living.

No longer did she feel safe, at all. Every shadow left her terrified that it held one of them waiting to drag her back to their pits. Every laugh sounded sadistic.

She wasn't sure if she'd ever feel right or normal again. If she'd ever get rid of this feeling that every nook and cranny held danger for her.

Cameron had thought her childhood had left her traumatized

and defensive, but that was nothing compared to the latest horrors of their enemies' tender, loving care. It was a nightmare she'd wish on none. And definitely not on someone as decent as Mr. Dupree.

Most especially not after he'd allowed Thorn to cut his throat and had sacrificed himself like a slaughtered lamb to spare her and her brother, Paden, from the merciless cruelty of their enemies.

Cameron was brutally aware of the fact that, for every minute she wallowed in safety, he suffered in agonizing hell.

Why, Mr. Dupree?

Why?

But then she knew the answer. He held himself to blame for his own brother's murder. That single event had scarred him to the bitterest depths of his soul. And no doubt he shouldered equal blame for her being taken by their enemies under his watch, even though it wasn't his fault at all. None could have saved her that night—which was the source of her current unending nightmares—and he'd tried harder than any other would have even attempted in his fins.

Wincing, she could still hear his agonized shouts as the water sprites had swept her overboard from their ship during the storm. See the anguished expression on his face. He'd lunged for her, trying his best to keep her from their grasps.

In the raging sea, he'd taken her hand, and for one instant, she'd thought herself saved. Thought that all would be fine again.

His grip had been so firm and steadfast that she'd let herself believe the impossible.

That she was safe in the icy water.

"I won't let you go, Cameron! So help me!"

Until their enemies had overwhelmed him, prying his hand away from hers. Even then, he'd fought against them with a fury the likes of which she'd never seen before.

"Nay! Nay!" The insanity in his pale eyes as he'd desperately swum for her had been the last thing she'd beheld. His agonized cries as he searched had stayed with her every minute she'd been gone.

Tears choked her as she clutched at the necklace he'd given the captain for her to keep in his absence.

Tell her to pray for me brother's soul.

Not his. He thought himself too damned for redemption.

Some days, so did Cameron. For Kalder held a darkness inside him that made a mockery of Captain Bane's. A deep, soul-wrenching blackness that said it wouldn't take much to lose him forever to the Cimmerian forces they fought against. But no one deserved what they were doing to him. And definitely not after he'd done a favor for someone else.

Never be beholden. 'Twas what her parents and brother had raised her up on. It was what she lived her life by. And she owed Kalder a debt that could never be fully repaid. For he hadn't just freed her, he'd given her back her brother, too.

Closing her eyes, she could still see Kalder's body the day he'd died to liberate them.

Because of the torture and insanity, Paden had turned on her. His hands had been wrapped around her throat when all of a sudden Kalder had been there, pulling him back.

At first, she'd thought herself dreaming.

Until their gazes had locked in the misty nether realm between the worlds.

There in that dark, vacuous place where light and dark mingled into one—where it was neither day nor night—good nor evil—Kalder had reached for her. And for the slightest second they'd almost touched.

But just as his hand brushed against her skin, he'd faded from her reach like a whispered blur—torn from her side so fast that she couldn't stop it.

She'd awakened back in this world to find him on the ground at her feet, lifeless and cold in a pool of his own blood where he'd allowed Thorn to cut open his throat to steal him from the realm of the living to take her place in the hell hall of the dead.

For her. To spare her life and save her soul. And this even though his worst fear had been to die alone and have no one mourn his passing.

Again.

But she refused to mourn him now, because she refused to let him stay there in torment, in her stead.

We're coming for you, Kalder. Hold on. . . .

Hell or high water. Ain't none what'll have you on our watch.

Vine attacked the Dark Seraph as soon as she returned to the cell that made up their vile cage of a home. "Why did you call me back? I had them!"

Clad in her ancient bloodred armor, Gadreyal laughed in her face. Her wings flared out to punctuate the anger in her eyes as she towered over Vine with a twisted expression that said she was imagining the taste of Vine's blood on her lips. "He was kicking your scrawny arse, Deruvian whore. Make no mistake about it. Another minute and all that would have been left of you was a stain upon the floor. You should be thanking me for saving your putrid life, such as it is."

"I had it under control."

"Until you let your arrogance take over, and outed yourself to him. Why did you tell him you live when we were planning to use that to our advantage? *Why?*"

"To rattle him."

"Rattle *him*? Are you insane? Nothing rattles that beast. He feels nothing. Of all creatures, you should know this."

Those words struck their mark and brought a wave of unexpected pain to Vine's heart. Damn the worthless trollop for it! And for the reminder that for all the years of her marriage to that black-hearted bastard she'd never once been able to make Bane love her. No matter how hard she'd tried or what spell she'd used, the beast was forever devoted to her sister.

Her sister!

Never her.

His wife. She was the one who was his equal in brutality and cunning.

And beauty.

Not Mara, the milksop. Duel should have loved her more than any other.

Instead, Mara-the-hag had ranked first in his affections.

Damn them both for it!

It'd never been fair that, in spite of her greater beauty, grace, and intelligence, Vine had never been able to win him over. That he'd pined for Mara even while he'd been in her bed and body. And the last thing Vine wanted was a reminder of her failings. In her past life.

And especially *this* one!

Shrieking, she blasted the Irin and knocked her back.

Gadreyal returned the blow with one of her own that caught Vine across the face and left her on the ground with her entire cheek stinging. Her eyes watered until she could scarcely see.

"Care to continue?" she taunted, arms akimbo.

Not really. Especially given how much the blow burned and ached through her entire being. More than that, Vine wanted to wipe the smirk off the Irin bitch's face. But Gadreyal had made her point. She was the warrior who had spent centuries battling the Sarim and the Light Seraphs of the Kalosum army they fought against.

Vine wasn't.

She'd never been a fighter of any kind. It was why she'd married Bane. He'd been her attack dog that she'd unleashed on others whenever they displeased her. And before him, she'd relied upon her first husband and her sister for such unpleasantries, as they were far more vicious and accomplished in a fight than she was.

Nay, she preferred a much more elegant means of vengeance.

Deception and betrayal.

Treachery.

Poison.

So she smiled in the face of her enemy, and retreated. "We shouldn't be fighting with each other. Not when we have another to worry over."

Suspicion hung deep in her enemy's eyes, letting Vine know that

Gadreyal didn't trust her. But then, given that Gadreyal was the first among her kind who'd turned against the Sephirii and tempted them to betray their own brethren into the hands of their enemies, hence why she was now known as an Irin and not a true Seraph anymore, it made sense. Gadreyal knew how quickly betrayal came. And how likely and unlikely the source of it.

Crossing her arms over her ample bosom, she narrowed her gaze at Vine. She would get this bitch back in time. Patiently, and on her own terms. "They'll be on guard now. Ten times harder to defeat."

"Aye, but we still have what they want." She lifted the chain from around her neck that held the medallion they'd both risked their lives to collect. "And another secret I didn't say a word about."

Paden Jack's Seraph medallion. Something Vine had pinched from Cameron while they'd held the chit in their custody. Neither Paden nor his sister knew she possessed it.

Nor did they know what she'd traded out for it—that was going to be a great surprise if Paden Jack attempted to use his enchanted family sword against them.

And with the soul of the Jacks' ancestor in her possession—the direct link to Michael—she could control them both. Corrupt them much easier now.

Aye, Duel had no idea what was coming for his crew. But she did, and it was about to get fun.

Vine smiled at Gadreyal. "There's an old wizard we needs see."

"I don't follow."

Laughing, Vine clutched the medallion tighter in her fist. "Of course you don't. You weren't born to our world. But there's history between Duel and the Myrcians. Legends of Tintagel you've never been told. I will have him and my bitchtress sister yet for what they've done to me. Before our masters are set free from their prison realm, I will take what I want and none shall stop me this time." Not when she was so close to having everything she'd ever wanted.

Nay, none indeed.

She hadn't thwarted death itself and defied all enemies to fail now.

Gadreyal and her masters might have thought they had her quelled, but they didn't know her resolve or the source of her powers.

Nor the bargain she'd made . . .

Beat to the quarters, dearest. I'm coming for you, and this time, I'll be dancing on your grave.

And she knew the perfect vengeance on them all. One Duel would never see coming, and one not even the mighty Thorn could thwart . . .

3

Beware the course of faith.
It haunts. It daunts.
Most of all, it betrays . . .

"Kal?"

Weak and aching, Kalder froze at a voice he'd never thought to hear again.

Nay . . . it wasn't possible. It was only more torture wrought by the very bastards who'd been mercilessly tearing at his flesh for so long now that he'd lost all concept of time. All concept of reason. Because of their cruelty, his mother had become pain, and punishment his sole nourishment.

Shaking his head to clear it, he reached out to steady himself.

Someone took his hand.

Startled, he clenched his fist to strike out at them, until his gaze focused on the face of the man in front of him. Only he didn't see a man there. He saw a boy. A boy who'd once run after him with the kind of soul-deep adoration in his sea blue eyes that only a younger sibling could give.

Kal! Kal! Wait for me! Can I come with you? Please, brother! Please!

And in that single heartbeat, he felt himself mentally breaking at the onslaught of memories he'd done his best to bury and forget. "Muerig?"

His brother tightened his grip on his hand as he nodded.

Still, Kalder didn't believe him. How could he? "You're dead."

"So are you."

"Aye, but I was damned and forgotten."

Muerig wasn't. Unlike him, his brother had always been a good and decent man. Honorable. Loved by everyone who'd had the pleasure of his kindness. He'd never whored. Never lied or cheated. Never gambled.

Or broken their mother's heart.

While Kalder had schemed and drunk his way through life, Muerig had studied and labored hard. Ever sober and serious. Forever generous in all things, especially his heart and with his compliments.

Kalder had only been generous with his insults and scorn.

And Muerig had died because Kalder was a worthless piece of scytel.

Sadness turned his brother's gaze stormy an instant before a twisted demon grabbed him and flew off.

"Nay!" Kalder jumped up, but was unable to reach them to stop it. Or reclaim his brother from the demon's clutches.

Feminine laughter rang out around him. "So you do love something. . . ."

Horror filled him as he realized what he'd just done. He'd betrayed himself once more.

Worse, he'd betrayed his brother. Again. But that horror was quickly replaced by a resounding fury over the trick they'd played upon him.

"Damn you, Vine!"

When he spun to attack her, she tsked. "Strike me and your brother will bleed in ways you cannot imagine."

She was wrong there. For he possessed quite the imagination when it came to ways to make others suffer. In that, he'd give even the great she-bitch herself a run for her money.

Aye, there were good and sound reasons he'd been damned.

He'd earned it, with both fists, brawling his way straight to the devil's throne. Not a source of pride. Merely a statement of fact. One he was more than eager and willing to educate her on.

Yet her cautionary words stayed his hand better than any assault ever could. Because Muerig was one of the exceptionally few things in his life he'd ever cared about. One of the exceedingly rare things he'd ever been willing to protect and bleed for. "What do you mean?"

One moment he was in a searing, infernal pit, and in the next, they were both outside a smutched, bleeding, besmottered hole. The odor here was even worse than the Hadean pits where the demons had been chasing him. The walls around them appeared to breathe, and oozed with a viscid substance that could only be blood.

"Kal?"

He heard Muerig's weak, tear-filled voice, and that tone iced his fury. While he'd been born an angry, intolerant brawler ready to die over any imagined slight, his brother had never been a fighter of any sort.

And in that heartbeat he was taken back to a time and place where everything was simply complicated. Back to the horrors of that haunting nightmare when he'd found Muerig's battered, lifeless body and everything had coalesced into one single reverberating pain as all the sins of his life had viciously come home to drive a stake straight through that most vital organ that served only to pump venom through his hardened veins.

This . . . *this* was so much worse than seeing himself for what he really was.

For what they'd made him.

Held above Kalder's head, just out of his reach, Muerig was fastened to a narrow ledge. His skin had peeled back from lack of water. Agony bled with every ragged breath he struggled to take. But worse than the torment in those eyes that were so similar to his own was the deep resignation that hovered there.

That unspoken wish for death to end his suffering.

It was a silent, echoing scream that Kalder knew intimately. One his own soul had been shouting since the hour of his unfortunate birth and the one that bitch Mercy had never seen the decency to oblige. Indeed, she took a sick perversion in allowing him to suffer more with every passing year.

With a furious war cry, Kalder tried to climb up the sheer volcanic rock to free his brother, but he slid down the slick, bloody surface that sliced open his hands and left them ravaged.

Muerig cried out.

Too late Kalder realized that somehow his brother's nerve endings were tied to the surface of the very ground and rocks around him. And every step or movement he made caused his brother more agony. He shuddered at the horror of it all. "Forgive me, Muerig."

Muerig groaned even louder.

Afraid to move lest he cause his brother even more harm, Kalder held his breath as he considered ways to free him from his prison. Yet every shift in weight drove more agony through Muerig's body. This was a maniacal lair built by the unholiest of monsters.

Damn the Cimmerian army for their cruelty! They had thought this through far too well. There was nothing to be done that wouldn't harm his brother more.

And none of it would kill a man who was already dead. So there was no release for Muerig whatsoever.

It was sickening. Tangled weeds had grown through Muerig's body, planting him to the underside of the ledge over Kalder's head. Worse were the demonic hands that held him, particularly the one at his throat that tightened any time Kalder moved closer.

"Whose life do you value more?"

Kalder tensed at the sudden question that came from a voiceless, heartless whore. "What?"

"You heard me, mermaid. You traded your life force for

Cameron's to get here. Tell me whose life you would trade for your brother's?"

"Mine."

Gadreyal laughed before she materialized to hover in the air near Muerig's perch. Her wings fluttered with the memory of when she'd once been on the side of good.

But that had been aeons ago.

Now, she was a soulless, pitiless creature of absolute evil. "You think we'd make it that easy on you? Nay, little fish. Never. Besides, we already have *you*. What we seek is something a lot more important than your worthless scaly hide."

Vine materialized at his back. Like the Deruvian monster she was, she wrapped her thorny branches around Kalder and tightened them so that he couldn't move. They bit deep into his flesh, drawing blood. His arms and legs throbbed even more as he fought against the restraint. He should have known that Vine would be part of this. Her species was grown from the earth. Made up of wood, her sylph ancestors were the worst sort of magical beings once they ceased to be protectors who guarded mankind. Their withered hearts turned black with their Wintering disease and they became predators who preyed on human blood and souls. . . .

So asking her for mercy was as useful as trying to milk a stump for sustenance. And fighting against her would be more useless still. She had him and there was nothing he could do, except bleed more. Never had he felt more powerless. Or weaker.

And he hated her for it.

This must have been how they'd trapped Muerig. And how they planned to eternally torment him. To tie him here to the ground with her limbs so that she could feed and he could watch his brother suffer and know that he was the very cause of it.

There was no worse hell to be had.

"Vine! Release him. Now!"

Kalder gasped as he heard Thorn's thunderous voice cut through the air between them. Even though it was sweltering here, that tone sent a chill over his body.

The ferocity was enough to cause Vine to immediately let go and step back. But only for an instant. Then she recovered herself and gripped him again. "You do not command me, you whelp of a whore!"

Thorn appeared right in front of them with an expression on his face that said she had to be the dumbest creature to ever draw breath to challenge him so. "Oh, foulest bitchington, please . . . in the mood I'm in, you truly don't want to press this issue." He smirked. "Or mayhap you do. Please"—he smiled coldly into her face—"tell me that you do. For you, I would be willing to dine on blood. Consequences be damned."

His green eyes flared to red.

Vine let go one last time and withdrew. Gadreyal started forward, but Thorn quelled her advance with nothing more than one arched brow. A truly impressive feat.

Even so, the Irin shook her head. "You have no authority here, demon. He belongs to us."

"There you would be wrong. He's earned his release. Harm him further and I'll be glad to take it from your hides." He passed a cold stare to Vine before he returned that glare to Gadreyal. "Care to press my patience further?"

Gadreyal's breathing intensified as she landed and stepped close enough to stare up into Thorn's eyes. "I know not what bizarre relationship you have with our masters or what powers you wield here, but the day will come when my hand will not be stayed so easily."

"Nor will mine. But remember, Gaddy, when that time comes, I won't be protecting your back. I'll be cutting your throat." He stepped around her to collect Kalder.

Aghast, Kalder couldn't believe that Thorn was here to liberate him again. The very demon who'd freed him once to serve on Captain Bane's crew.

The same demon who'd opened his throat to bleed him out so that he could be damned here to this hell and replace Cameron and her brother.

Vine sputtered indignantly. "What? Are you serious? We're really to free him because this lickspittle says it?"

Gadreyal nodded. "Let the mermaid bastard go. Trust me. You can't win this."

Cursing, Vine stepped back, then hissed at Kalder. "This isn't over, whoreson. I will have my flesh from your bones."

Thorn snorted. "From the looks and smell of him, I'd say you already have."

Completely offended by that unnecessary insult, Kalder gaped. "Let's see how you'd smell and look after they tortured you."

Thorn cracked an evil grin. "Like blood, piss, and shite. 'Cause I'd be covered in theirs to pay for their attempts at it. And I'd revel in the violence of it all."

Aye, he was a sick bastard. He most likely would at that.

As Thorn started away, Kalder stopped him. "Me brother's here. I won't leave without him!"

Thorn followed his gaze to see Muerig's tortured body up on the cliff. He winced in response to the grisly sight. "Sorry, lad. I can only take you from here. Not him. He's not part of my bargain."

"Then you can keep it. I won't leave him here, suffering like that."

"You have no choice."

Kalder had been told that the whole of his life, and he was done with it. "Nay! He stays. I stay."

He'd barely finished those words before he found himself on the shores of a foreign beach. Shocked and repulsed, he turned around in a circle, seeking some sight of his brother. "What is this?"

Thorn sighed heavily. "I told you, we had no choice. I was lucky to secure what they owed *you*. And make no mistake, there won't be a third time, so please don't do anything else so stupid with your freedom."

It was only then that Kalder saw the condition Thorn was in. Or rather, the condition he was *hiding*. Pale and weaker than he'd ever seen the demon, Thorn could barely stand on his own. Indeed, he looked as if he'd fall over any moment.

"What did they do to you?"

Thorn's eyes turned red again as he straightened. An unholy fire burned in the depths of that rock-hard gaze. He grabbed Kalder by his ragged shirt and jerked him forward. "Know that your freedom, though earned, came at a high cost. Do not squander it." And with those words, he threw Kalder back.

Kalder expected to land on the sandy beach.

Instead, he kept falling through a darkness that had no substance or form. An endless night that was cold and vacuous. As bereft as his soul that wanted them to correct the injustice of leaving his brother behind.

When Kalder finally came to rest, it was against solid board. The unexpected impact knocked the air from his lungs and left him gasping for breath and dazed, with stars dancing in his vision to the point it near blinded him.

Stunned, he rolled to his side, ready to battle in spite of not being able to see clearly. But as the dancing images came into focus, he realized that these were demons he knew.

Demons he called family. And the sight of them made his heart lighten as unshed tears choked him.

"Bart?" Kalder blinked, unsure if he could trust his eyes. Or if this might be another vicious trick Vine was using to weaken his resolve.

The Simeon Mage's long brown hair was loose from its queue as his merry blue eyes sparkled with relief. "Kalder!" He stepped forward to lend a shoulder and help him stand. "You look like hell itself swallowed you whole and shat you back out."

"Pretty sure it did, mate." And still Kalder couldn't believe he was back among the insane crew that called this ship home. That this was real and that they were here with him again.

How could it be?

He kept waiting for it all to vanish. But as each second passed and he remained, as each crew member came forward to welcome his return, he knew it wasn't a dream.

Especially when he saw Bane in all his dark, venomous glory.

Aye, there was no missing that amount of sinister power. It thickened the air and sizzled with an electricity that caused the hairs on his neck and arms to rise. No one commanded the unholy authority or powers this creature did.

Without a word, Bane jerked him forward into a tight embrace and pounded him so hard on his back that it, too, knocked the wind from his lungs.

Shocked, Kalder felt his jaw drop as Bane released him and stepped aside to greet Thorn, who'd materialized by his side. All signs of weakness were now masked. The demonic bastard appeared as hale and hearty as ever. Yet Kalder knew that for the illusion it was.

He swallowed hard as Bane inclined his head to Thorn. "I would say thank you, but I know how much you despise gratitude."

Thorn snorted a prim dismissal at Bane. "Told you I'd get him back."

"And I trusted you would. Arsling you might be, but you were ever good to your word."

"That a compliment?"

Bane scoffed. "Never. Just a statement of fact."

Smirking, Thorn rolled his eyes as Bane's wife, Mara, joined them on deck. As a Deruvian—and Vine's sister—she was born from a race of wood sylphs and was the very enchanted ship they sailed upon. Yet unlike Vine, she wasn't possessed of their Wintering disease that had stolen her sister's soul and sanity. She was still a protector for Man, and held her soul intact. Her Deruvian vows were sacred to her, as was the safety of every person she housed inside her hull.

And just as Kalder's brother had been bonded to the ground,

Mara was part of the ship itself and knew everything that happened aboard it. Every piece of wood was tied to her in much the same way the ground had been melded to Muerig. She could sense every swipe of the ocean water or step of foot against the planks. They were all part of her body and being.

With the palest golden-brown hair that was liberally laced with strands of pure ice white, she was lithe and angelic—more graceful and beautiful than any woman Kalder had ever seen.

Except for one who was conspicuously missing at the moment.

Mara moved to stand next to Bane while Thorn scanned their crew with a warning grimace. "And with that, I should warn you that the Carian Gate fell open completely a short bit ago. The entire Sarim Council, including Michael and Gabriel, are holding the battle line with their armies as best they can, but . . ."

"All hell's breaking loose?"

Bane and Thorn both passed a droll stare at Will for his unsolicited comment that caused half the crew to groan out loud over the bad jest.

Bartholomew Meers, or Blackheart Bart as most knew him, shoved Will forward. "You're ever a daft wanker with ill timing. Read the room, man. Toss him overboard for you, Captain? Do us all a service?"

"Maybe later. We might could use the entertainment."

Unamused, Kalder froze as he felt a presence behind him similar to warm sunshine brushing over his naked skin. It was hot and tantalizing.

And it left him breathless.

Knowing instinctively that it was Cameron, he turned to see

her in the shadows of the hatch. Tears glistened in a pair of pale sea-colored eyes that widened with disbelief. With her arms braced on each side of the doorframe to steady herself on the rocking ship, and her breathing labored, she chewed at the bottom of her lip. A habit of nervousness he found absolutely charming.

Still dressed in the breeches and tunic of a boy, she was the most beautiful woman in the world to him and he'd gut anyone who said otherwise. Especially when she launched herself forward at a dead run across the deck for him.

Her laughter rang out like a song.

Catching her in his arms, he was completely unprepared for the ferocity of her assault. She wrapped herself around him and cradled his entire body with hers. Never had anyone greeted him with such reckless abandon and enthusiasm. And he'd never thought to have a homecoming like this from a woman of such fine and upstanding character and nature. Usually, people were only this happy to see him go.

Kalder couldn't breathe as the almond scent of her skin hit him hard and he fisted his hand in the silken chestnut strands of her hair. "Take it you missed me, lass?"

Cameron wanted to beat him for that question. But she was too grateful to have him back to taint it, even if he did deserve it for baiting her so. "How could I miss anyone as thoughtless as you?" she teased. "You're a feckless beast. Worthless from your first breath to your last!"

He flashed a charming grin at her. "'Deed, as is evidenced by your reluctance to loosen that Herculean death grip you've got about me throat."

Cameron felt her cheeks stinging as she realized how right he was. Her arms ached from the tightness of her grasp. "Only because every time I let you out of me sight, Mr. Dupree, you get into all manner of trouble."

Reluctantly, she released him and stepped back to stare up into those eyes that defied her ability to name their stormy pewteresque color. And how could she have forgotten just how handsome he was? Or tall?

Or how incredibly massive and refined for a bloke!

Only Captain Bane was larger in size.

Even bruised, Kalder was still the most handsome creature she'd ever seen in the flesh. And the sight of him there before her left her breathless and hot in a way that really should be illegal, and probably was in most colonies. In truth, she hated how much he affected her, and he wasn't even trying. That was the worst part of it all. She had none to blame for her untoward thoughts but herself.

And if her heart didn't quit pounding, it would soon beat a hole from her chest and be skiddling along the deck at their feet. The sound of a gruff male clearing his throat interrupted her appreciation of Kalder's finer assets. Too late, she remembered that her older brother was now on board their ship, sailing with the crew.

And staring angrily at them in a state of obvious distemper over her overt ogling. Never mind the overt groping.

Her face heated up even more.

Stepping away from Kalder, she turned toward her brother, who was as fair-haired as she was dark. "Paden . . . may I introduce you to Mr. Kalder Dupree?"

A tic started in Paden's jaw as he crossed his arms over his chest and took up that stance he had anytime a male came near. "I thought you and he were *just* friends."

"We are."

The annoyed scowl he cast toward her hand that was still tucked inside Kalder's accused her of lying.

Offended that he'd dare such, she arched a brow. "Don't you even now, me boyo. Won't be having none of those lectures from the likes of *your* sorry hide, given what you've gone and put your poor Letty through. And how you left her when you pulled out your sails last. You're a fine one to think to be lecturing me on me behavior, Patrick Michel Alister Jack!"

This time Paden's cheeks turned rosy, at the mention of his pregnant fiancée who waited for their return in Williamsburg. Aye, poor Lettice was in a pickle because of his thoughtlessness. He had no right to be sanctimonious when all she'd done was have long conversations with Kalder.

In the most public of rooms and spaces.

Filled with witnesses!

Truth to that. Never once were the two of them alone. Though to be honest, there was a part of her what wouldn't mind a bit more than friendship, and that part terrified her. Because she'd seen the darker side of Mr. Dupree's nature whenever he let down his guard. And still, even though she knew what he was capable of—knew the darkness what lived deep inside him—she found him more compelling than any man she'd ever met.

He's not a man, Cam. You know this.

Kalder was another beastie altogether. A dangerous water kelpie. The kind that could easily lure her in . . .

Forevermore.

Trying not to think about that, Cameron lowered her gaze, then froze as she realized something.

With a gasp, she took Kalder's hand in hers and pulled his dirty sleeve back a bit so that she could get a better look at his forearm.

"Hey!" Paden snapped indignantly at the way she pawed at Kalder.

She ignored him completely as she saw the most miraculous thing of all.

Kalder's mark was gone.

"Where's your Deadman's Cross Ribbon?"

Bart and Will came forward to look at his arm with her. Then they turned in unison to stare at Thorn, waiting for an explanation of its absence.

He shrugged. "When he traded his soul for you and your brother, Miss Jack, he redeemed himself." Thorn jerked his chin at Kalder's wrist. "Means you can die again, Dupree. For real, now. Beware and take care. One resurrection after your redemption is all I can manage. There's no hope for you after this."

Shock hovered in his eyes. "Why didn't you tell me?"

"Just did."

"That how you freed him?"

Thorn ignored answering Devyl's pointed question straight out, but then that was normal. The bugger never liked to answer much of anything. "You'll never know, mate. The devil's son works in mysterious ways."

Sancha Dolorosa sucked her breath in sharply at his take on the common phrase. "That's blasphemy!"

He passed a droll stare at the ship's pilot. Tall and thin, she wore a long, curly black wig that set off her dark patrician features to perfection. "Really? You're going to chastise *me* for *that*?"

Before they could comment on whether or not he had a right to it, something struck the hull of the ship. Hard and with a vigor that sent the ship careening. Mara turned pale from the pain of the blow against her hull, as she staggered and Captain Bane caught her to his side.

"My lady?"

"There's a lusca in the water." Her breathing turned ragged as waves rushed over the decks from where the sea monster was attacking them, and hammering more blows against her.

Both Cameron and her brother shifted instantly from their "human" appearance into their Necrodemian bodies—something that happened any time true evil came near them with ill intent. Their hair became as white as Mara's and Sancha's real hair that she kept hidden beneath her curly black wig, and their skin turned a ghostly, glittering pale. Likewise, their wings expanded and fluttered out.

Though why this eerie transition happened to her now after Paden had been returned from Vine's custody, Cameron couldn't imagine. Paden was the one who'd inherited their mother's sword and her powers, and calling. Not her. Technically, she should have gone back to normal once they were freed. Yet why Cameron would change around evil this time when she hadn't changed earlier in the tavern when they faced Vine and her minions, she couldn't imagine.

Like Paden, she had no control over her shifted forms. It came upon her without any warning.

Captain Bane handed Mara's care and protection off to Will. "Guard her well, Mr. Death!"

Mara cast her husband a chiding glare, but didn't speak, as they were all accustomed to his overprotectiveness when it came to his wife's safety.

Kalder started for the side railing, but the captain stopped him.

"You've been restored now, Mr. Dupree. Stay on board and don't risk yourself."

Kalder scoffed at his order. "Not while there's a threat to this crew, Captain. Me life makes no never mind to me, you know that. They want a brawl and blood in the water, I'm in the mood to give it."

Cameron started for him, but Kalder was over the side and in the raging seawater before she could stop him from his recklessness.

Paden pulled his enchanted Seraph's sword from its sheath, and went to take a station with the rest of the crew. As Cameron headed to join them, Thorn took her elbow.

"They fed you blood while they had you?"

Cameron hesitated at his question. "Pardon?"

"Did you drink blood while you were held by Vine, lass?"

She winced involuntarily as her mind flashed on the nightmares she'd survived at the hands of Vine and her unholy alliance of misshapen adulators. No matter how hard she tried, she couldn't erase the trauma of it all. "They poured it down me throat. Aye. And Paden's too."

He looked as sick as she'd felt when they'd done it.

And the curse he let out made her stomach draw tight.

"Why, Lord Thorn? What did they do to us?"

"They've bonded with you." He glanced over to Paden. "And your brother, no doubt. I should have thought of that."

"What's that mean?"

A tic started in his handsome jaw as his eyes turned a deep, flowing green that reflected like iridescent water. "It depends on whose blood they used . . . and the binding spell." Thorn winced as if some nightmare just occurred to him.

"What aren't you saying, my lord?"

"You've the blood of Michael in your veins, girl. While the others are strong, he's one of the most powerful of all. His blood is straight from the Source itself. There's no telling what such a bond could cause. The damage not just to you and your brother, but to the entire world."

A shiver went down her spine as she considered his words. "You're terrifying me."

"Good, lass. You need to be scared. More than that, you need to be vigilant. Because like it or not, you're no longer simply a protector, born of the light. With what they've done to you, you're now a creature of darkness, same as the rest of us. And you will be pulled toward that pit with a hunger the likes of which you've never known. As bad as it is for us, it's nothing compared to what it'll be for someone like you who's never known its lure before. May the gods help you, little one. I've yet to meet the soul who hasn't been damned by those flames."

4

Kalder hit the ocean water and soaked it in with a
sigh of relief as his gills finally opened and he was
able to take his first real breath in weeks.

Or maybe it was months.

To be submerged again . . .

It was second only to an actual orgasm.

Although, it'd been so long since he last had one
of those that they might actually feel the same. Honestly, he couldn't remember anymore.

The unexpected and sublime sensation was so

immediate and intense that he sincerely forgot what he was doing. That they were actually in the middle of the ocean and under a violent attack.

Until the sea monster rose up and slapped him hard with one slimy, nasty tentacle. That stinging blow brought him out of his stupor and reminded him of their imminent threat.

And his own place in the world.

He was here to slay.

Slamming his fists against the waves, he summoned his powers and felt them wash through his body like lava. Thick and hot. They contrasted sharply with the cold seawater.

The huge sharklike octopus beast bared its fangs at him as it turned away from the ship to attack Kalder full frontal. Aye, he had its ugly attention now. Full on. Complete and utter.

The stench of it was tantamount to a rotting corpse that had lain for weeks in the sun. It hung in the air and choked him as the beast came about for another attack.

"That's it, me smelly friend. Come get some."

He shot a fiery blast at the creature that caught it across the face. It recoiled from the fire and dove under the waves. The *Sea Witch* turned in the water to head back in their direction and render support to him. Her long nines rolled into place while their aeromages scrambled for assault. The sound of metal scraping against the wood rolled like thunder over the ocean and caused Kalder's blood to pound with delight at the smell of war. This was what he loved most in this blackened world.

The fight. The blood.

The massacre.

Except for one thing.

Back in the day, balling had been the sole activity he'd partaken in more than brawling. So much so that his parents had threatened to harpoon him to the wall of his bedroom if he didn't learn to restrain himself from the company of loose human women. While it'd been oft said that the females of his people were seductresses sent to lure mortal men to their doom, he'd argued that human women were much more attractive than any mermaid ever born. For he could normally turn away even the most beautiful of Myrcians.

Put a human woman in front of him . . .

His breeches had fallen straight to his ankles as if controlled by magic. He'd been more wanton than any harlot imaginable. And yet with all those women he'd never known real desire or hunger.

Until Cameron Jack.

It was why he shouldn't have come back here, he realized as he saw her standing on deck with the others, and he felt a rising panic at the thought of her being harmed in this fight.

Or worse, her being taken again by their enemies.

I kill everything I love.

Just like his father. The only thing that had saved Kalder from his family's curse in the past was the fact that his father hadn't loved him at all.

Not that it mattered. Kalder had never been particularly sentimental about anything or anyone.

And right now, he needed to be focused on this fight, as the lusca was currently kicking his arse and would kill him if he didn't get his head off the lass who was watching him and back in the fight he was supposed to be having.

The beast lifted up in the sea and squalled out with a tremendous shriek.

Kalder pulled back, expecting another attack to rain down on him. Instead, he saw a cannonball land squarely against the creature's hideous neck. Followed by two more powerful shots. Blood and sinew spewed out over him and the creature. He felt good about that.

For about a minute.

Then it exploded and sent all manner of nastiness coating his body and clogging up his gills.

Screwing his face up, he silently cursed every member of the now cheering crew.

Until he heard the sounds of someone sputtering in the water near him.

At first he thought one of the Deadmen had fallen overboard, and was drowning. It was a normal enough occurrence in battle, as many of them couldn't swim since they had never been near deep bodies of water in their human lifetimes. For that matter, most had never been near even a modest bath by the smell of them.

He'd always assumed that was the primary reason Bane had wanted him for their crew. Made sense, as Kalder usually fished them out and returned them to the ship during battle.

But as he neared the man who was struggling in the water, he drew up short at the unique sight of silvery skin and dark hair that marked him as something other than human.

Not a fellow Deadman at all.

This was a Myrcian.

And not just any Myrcian . . .

"Muerig?"

His brother coughed and wheezed as if trying to get his bearings. "Kal!"

Shocked, amazed, and not quite sure if he could believe what he was seeing, Kalder grabbed him in the water, and pulled him closer to his chest. "What are you doing here?"

"I don't know. Where am I?"

Dumbfounded, Kalder tried to make sense of this. "You're back in the world of the living."

Surrendering his weight to Kalder, his brother scowled as he looked around in disbelief. "I don't understand."

Neither did he. But right now, that didn't matter. Only getting them both back to the ship did. "Come on." Thrilled and confused, he wrapped one arm beneath his brother's armpits, and swam with him toward the *Sea Witch*.

Kalder climbed up the side and lifted his brother over the edge first, then made his own way to the deck.

Bane seized him in one angry, malevolent fist and lifted him with a disturbing amount of ease given Kalder's immense size and amount of muscle weight and saturation. *No man should be this strong.* "What were you thinking, you wee daft fish?"

Kalder blinked at the new insult Bane had found for him. "That you needed someone in the water."

"You defied my orders!"

So what was new? Bane acted as if he'd never done such before, and Kalder would have said that out loud, but wasn't quite so suicidal given the rage on his captain's face. Nor could he fathom it. As noted, he wasn't exactly known for following anyone's dictates.

Not even Bane's. So why the captain was surprised by his insubordination, he had no idea.

For once, he stilled his tongue and merely arched a brow at Bane's distemper.

Rather, he gestured at Muerig. "Have you met me brother, Captain?"

That at least succeeded in causing Bane to loosen his death grip enough that Kalder could breathe again.

"Pardon?"

Kalder cleared his throat as he extracted the last of his shirt with an exaggerated grimace from Bane's grip. "Me brother Muerig." He moved to kneel by his brother's side so that he could check on him.

While Kalder tended him, Thorn and Belle came to help. Though the expression on Thorn's face said he was suspicious enough that he might be considering tossing them both overboard again and summoning another lusca to have them.

Thorn narrowed his gaze on Muerig. "How did you get free?" Aye, there was pure venom in that tone.

Muerig wiped a shaking hand over his chin. "They let me go."

Thorn laughed bitterly before he met Bane's equally suspicious glare. "Gadreyal never lets anyone go."

"Truth to that." Bane stepped forward. "Unless she has mischief intended. Or they're in league with her."

Well aware of where this was headed, Kalder rose to his feet to defend his brother, and even though he knew it for the folly it was, he stood his ground on this matter. They weren't about to harm his kin. Not while he was there to stop it. "He's me baby brother, Captain."

Thorn and Bane passed a look between them that shriveled his stones a bit, as he had no doubt they were questioning his sanity, and debating whether or not to geld him, and cast his brother, *and* his stones to the sharks.

But after a long pause the captain let out a deep sigh of resignation. "Keep a weather eye, Mr. Dupree. People, even beloved brothers, change. Seldom for the better. Usually toward the worst." Bane glanced over to his younger sister, who'd come back to him after her own death at the hands of Bane's enemies. "But I know the pain of losing what you hold dearest, and I won't be depriving you of your family. Just remember the first rule of betrayal."

That it never comes from the hand of a stranger or enemy.

Only the ones you trust can betray you.

It was a lesson Kalder had learned before he'd been weaned from the teat of the whore who'd whelped him.

"Aye, aye, Captain." Kalder's gaze went to Cameron and his stomach tightened as he realized that he had a lot more to lose now.

This time, he cared.

"I'll be on me guard."

Thorn's tic picked up its pace in his cheek. "What did they say when they freed you?"

Muerig shrugged. "Nothing. They just let me go."

Holding out his hand, Thorn helped him to his feet. He kept his expression guarded.

"Take him below, Mr. Dupree. See him settled." Bane stepped toward Thorn. "And welcome to the Deadmen."

Kalder didn't miss the icy undertone in those words. Not that he blamed him. Bane knew nothing of his brother. Or his loyalty. But he'd learn . . .

Thorn watched as Kalder led his brother away and the Deadmen returned to normal. Or at least as normal as this crew of miscreants could manage.

Though to be honest, there were now members of the crew who weren't technically Deadmen anymore.

Kalder, of course.

And Devyl and his sister Elyzabel—an ancient magickal Deruvian like Mara. Elyzabel was a slender woman with long brown hair and amber eyes, and was a balm for her brother Devyl's most cruel nature. Because of her brother's care and sacrifice, Elyzabel had never given in to the darker side of their people. As with Mara, she was a creature of pure light and, thanks to her brother, she would forever remain so.

Yet Thorn saw in all their gazes the same suspicion about Muerig that he held. "You don't trust him either."

Devyl shook his head. "Something about him's not right. I can feel it with every instinct inside me."

"Aye," Elyzabel agreed. "Gaddy would never release him without nefarious cause. Kindness is as alien to her as trust is to you."

When she started after them, Devyl gently took her arm to keep his sister by his side. "You're to stay clear of them, at all times."

She chided at her brother. "Duey—"

"I mean it, Elf!" His tone was brittle and sharp. "I lost you once. Don't make me set fire to them for looking askance at you. Especially not Kalder. I'll gut him as sure as I'm standing here to protect you."

Her expression softened. "Fine, but only because you asked me so kindly." Her sarcasm was quite impressive. She glanced past his shoulder to Mara. "However, my dearest brother, I would caution you to remember that I now have a secret weapon."

Devyl arched his brow. "And that is?"

She jerked her chin toward his wife. "The one thing you'll never say nay to." And with that she cast him a most impertinent smile and sashayed off to join Belle.

Thorn laughed.

As did Mara, before she smiled up at her husband. "Have I said how much I love your sister, Du? She's as precious as the day is long."

He let out an exasperated breath as he passed a droll stare to Thorn. "I curse the day the two of them ganged up against me. I haven't had a moment of peace since."

Thorn snorted at his dire tone. But he knew the truth. Devyl loved every minute of having those women near him. "I hear the lie in your words, and I call you on it."

Thunder clapped overhead, punctuating his pronouncement.

"Storm's a-coming," Blake Landry called out from the crow's nest.

"Thank you, Captain Obvious, for your astute observations!" Will snorted as he drew near them. "So glad he's on watch for us. Whatever would we do with a more competent pair of eyes on the horizon, I ask you?"

Ignoring them, Thorn returned to his conversation with Devyl. "When I freed Kalder, they were torturing his brother and making the Myrcian watch."

"Sounds like Vine."

"Aye, but freeing him out of the goodness of her heart doesn't."

By his hooded expression, Devyl had to bite back an excessively caustic retort over that. "Am thinking to borrow Mr. Death's insult for you, Captain Obvious."

With a mirthless smirk, Thorn crossed his arms over his chest. "You know Vine better than anyone, Duel. Tell me where her head was when she freed him."

Up her arse. He knew that for a fact. She was about mischief most foul, and as usual, he was the target. Sad thing was, poor Kalder was caught in the snare this time, and for that, he was truly irritated. "There's a debt I owe, from long ago. One I promised to keep sacred."

"And?"

"And I failed. Vine knows the source of it, as she was there when the bargain was struck between us." Devyl should have killed her then. Too bad he'd been married to her at the time, and had thought to keep his family intact. Stupid him for being sentimental.

"Care to fill me in on it?"

Not really. Devyl didn't want to confide in Thorn. Long ago, they had been the bitterest of enemies. It was hard to get past that. Hard to trust someone he'd once spent years trying to slaughter.

But they were allies now.

More than that, he owed Thorn his life.

His current marriage.

And his sanity.

Had the bastard not saved him, he'd still be in hell and not married to the only woman he'd ever loved. So perhaps he could find a little faith in the beast even if Thorn was the son of all evil.

So Devyl decided to take a little leap. "Do you know who Kalder's father is?"

"A Myrcian, of course."

Oh, with that level of sarcasm the wee bastard made it hard not to gut him where he stood. Harder still not to slap him. Akantheus Leucious of the Brakadians sorely tried what little patience Devyl managed. And the smug gleam in those green eyes said that he took entirely too much pleasure in his taunting. No wonder he'd cast off his old name and started going by Thorn instead. It was definitely apropos, as the man was certainly a thorn in everyone's arse.

Letting out a disgusted "heh," Devyl shook his head. "King Daven."

Unlike Leucious back in those dark, fun-filled days, Daven had been one of Devyl's friends and allies. One of the sad, tiny handful he could trust.

Well, mayhap "friend" was a bit much, as neither of them were exactly friendly. But they'd drunk together and spent cordial time without fighting.

That was as close to friendship as either of them could manage.

Daven Dupree had possessed his own mental issues with those around him. Myrcians by nature were a warring lot. Treacherous and slanderous. And his own family had been quick to sell him out to their Roman adversaries. Even quicker to betray him to the fey bastards out to end them.

So the two of them, as warlords, had allied together to secure their borders, and protect their lands and people from family and enemies.

Better still, Daven had united his forces with Devyl's to fight against Leucious's sanctimonious army. And had treachery not ended his old ally's life, Daven might have succeeded in putting Leucious out of Devyl's misery for good.

As it was, the mention of Daven's name at least succeeded in taking the smugness from the prick. Indeed, Thorn actually choked. "You're not kidding?"

He shook his head. "Surprised you didn't recognize him. Kalder looks just like his father."

Leucious cursed under his breath. "I've had so many enemies throughout the centuries . . . hard to keep track of them all."

"True. Sooner or later, we all want to kill you."

Thorn glared at him.

"What?" he asked innocently. Not like it was his fault. Leucious Thorn had a way of getting on pretty much everyone's kill list. And he'd once been at the very top of Devyl's.

Some days he still was.

Letting out an irritated breath, Thorn shook his head and continued their conversation. "So it was Queen Bron who gutted him, then. I'm shocked she'd kill her own child."

Devyl laughed bitterly. "His mother isn't the bitchington what gutted him."

It took Thorn a moment to catch on to what Devyl meant by that. When he did, he gaped. "What?"

"Aye, you heard me. Bron was the Myrcian queen and Daven's wife, but she didn't birth Kalder. She only raised him at his father's behest and led the boy to believe she was his mother. Kalder never knew any differently—per his father's dictates. After his father died, and so long as I lived, I was the threat that stayed her hand from the boy. She didn't dare harm him for fear of what I might do to her."

Tragically, when Vine killed Devyl, she'd left Kalder without a protector. The boy hadn't lasted a year before Bron had found a way to legally murder him. There'd been many a day when Devyl had wondered if Bron had placed her own son in harm's way just for the excuse of slaughtering Kalder with impunity. He wouldn't put it past her.

Women were treacherous that way, and none more so than Daven's chosen queen.

She and Vine had had much in common that way.

"If Bron wasn't his mother, then who was?"

That was the real rub of it all. And the true source of Kalder's powers.

And Bron's true fears.

"Melusine."

Thorn choked again at a name Devyl knew he wasn't expecting. "As in the river goddess?"

"Aye. One and the same."

"And Kalder has no idea?"

Devyl shook his head. "None whatsoever."

"Does Vine know?"

Crossing his arms over his chest, he shrugged. "That would be the question of the day, wouldn't it?"

Aye, it would. Because if she knew . . . "Why would she let him go if she had knowledge of his real birth mother?"

"Indeed." Devyl paused to give him time to consider the gravity of it all. "Whoever has possession of Kalder has a direct line to one of the oldest and deadliest of ancient powers. A power that Vine could use to destroy not only you, but me as well, and the entire world as we know it."

Thorn cursed. "If Kalder has no idea what a critical piece he is in this game, then we need to assume that Vine *does* know and that his brother is her lure to get him back to her side of the veil."

"I'll do you one better."

Thorn scowled. "What's that?"

"That his brother's here to get our Miss Jack to their side so that she can deliver Kalder over to them with a bow around his neck."

Thorn let out a low growl of agreement at the insidiousness of such a plan. "Double jeopardy."

Devyl nodded. "Vine's specialty. Either way, she wins and Kalder loses."

5

"So she's a doll made entirely of straw?"

Kalder scoffed at Muerig's oversimplification of Valynda Moore's inhuman state and bitter plight. A conclusion too easy to draw whenever one first met the woman and saw her poppet-like appearance. "Not exactly. She was a lady bespelled by a man who was in love with her and wanted to force her to love him. Because he didn't understand the magick he invoked, her soul was accidentally pulled from her body, and her body destroyed before she could reclaim it. For now, to keep her from dying, her soul was placed in this current straw form to hold it safe and secure, but if she redeems herself, she'll be returned to a flesh state so that she may live out her life as a living woman again."

Muerig appeared to be unable to grasp the concept of it. "How is that possible? Surely you can see that it defies all logic!"

No more so than his brother being returned to this realm when he'd died so long ago.

Or, for that matter, Kalder being brought back from the dead, not once, but twice. Face it, there was much in their world that made no sense whatsoever. Who was he to argue the logic of Valynda's current form? Never mind, for Muerig to play the skeptic.

At this point, Kalder was willing to believe just about anything.

Even in Santa and flying reindeer.

Valynda laughed at Muerig's brother's befuddled expression. " 'Tis a long story, good Muerig. And we don't ask those questions on this ship. Just accept that things are unusual here and you'll get along quite well." Chucking him playfully on the arm, she skipped out of the room so that she could join Belle and Janice for their regular game of chance that usually involved fire, a lot of cursing, and enough bloodshed that it made the captain rather grateful the Deadmen couldn't perish from actual blood loss.

And this was from the women of their crew.

The men who made up their family were far more tame by comparison.

Dumbfounded, Muerig gaped at Kalder, who shrugged nonchalantly. "Don't stress yourself over the matter, little brother. It's all good."

"I'm so confused by all this. Just when I think no one onboard can be any stranger, they surprise me with another tale of oddity."

"Says the boy who breathes water and farts bubbles. And just wait until you meet Sallie. He keeps his soul in a rum bottle."

Muerig gaped. "You're serious?"

"Quite." He flashed his brother a roguish grin. "And whatever you do, don't be opening that bottle. You'll unleash said soul, which is the last thing you want. That will wreak unholy mayhem on us all, as it tends to go a bit berserk." Kalder winked at him. "You'll find our Deadmen unlike any other crew you've ever met. A motley band, for sure, but it works for us. Most days."

"Am thinking you're all insane."

"There's no denying that." Kalder watched Muerig stretch out on the bunk and sigh as if he were in heaven. "Are you all right?"

"Just grateful to be away from those she-bitches. And, in particular, their claws."

He certainly understood that. "You know I didn't want to leave you there. I did me best to stay."

"I know."

Kalder swallowed hard as a most bitter wave of guilt tore through him. "You hate me for it, don't you?"

Muerig scowled. "Pardon?"

"You've every right to. I got you killed. And tortured. It's all me fault what happened to you. Then and now." He had to steel himself not to flinch as an involuntary image of his brother's body went through his mind, the way it had looked when he'd found him on that ledge. He still couldn't imagine the pain they'd put Muerig through because of him. "How did you end up in their hands, anyway?"

"In all truth, I know not. I was in paradise and the next thing I knew, they had me pinned and rooted there. It was horrible."

"Well, you're safe now." Kalder wasn't sure whose benefit he said that for—his or Muerig's. "I won't let them take you again. I swear it."

"Good thing, that. I for one would definitely appreciate it, brother."

Ignoring his sarcasm, Kalder hesitated as a million different emotions went through him. While he'd never really gotten along with his older siblings, Muerig had been different. Since the moment he'd first laid eyes on the newborn infant, he'd been protective of the boy. For no other reason than Muerig had been the first person to ever really smile at him. To look at him as something more than an inconvenient nuisance.

And he'd been the only one Kalder had never lost patience with. Not even when he'd broken Kalder's toys or tattled on him to their parents. Not that Muerig had done it often. Only when their father had cornered him, and Kalder couldn't really blame him for that. Daven Dupree had been a Myrcian renowned for his fierce temper and immense size.

Even seasoned warriors had wet themselves in their father's terrifying presence. Only Kalder had ever stood toe to toe with him, and that had amused his father to no end.

"At least I have one courageous son cut from me fin and bones." He'd often raked a sneer over Kalder's older brothers that would cause hell to rain down on him later for such praise, after his father left them alone. But while they were together, his father's golden eyes would shine bright with pride for him. A rarity he cherished, in spite of the consequences. "You're the one I know will lead our people to glory, and not cower before our enemies. I can depend on you, Kal. You won't flinch or falter. May the gods help us with those milksop brothers of yours at your back."

"Daven!" his mother would chide every time he'd start in on them. "No need to berate your boys so. They're fine warriors—one and all—and will do you proud. You'll see."

But his father had been right. His brothers would scurry from their father's approach, while Kalder would meet him without flinching. Even when he beat him, he'd beg him for more and to hit harder. It'd ever been his contrary nature.

Show no pain. Let no one see me break.

Just like his father.

They said that Daven had died laughing in the face of his enemies as they gutted him on the field of battle. That was how Kalder wanted to go.

Forever strong.

Trying not to think about that, Kalder rubbed his hand over his forehead and focused on his brother. "Are you hungry?"

"Famished."

"Then, I'll get you something." He left him on the bunk, and headed for the galley at the other end of the ship.

Kalder hadn't gone far before he ran into Cameron beneath the cramped decks as she made her way toward the women's quarters.

Awkward silence hung between them while he searched desperately for something to say. This should be easy, given all the conversations he'd had with her in his mind during the weeks they'd been apart. All he'd done was dream of her while he'd been in hell.

Dreams of her, alone, had kept him sane. Had given him comfort in the utter madness of their bitterest torment. She was the only succor he'd known during their cruelest punishments. And the sole thing about this world that he'd missed. He'd called himself all kinds of a fool for that weakness. Yet he couldn't help it.

Cameron had become his one and only talisman for sanity.

All he had to do was remember the way she looked at him—as she did right now—and they could do their worst to his body. None of it mattered. None of it compared to these feelings she stirred within him. For in her eyes, he was worthy.

Heroic.

Desired and special.

When she looked at him, she didn't see a sorry piece of shit. And that was why he couldn't embrace her. Why he dared not ever sully her with his touch. Because she was such a fine and decent noble lady and not meant for the grubby likes of him.

With a kind and gentle smile, she held her hand out toward him and opened it. " 'Tis your brother's necklace, Mr. Dupree. I'm thinking you'll want to return it to him now that he's back."

Honestly, he'd rather she keep it. Had it been his, he would have insisted. She had so very little that belonged to her personally, and she deserved beautiful things. Things much more valuable than that bit of silver in her palm. 'Twas a pity her brother hadn't provided better for her, as he should. Truth was, it angered him that Paden had forced her to dress as a lad, instead of bathing her in the finest silks and every dainty lace and toiletry that women preferred. Indeed, he'd seen the way her gaze would sometimes linger on Lady Marcelina's gowns. Not with envy, but with aching hunger that said she'd like to have something so feminine to call her own.

Or how her hand would idly play with the fine velvet of Belle's and Sancha's gowns whenever they stood close to her. Though Cameron never said a word in complaint or jealousy, it was obvious that she liked such luxuries and would love to have them on her own body. And he would like very much to see her dressed in such finery. No doubt she'd outshine them all with her graceful beauty.

Yet that necklace had been sacred to Muerig, so he was honor-bound to see it back to his brother. "Thank you."

Her cheeks turned a bright pink as she stepped nearer to him and set the piece in his hand. The heat of her flesh seared him and sent a fissure up his arm that electrified his body and left him hard and aching with a needful hunger, especially when her sweet scent filled his senses.

Cameron gave him that sweet, precious smile that was uniquely hers. Damn, but she had a way of looking at him that was indefinable. Her hand lingered on his. "I missed you, Mr. Dupree. Glad I am to have you back, safe and sound, where you belong."

"I'm sure he's glad to be back."

He glanced past her shoulder to see her brother eyeing them again with his condemning censure, and he wanted to punch the irritating bastard for it. As if Paden judged his sister and found her lacking in morals or character. And that made his anger rise. Not so much that Paden was suspicious of him—he had every right to be, as Kalder's thoughts were truly salacious in nature where the lady was concerned. He wouldn't deny how much she tempted him. But Paden should never doubt the virtue of a woman as refined and noble, as damnably decent, as Cameron.

So, in deference to her, he decided to set the bastard back a bit with his words, instead of his fists. "Not really. Rather, I like being beat upon. Makes me feel alive. Keeps the circulation going. You know?"

Cameron choked on a laugh at Paden's shocked expression over Kalder's unexpected retort. That was the one thing about the Myrcian. He seldom reacted the way anyone anticipated.

In *any* given situation.

And with that, he pushed his way past them. "If you'll excuse me, I have me brother to see to."

Cameron's heart sank at the curtness of his tone and the underlying hurt it betrayed. And it angered her that her own brother had caused it.

"You shouldn't antagonize him so, Paddy. Especially given what we owe him."

"I don't care for the way he looks at you."

How odd, given that she craved it. Cherished it, even. Especially since Kalder was the only man who'd ever seemed to notice that she was a woman and not a mate or ugly hag. "And I'm a grown woman, not a child."

"You're still answerable to me."

Those words set fire to her temper and caused her to laugh in his face that he'd dare to say such to her, as if he were her lord and master. "I answer to no man, Patrick Jack. You'd best be getting your head on straight there, boyo. Make no mistake about it. You went out to sea long ago, gallivanting about what with no cares of home, and left me behind to fend for meself. If you wanted to keep me under your boot heel, you shouldn't have abandoned me in Williamsburg to me own means. So don't think for one heartbeat that you're going to come back now and put a saddle on me like some old nag you be owning and left stabled up with your neighbors waiting patiently for your return. Not going to happen, brother dearest."

"What are you saying?"

"I'm saying what I'm saying. And you'd best be turning your ears to hear every syllable of it."

He stiffened as fury darkened his cheeks and turned his blue eyes icy. "And I'm the one what loves you, Cameron Amelia Maire Jack. Been looking after you the whole of our lives. There's never been a day in your entire existence when me morning hasn't started with your welfare coming up as the first thought on me mind and your safekeeping being the prayer I whisper before sleep wrestles me into oblivion. So don't you be taking that shrewish tone now and giving me none of your impertinence in this matter. You think that fish-man loves you? Think again. I know his type. 'Deed I do. All he sees is a fertile, unplowed field he wants to sow and leave planted with his seed as soon as he can. And I'll be the one what's left to dry your tears while he's off on his merry way with another, and you're long forgotten to him."

Those words stung deep. Yet not nearly for their indictment against Kalder's character so much as for her brother's low opinion of her intelligence. Or her feminine wiles. "Mayhap what you say is true, but few are the knaves what'll let their own throats be cut open for a mere piece of trim. Virgin, fertile, or other. Believe me, brother,

I'm not that big a fool and I'm under no delusion to think meself so precious as all that, to any man. Even you. Especially a maid a man has yet to taste, never mind plow. I know *your* breed better than that. Ain't no woman held in such high regard but the most beautiful of our kind, and me looking glass don't lie whenever I care to look at it. I know exactly who and what I am, and what me true value is. Not a great beauty by any measure or quaffing of beer. Seldom am I even passable. And God knows I don't lactate ale, nor are the walls of me womb lined in gold. So have no fear that I be blinded by any sort of guile on his part or any other species of male. Me head has never been turned by any man's honeyed words. But I do know what I owe that man and what he sacrificed for me when he had no reason to, and for that I am grateful, and will always be so."

And with that said, she stepped around her brother and headed topside to put distance between them before she spoke words toward *his* character that couldn't be undone. Or worse, slapped him for the pain he caused her at the reminder that she wasn't a comely lass. She knew well enough that she didn't inspire men to forget themselves around her.

Rather, she inspired them to run for the door or into the arms of a more fetching bosom.

It was why she was virgin still, even though she'd worked in a tavern with disreputable rakes and blackguards. Why she was able to pass herself off so easily as a man. She wasn't the type of woman men wrote sonnets for or that inspired them to forget themselves, not even when they were neck-deep into their cups.

Sadly, she'd had far more women come after her, thinking her a man of prospect, than men trying to get into her knickers. Even some of the boys in her tavern had had a better record of men chasing after them than she had, and that was truly a blow to her ego.

Aye, Cameron Jack wasn't a head-turner in any sense of the word.

Never had been. Never would be.

But Kalder . . .

He was exceptional. There wasn't a woman on board this ship what wouldn't agree.

And a few of the men, too, for that matter. He had a backside for days. If ever a muse were born to be male, it would bear his face.

Every part of him was the perfection of male beauty. Masculine and strong, he rippled with refined grace and confidence. With swagger.

And that lyrical accent of his . . .

She could listen to it all day long. He could read a ship's manifest and make it sound like poetry. Never mind the way his voice carried whenever he hummed or sang in a low tone the ditties of the crew.

If only she were more comely.

Damn you, Paden! Damn your rotten hide straight to the Locker and then some!

"Are you all right, Miss Cameron?"

She paused at the other glorious accent that never failed to lift her spirits. Only this one was sweet and motherly.

Belle jumped down from the mast rigging to land beside her on the deck.

Cameron scowled at her nimble grace. "How is it you do that, woman, without breaking your neck or leg?"

Belle laughed. As a rigger, she was one of the best they had among the crew. "I think nothing of it. It's like breathing. You should try it sometime."

Cameron wrinkled her nose as she imagined herself tripping and falling to her death—and that while merely walking over the regular decks. "Nay. You've never seen me sorry attempts at sewing. I'd just tangle the sails and then the captain would have me . . ." Her words trailed off as she glanced up and a weird whispering sounded in her ears. Like rushing fire. Her hair fell loose from its queue and turned stark white at the same time as her wings unfurled from her back.

Writhing from the unexpected attack, she cried out in pain. Normally whenever the Seraphim blood took over, it didn't hurt, but this was excruciating. Agonizing. It felt as if the flames of hell were engulfing her.

Worse, she could hear the screams of the damned begging for mercy. The voices of those torturing them with their sins, reminding them of the evils they'd done. Loudest of all were the demons who taunted them, and the ones after more victims, promising them the world if they'd sell out their souls.

It was more than she could take. Pressing her balled fists to her eyes, she tried to blot the horrific images. She wanted to claw out her eyes to do away with what she saw. What she heard. To stab out her eardrums. Anything to make it stop.

Someone close by screamed and screamed.

Suddenly, someone held her in strong arms and rocked her like a babe with her head tucked beneath his chin while he stroked her hair. His heartbeat pounded against her cheek, soothing her and blotting out the voices as he hummed a soothing lullaby in a language she'd never heard before. Closing her eyes, she breathed in the comforting scent of sea brine and warm leather that was uniquely Kalder.

Cameron trembled at the thought of how they must appear. Her in her Seraph form, white wings draped limply over the wooden deck while she lay sprawled in Kalder's lap.

It was scandalous.

But he said not a word as he held her while the others stood in a circle around them. Even the water witch, Strixa, was there in her human form.

"Are you better, poppet?" Kalder asked in the gentlest of tones.

"Who was screaming?"

"You were."

Stunned, she lifted her head to look up at him for clarification. "W-w-what?"

"Aye." He cupped her face in his warm hand and brushed his thumb over her chin. "You said they were tearing you apart."

"I don't understand. Are we under attack?"

Kalder shook his head, then looked over to Thorn, who'd also come out to stare at her. "Why is she in this form while her brother didn't change at all?"

Thorn's features paled. "I'm not sure you're going to like the answer. Most of all I pray I'm wrong."

"What do you mean?" Kalder had yet to loosen his grip on her.

"There's only one reason I can think for any of this." Thorn glanced over to the captain. "And you can correct me if you think I'm wrong. You know Vine better than I do. But it suddenly occurs to me why she'd free Kalder's brother and send him here. If I had to lay odds, I'd say it was Muerig's blood she fed to the Jacks, and a binding spell that holds them here. One that won't let them both stay on this side of the veil."

Thorn passed a stern, harsh look to Kalder. "I'm going to bet, Mr. Dupree, that she will require you to make a choice on who to send back to her. Miss Jack or your brother."

6

Kalder glared at Thorn as fury filled him. "I can't make that choice!"

How could he send either his brother or Cameron to suffer at the hands of Vine?

Thorn sighed. "I know, lad. She's the worst sort of bitching-troll to ever lay a trap, and you fell right into her snare. For that, I am sorry. Misery most foul is what she peddles as her stock-in-trade. And you are her primary fare."

Paden cursed under his breath. "This is all my

fault. She'd have never known about Cameron had I not fallen into her hands."

Thorn laughed. "Evil comes for us all. Sooner rather than later. Doesn't matter how or what we do. None are immune. So get off the cross, brother. Someone needs the wood."

"He's right about that." Devyl let out a fierce sigh. "The gates are going down. The Malachai is rising. Vine is menstruating—"

"Du!" Mara snapped fiercely at her husband. "I can't believe you just said that!"

"She's your sister. Are you going to deny it?"

"Wintering isn't the same as *that*."

"So say you. Having been married to the witch, I beg to differ. Never could I tell the difference between them. Both conditions lead to the same degree of bitchiness and infestation. Besides, she's the opposite to most women. She's only kind five days of the month . . . if that."

Rolling her eyes, Mara cleared her throat and turned back toward Paden. "At any rate, what my husband is attempting to say poorly is that you don't shoulder any of the blame. My sister's moods are her own, and there's none to blame for them, except Vine. Same for the Malachai. The world's been topsy-turvy since the gates fractured. It's why we've all been brought together in this quest."

Thorn nodded in agreement. "I've been chasing the devil since before your ancestors were born. And before that, I led my army for him. The one thing I can tell you is that sooner or later, when you dance with darkness, you will succumb to it."

"So it's all me own fault?" Kalder's tone was icy and lethal.

"Not saying that, either. This isn't about blame. It's about survival. I didn't risk what I've risked or suffer what I have to see any of you go down without a fight. You want to keep them both and I want to ruin Vine's day. I say it's time we win one. Who's with me?"

Rather than rally, the crew began to grumble.

Thorn glanced about as if surprised by their reaction. "Really? No one's going to rise to my challenge?"

Devyl scoffed. "You never were much to rally your forces. Only threaten them, as I recall. Step back and let those of us with experience do the leading before you cause a mutiny, mate."

"I beg your pardon. You did far more threatening than I ever did. . . . And killing, too, as I recall. Not to mention, you drank the blood of *your* troops who didn't follow your orders."

His gaze unrepentant, Devyl grinned. "Kept them in line, you mean."

Thorn rolled his eyes.

Ignoring him, Devyl turned toward the Deadmen. "The bitch wants our blood. More than that, she wants the blood kin of our brother now that he's earned his freedom. We let her have him and what he cares about, and she'll be after the lot of us, twice as hard. Time we show her and the Cimmerian forces they can't take what we love. Not on our watch. And not without a fight so brutal the bards will be writing tales of it for centuries to come. We set them back hard on their heels with a lesson that rings not just in their ears, but so deep in their bones that their ancestors feel it. You with me, lads?"

This time, the crew shouted in agreement.

Thorn glanced at Cameron with a stern scowl. "How does he do that?"

It was Will who answered. "Captain speaks Deadman. You speak Stupidity, my lord. Big difference."

And still Cameron remained in her Seraph's body while Paden stayed human. That alone raised chills on her skin. What evil was afoot to cause such? It made no sense and defied everything they knew. Everything they'd been told.

"Why am I like this?" she asked Thorn.

"I don't know. Truly, I don't. Even if she fed you the blood, this makes no sense."

Cameron didn't miss the concern that Thorn attempted to hide behind that steeled expression. Which made her even more nervous. What had they done to her?

"I'll keep you safe, Cammy."

Kalder scoffed at Paden's offer. "Seems to me, you were the one what got her into this, mate. Perhaps you should step aside before you get her killed."

"And you need to mind your own business. She's me kin, not yours."

"Nor is she some poppet for the two of you to be fighting over." Sancha elbowed them apart and lifted Cameron to her feet. "Woman's got a mind of her own. Don't you two be forgetting that, with yer male cocks hanging out. Therefore, we'll be the ones what protect her from harm."

Before Cameron could comment, Valynda coiled her arm through Cameron's right elbow while Belle took her left bicep, and the two of them whisked her away from the men, and escorted her from the deck to their quarters, where Janice waited with a knowing smirk.

The Trini Dark-Huntress tsked as soon as she saw them. "I

heard the whole of it through the planks. Woke me from me sleep, it did. Damn shame, all of it."

Sancha shut the door behind them, then pulled her dark wig from her hair to free her snow-white tresses. Something she wore only because she hated the hair that had faded with the death of her daughter and served as a reminder of her lost child. "Can you believe the nerve of them, telling you what to think?"

"Aye," they said in unison.

Valynda let out a deep sigh. "Well I, for one, won't see her pushed about by them. Not after what such male fighting cost me." She held her straw hands up in hopeless despair. The anguish in her glassy eyes was tangible and brought a lump to Cameron's throat as she felt for the poor woman and her plight. "Why do they treat us so?"

"Fear." Belle crossed her arms over her chest as she jerked her chin toward the porthole. "They know the harshness of this world and what waits to devour us all. Like a child with a cherished toy, they seek to hang on to what comforts them, never realizing how much it harms us to be clutched and shoved into the darkness of their protection. As mothers, we know that sometimes, even though it pains us to do so, we have to watch what we love be harmed in order to learn harsh lessons so that they can grow—like a child that has to skin its knee when learning to run. Part of loving someone is letting go so that they can be happy. We are trained for it. They're not."

Belle stepped closer to Cameron. "When first the captain freed Kalder from his damnation to join our crew, I thought him mad for the choice."

That shocked her. "Why?"

"There's a burning hatred inside that boy so intense, it's like a living, breathing creature waiting to rise up and devour everything in its path. When first I encountered it, I thought it directed at the world. Only after getting to know him, I realized it's not the world he hates. Rather, 'tis himself."

Pouring herself a drink, Sancha nodded. "Like many of us, he's on a path of self-obliteration."

Cameron knew Sancha spoke from her heart, because she blamed herself for her young daughter's death at the hands of her callous husband while she'd been out carousing with her friends. To this day, the woman had no peace from the guilt and sought to drown it all in as much rum as she could manage. Especially since she'd murdered her husband over the fact that he'd shaken her child to death simply for crying over her absentee mother.

No one knew the source of Belle's darkness. They could only sense it. That sadness that hovered behind her eyes as a constant companion.

The same with Janice. They kept their pain secluded and private as if too afraid to let it out, for fear that the mere mention of it could undo them. It pained Cameron that they wouldn't share with them. For they knew better than to judge. There wasn't a soul on this ship who hadn't been through it. Phantom wretches all.

Besides, such wasn't in her heart. She'd seen the truth of these women and she loved them regardless of their pasts. Regardless of whatever crimes had caused their damnation. Or perhaps she loved them because those pasts had made them who they are, and what they had become because of it.

Cameron . . .

She went ramrod stiff at the strange voice in her ear. A husky deep tone unlike anything she'd ever heard before. Neither male nor female, it was a summons that was almost impossible to resist.

Blinking, she glanced to the others to see that none of them had heard it. Or if they had, they gave no clue. Rather, they continued chatting amongst each other, oblivious to the call that came for her ears only.

Unnerved and spooked, Cameron tried to ignore it.

That was easier said than done. The intensity of the voice picked up volume. It grew in intensity. Louder and louder. A thumping heartbeat that resonated through her entire being.

Belle turned to face her, then gaped. "Child . . ."

"What?"

"Holy mother of God!" Janice crossed herself.

As did Sancha and Valynda, who stared on wordlessly.

Taking their panic as her own, Cameron turned about, trying to understand what had them so concerned. "What is it?"

Belle dragged her toward the small looking glass in the corner that they used to dress their hair. There, in the dim light, Cameron saw what had them all pale and trembling.

Her hair was no longer white.

It was now silvery and it shimmered in the shadows.

Holy of mother of God, indeed!

MICHAEL'S
KEY

7

Kalder left Muerig to rest on the bunk and returned the soiled dishes to the galley. Yet even so, he couldn't shake the peculiar feeling he had deep in his gullet that something wasn't quite right. It didn't matter that the moon appeared perfect in the sky above, or that the crew acted as normal as they could while they went about their business. Or that nothing seemed out of the ordinary.

His unsettled feeling was undeniable.

You're being ridiculous.

He was free. His brother was alive again and Cameron was back where she belonged. What more could he ask for?

And all the while Thorn's warning about him having to choose between them stayed on his mind like some drunken bloke who could only remember a single stanza of one song—and even then it was with the incorrect words. Driving him to madness because he knew the truth of what the demon had warned. It was just the sort of treachery the fey bitch would play on him as punishment.

Nothing in his life had ever come easy or without the harshest price imaginable. It was why he'd settled for being a rake and a scoundrel, and nothing more.

Hard to trip and fall from grace when you lived your entire life on your belly, in the gutter. He'd learned to keep his head down and stay out of the line of fire of his ever-feuding family. Especially after his father's death. No need to declare a side when his brothers shifted their alliances faster than the ocean tide reversed direction. One moment, he'd been protecting Darcel's back, only to find himself Darcel's enemy when Darcel aligned himself to Varice, and they both turned against *him* because he'd gone against Varice on Darcel's behalf. All this when just hours before the two of them had been mortal enemies, vowing to see each other in their graves. 'Twas enough to make his head ache and stomach heave.

Ever the hated asshole—that was his one true role in his family. No matter what he did—even if he stayed out of their never-ending drama—he came up the short for it.

Only Muerig had been immune from their brothers' feral and mutinous wraths, and that only because their mother protected him.

As the youngest, he'd held a special place in her heart that the rest of them had never quite managed.

God knew she'd never spared Kalder a single moment of her hatred or blistering tongue. For whatever reason, she'd borne a special grudge against him from the moment he'd drawn his first breath and had held it against him the whole of his life.

Don't think about it.

There was nothing to be done for it. All that was long ago. Centuries past. This was a different time and place. He was a different man now.

Different creature entirely.

One who knew his place, and was comfortable with the fact that he was alone in this world and wanted nothing from anyone. Ever. Not even Cameron. He meant it. In spite of what his other regions might be thinking and wanting.

Determined to stay in control of his mutinous body, he made his way topside, where he found Sallie repairing a sail that had frayed a bit.

Kalder paused to watch the expert way the older man's hands worked with the rough material. Like his own treacherous body that cared not a whit what his brain told it to think, they appeared to have a life of their own. And their graceful movement was a stark contrast to the gruff sailor's appearance.

But then Absalon Lucas, or Sallie as they called him, was one of the few members of the crew who'd actually been a sailor before Devyl and Thorn had recruited him for this madness. And his expertise was more than evident, even as he scratched at his scraggly, graying beard.

"How did you get crossed up with a sorcerer, anyway?" The question was out before Kalder could stop it. Oddly enough, he'd never thought to ask it before this.

Sallie paused to look up at him. "Interesting way to open up a conversation there, Mr. Dupree. No finessing at all. Just jump right to it, do you?"

Kalder shrugged. "Never been one to mince words."

He tugged at the ropes to test them. "Makes two of us." Sallie pulled his rum bottle from the waistband of his breeches and held it out to Kalder.

He took it, thinking it was the one that held the man's soul. Until he realized it was a much smaller bottle, and that Sal was offering him a drink. Laughing, he obliged himself, then returned it to the strange middle-aged man.

Sallie pulled a kerchief from his pocket to wipe at his lips before he took a drink himself.

With a sigh, he savored the fiery liquid then put a keen squint to Kalder's form. Not censuring, just measuring. Comparing. "You know, Mr. Dupree, I'm a fine, handsome man in me real body, I am. Give even a dandy like you a run for the folderol skirts, I would. And like you and Will and Bart and the captain, I had even posh birds aplenty who turned their heads any time I entered a room and watched me every move with wanton eyes, they did. Thought nothing of it, I did . . . until it was gone. Damn shame, that. The things you take for granted that leave your company far too soon, mind you. We should all take a minute to appreciate our moments in the sun before they fade bitterly to night."

Kalder didn't comment, as he knew just how right the man was. Life had a nasty habit of turning from kind to vicious on the breath of a breeze. Honestly, he was sick with the unpredictable treachery of the bitch.

She'd bitten him personally one time too many.

"Anyways, so there I was with this comely dainty vixen, just minding a bit of me business with her as most men would. Drinking me fill of her lips and taking a bit too much freedom with her ample charms, when all of a sudden her father shows up, a bit vexed and chafing over me dalliance with his daughter, as any good father would be. He hit me and I hit him. Some harsh words we exchanged. And an insult I never should have said about his daughter. Next thing I knows, I was turned into this short, hideous thing you see before you now, and me soul was handed to me with a warning about attacking any man e'er again." Sallie shook his head as he fidgeted with the bottle that did hold his soul.

"That how you died, then?"

Sallie's eyes turned dark and grim. "Nay, lad. What soft, for that, I killed meself to escape the nightmare what was me life thereafter. Couldn't stand the pain of it all. But you see, before the final act that damned me eternally, I'd been a mercenary bastard. That was the deed what cost me the soul dearest. For I'd wandered for years, murdering for gold, without conscience. Thought to battle meself into Valhalla, I did. Forgot that me mother was just Christian and vindictive enough to hex me to both me parents' hells for me wanton and vicious ways. Aye, she got the last word on that, she did. What with bitter, bitter clarity."

No one could miss the pain in that aged voice. It branded Sallie's soul as deep as the scars that marred Kalder's, and he hated that he'd dug into the man's past wounds.

"Sorry, Sallie. I didn't mean to pry."

He shrugged with a nonchalance Kalder was sure was for his benefit only. " 'Tis what it is, lad. When you go a-viking, you know the consequences of your actions. Especially when you're raised by Jutes."

Perhaps . . . But then Kalder hadn't known many Jutes in his day.

Sallie paused to give him a gimlet stare. "So what's really on your mind, son?"

"How do you mean?"

"We've been on this ship for months. Never once have you shown so much interest in me, or any other. Been keeping to yourself, you have. Saying little as possible to anyone—not that that's a bad thing, mind you. Especially what with this misbegotten crew, and all the secrets what's kept here. But now you have your brother with you and instead of passing time with him who you've missed so dearly, you're out here wasting the night with me? Mite peculiar it is, if you ask me. Can't help but wonder why this sudden and critical interest in me past that has a burning hole in your patience, laddie."

Kalder snorted. Sallie was far too astute, and there was no need in keeping another secret when it was clear the older man already knew the answer. "A peculiar feeling in me gut, Mr. Lucas. That is all, and nothing more."

"Sounds like you been eating some of Cookie's stew, then. That'd give anyone a peculiar feeling in the gut, 'specially what with these rocky seas we're having. You're lucky you're not tossing it all overboard."

Kalder laughed at a very true statement.

An ill wind blows ill things.

His humor died as he recalled one of his mother's favored sayings. It was something she whispered often in his father's court. Most often because she was the source of the bad tidings and maleficence.

And his father had reacted swiftly and with an equal measure of rancor. *Stop that, Bron! You'll be calling down bad humor upon us. The universe has ears and it listens to the words you speak. Careful what you say, woman! Hex us and I'll see that you pay for it with your tongue! And your life!*

His father had believed that wholeheartedly. As a boy, Kalder had thought it the greatest superstition.

Now, as a man, he wasn't so sure. Like his father, he'd seen a few things that made him wonder if perhaps the universe didn't listen and set into motion the very things that people spoke out loud.

The very things their minds whispered in fear.

Almost as if the universe was sick that way and took perverse pleasure in manifesting the very things that terrified people the most.

There was whisper magick, no doubt. Powerful and undeniable. This ship was proof of that.

As was Sallie's fate.

His own. The captain, and all those who lived here. So why was it so hard for him to believe in his father's proclamation?

But then, he knew. And it was something he really didn't want to face. Because at the end of the day, the thought of the past coming back to harm him was the most terrifying thing he could imagine, indeed.

The universe shouldn't have ears.

It shouldn't be listening. And it damn sure shouldn't be vindictive or spiteful.

Yet what if it actually was?

What if it could?

That thought drew his stomach even tighter and made him want to heave.

Cameron froze as she met Kalder in the cramped hull. His eyes widened as he took in her new pale hair color.

"Are you all right?"

She felt the heat in her cheeks rise the moment he reached to touch its awkward paleness. Clearing her throat, she quickly explained before he asked about the matter. "We've no idea what caused it to do this. But at least I finally got me wings to recede."

Guilt simmered in his steely eyes. "If I'm the cause, Miss Jack—"

She shook her head to cut off his words at the guilt his tone betrayed. He had nothing to feel bad about, and she couldn't stand the thought of him suffering for it. "You're the only reason I'm here, Mr. Dupree. Make no mistakes about that. Or apologies, either. I won't have it." Smiling, she took his hand into hers. The strength of that one member was absolute and undeniable. He was a creature of utter brutality. Paden hadn't been mistaken about that, and she knew it for a fact.

Still, he was also a creature of compassion. One who never hesitated to protect what he cared about.

"I don't know why you did what you did for me and me brother,

Mr. Dupree, but I can't thank you enough, and I'll never forget that kindness."

Kalder couldn't think straight as her fingers danced idly across the flesh of his palm. Most likely, she thought nothing of the gesture. A simple act of friendship or nervousness that was common in her world. But in his, it was a rarity to be touched without pain. To be offered even this small token of kindness. It was why he'd always been partial to human women. They liked such trivial gestures of affection, even when there was no real feeling behind them.

At least that was true of strumpets.

Ladies like Cameron and Sancha, Belle and Janice and Valynda, Elyzabel, and Mara . . .

They were a different breed. Ladies placed a great deal of meaning behind the slightest bit of touching. A man didn't lightly caress one.

Kissing was off-limits completely.

A harsh lesson learned his first day on dry land, when his father had demanded a public beating over a stolen kiss that would have meant nothing in the underwater city where he'd been raised. That degradation and mockery still rang in his ears. Barely fifteen, he'd known nothing of the human world and had been captivated by the blond lady whose flaxen locks had been unlike anything he'd ever seen in Wyñeria, where they were all dark-haired.

More than that, the human woman had smelled of sunshine. So to kiss her had seemed the most natural thing for him to do.

To share breath in Wyñeria was the highest form of a compliment.

In the world of humanity, it was a gross insult that had resulted in first the lady slapping him, then shrieking in outrage.

Stunned, he'd looked to his older brothers, who'd laughed at his mistake. The bastards had failed to warn him about human customs, and instead had been the first to tell their father of his innocent transgression.

Varice had immediately stepped forward with a dubious smile. "Let me be the one to whip him, Father. 'Tis a lesson I'm sure he'll never forget."

A promise his brother had well delivered on.

It was why Kalder didn't understand Cameron's kindness toward him now. It was such a foreign concept for him.

While he was used to loose women throwing themselves at him anytime he ventured near one, women of standing tended to stay away because they knew nothing of his social status. All they saw was a dark, mysterious loner who avoided others. An intriguing puzzle they wanted to explore—at least for a few hours, until he'd sated them. As a rule, those women thought him a ruffian of low character and little prospect.

The truth was, his father had been a warlord and king who ruled a vast empire of immense wealth. Had his mother not killed him, he would have stood to inherit the southern borderlands and lived a life of privilege that would make the kings of England, France, and Spain weep with jealousy. Never mind what his brothers had taken.

But Kalder had never cared about such things. Perhaps because he'd been raised with servants fawning over his every frown and seeking to please him, and more wealth than anyone could ever spend. It held no value whatsoever.

Nay, the only things he'd ever craved had been the most elusive and precious of all.

Friendship. Loyalty.

Kind words.

And, most of all, the look on Cameron's face as she stared up at him right now.

It humbled *him*, the son of a king. More so because she had no idea who and what he really was. Where he came from. She knew nothing about his past at all. To her, he was just another sailor. Same as Sallie or Roach or Simon. A commoner no better than the bilge water they pumped from the hold.

Yet she treated them all with the same deference she would show a king or emperor. Total kindness and open friendship and warmth. Never in his life had he met her equal.

In the clothes of a common, poor man, she was a grand lady in every sense of the word. And while she might not know his origins, she knew him better than anyone ever had.

Because she alone actually saw him.

Cameron cleared her throat nervously. "Are you going to say anything, Mr. Dupree? Or just continue to stare at me with that unnerving intensity?"

He softened his gaze and fought against the urge to laugh at her chiding tone. "I can't seem to help meself, Miss Jack. Your beauty and grace always leave me awestruck."

She let out an adorable scoff. "You flatter me, sir."

"Only if the truth be flattery."

And still doubt shone in the crystal depths of her eyes, toying with him and making him harder than a full-on caress could. He'd never understand how she could seduce him so easily when she didn't even try for it. Yet there was no denying the way he craved her every time she came near. It was madness, truly. Recklessness of the highest magnitude. And yet he was helpless before her.

She wrinkled her nose. "You're the only one who thinks it, Mr. Dupree, I assure you."

He savored the scent of her hair on the breeze as it stirred him even more. "Then the rest are fools not to see what's before them. I can't imagine how any could miss seeing the gem that is uniquely you."

Cameron bit her lip at words that brought a lump to her chest. More than that was the hot look in his beautiful, pale eyes that made her throat go dry and her heart pick up its pace. Goodness, it was difficult to be near him whenever he teased her so.

But she knew it was just his way and he meant nothing by it.

How could he?

So she sought to make light of it and chase him away. "Do you always charm women like this?"

Kalder leaned down as if to impart a secret to her. "How can I when I seldom speak to any?"

He had a point.

More than that . . . the warmth of his breath fell against her skin and sent chills over her entire body. The contradictory sensation titillated her, and left her limbs shaking and weak.

Seeking some smidgeon of sanity, she forced herself to any topic other than those delectable lips that hovered far too close to her own. "Why did you rescue me?"

"Because I more than earned me damnation, Miss Jack. You

didn't. It wasn't right that you should suffer when you'd done nothing to be punished for."

How strange that those words wrought disappointment in her breast. They should bring her happiness. Yet a part of her had wanted something else. She wasn't quite sure what, but there was no denying that in her heart, his answer hurt. "Is that the only reason?"

"Honestly?"

She swallowed in expectation before she nodded. "I prefer it to a lie."

"Then nay, 'tis not the only reason I saved you, for I'm a much more selfish bastard than that. Thinking of others has never come easily for me."

Her heart quickened again as her mind went to a place it shouldn't and she warned herself against hoping for something that was ridiculous and foolish. Something that could only lead her to more hurt and disappointment. Still, she couldn't help wanting the impossible. Dreaming of things she knew she didn't deserve. Things that were beyond her reach. Things not meant for lowly tavern wenches who'd been kicked down by life since the hour of their births.

"Why then would you risk yourself for me?"

Kalder hesitated as every last vestige of decency inside his vacant and hollow soul screamed for him to walk away and leave her in peace. To do what was right and not taint her by words or actions.

It was what he *should* do.

But never once in his life had he done what he *ought* to do. Never once had he lived his life by anyone's expectations or societal rules. Such things weren't in him.

Now he was too old to change his ways.

Fuck it . . .

His most commonly uttered phrase and thought before making any life-altering decision.

And with that, he lowered his lips to hers and tasted the one thing he'd been craving above all. The one thing he'd never known. Not even as a child.

Pure, sweet innocence.

More than that, Cameron's unique flavor that was sweeter than any bit of cake or heaven. Her warmth that fed a part of his soul he hadn't even known was cold until she'd touched it and made it thrive. It was like that summer day as a boy when he'd first discovered his legs, and had learned to run. Before that, he hadn't missed what he'd never known.

How could he?

Yet once he'd learned to run, he'd needed that freedom with a madness that still coursed through his blood like wildfire. It was as intrinsic as breathing.

And a part of him needed her that way.

Aye, this was crazy. But then so was he. He'd died for her, for no real good reason, other than he'd wanted her to live more than he'd craved it for himself. Against all common sense, really. Against his true, surly, contrary nature.

Was it so much to ask for this one wee bit of comfort, when nothing else in his screwed-up life made sense?

Cameron trembled as she felt Kalder's tongue sweep against her own. She'd never tasted a man's passion before. Never known a man's embrace other than that of family. While she'd suspected

Kalder was well experienced, this left no doubt to the extent of said expertise. He was a master of the craft and she was helpless in the face of the overwhelming desire that raced through her entire being.

Every part of her turned hot and molten. Alive. Breathless, she wrapped her arms around his shoulders and delighted in the way his muscles bunched beneath her hands in a wicked symphony.

When he finally pulled away, they stood nose to nose so that he could stare down with that piercing steel-gray gaze that defied her best attempt to define its true stormy color.

A teasing grin spread across his face as he cupped her cheek and placed a much more sedate kiss to her lips. "Well now, me *phearse*, not sure what it says about either of us that me kiss turned your hair back to its normal hue. Think I'll take it as a good sign, though."

Gasping, Cameron looked down to verify that he was right. Her hair was again its true chestnut shade. "How is that possible?"

"Not sure. Me guess is that me evil ways rubbed off on you and took away some of your pure Seraph blood from you."

She scoffed at his reasoning. "Doubtful."

"You think not? I've corrupted . . . well, I can't really say *better* souls than yours, as I've never met your equal in me life, but they were decent enough before they took up company with me sorry hide."

She shook her head at him and his deprecating humor. "No one can be tempted to anything that isn't already in them. You can trust me to that. Good or bad. There are lines that no one will cross, no matter the seduction."

Sadness returned to his gaze. "Wish I could believe that, me *phearse*. But too often I've seen much proof to the contrary."

"And I respectfully disagree, Mr. Dupree." She folded her arms over her chest, then cocked her head to scowl at him. "By the way, what is that, that you keep calling me?"

"What? *Phearse*?"

"Aye. 'Tis a term I've never heard before."

That wicked grin returned to tease her. "It's Myrcian. Our term for our queens. The word means a ferocious wise woman or counselor."

His words caught her off guard. "Why would you call me that?"

" 'Tis how I see you, me lady. For that's what you are to me."

She would think he was using it to mock her, but there was only sincerity in his gaze. Even so, she found it impossible to believe that a man like him would see her as someone so special. "I'm not so fierce."

"You think not? A woman who crosses an ocean alone to track down her errant brother and wrestle him from the hands of the devil himself to get him back alive? How is that anything else?"

"Well, when you put it that way . . . it sounds more akin to stupid, if you ask me."

He laughed. "I would never say such about you."

Suddenly, they heard the faint strains of music drifting through the boards.

Cameron grinned as she recognized the familiar voices that began to accompany it. "Sounds like Roach and Will found their fiddle and flute."

"And Kat his drum."

From the distant sounds of it, they were playing a lively jig. The kind her parents used to play to entertain her and her brother when they were children.

Kalder didn't miss the longing in her eyes as she savored the strands. "Would you like to dance, Miss Jack?"

His offer surprised her. For some reason, she wouldn't have thought him the sort of male who liked to partake of such things. "Are you obliged for it?"

He shrugged. "Well, it is 'All for Me Grog,' after all. You've got to dance to *that*. The gods might rise up from below and strike us down if we don't. Only thing more demanding of our respect would be 'Whiskey in the Jar.'"

Biting her lip in sudden enthusiasm, she couldn't resist his offer. "Well, I am Irish and French, and raised up in taverns and inns. There be nothing more I love to pass me time with than dance and music."

Before she could blink, he led her up to the deck, where the others had already begun their gaiety that they'd oft break into for no apparent reason whatsoever. It sprang up as regularly and unexpectedly as crew fights and vicious preternatural attacks.

Cameron wasn't sure why. Perhaps because they were a crew of Deadmen who appreciated the brevity of life, or because, having been betrayed by those closest to them, they knew to appreciate what little happiness could be found in something as simple as a song. Whatever it was, the crew never failed to play as hard as they fought. To laugh as deeply as they brawled.

And the sight of their merriment made her own heart light.

Elyzabel and William were already dancing together while Kat played his drum in time to Will's fiddle and Roach's flute. Meanwhile, Simon and Sallie sang the tune in a harmonized round that was quickly being taken up by the others as they swapped drinks and laughter.

Kalder turned her around with an unexpected grace and expertise before he led her into a flawless jig. Her jaw went slack as she watched him keeping pace with her. If she didn't know better, she'd swear the man was as Irish as her father had been. He didn't miss or hesitate at a single step.

"You've been keeping talents hidden there, Mr. Dupree."

"I hide a lot of things about meself, Miss Jack."

That was true enough.

As they spun about the deck, Cameron froze at the sight of Paden and the fury in his eyes while he glared utter hatred for Kalder. It sucked every last bit of humor from her.

The moment he caught sight of the blistering venom, Kalder let out a tired sigh and stopped their dance. He straightened his clothes with a sharp tug then cleared his throat. "Thank you for the dance, Miss Jack. I should get back to me brother, and you should see to yours before I give in to me urge to beat him for that undeserved glower."

Fury scalded her cheeks as she struggled not to murder her brother for him.

When Kalder started away, she caught his hand in hers. "He's not me father, Kalder. No one controls me mind save me, and I'll not have the likes of Paden or anyone else dictate me life."

He lifted her hand to his lips and placed a tender kiss to her knuckles with a savoring longing that brought an ache to her chest.

"Don't alienate him, me *phearse*. Not for the sorry likes of me or anyone else. Take it from someone who's lost and buried every member of his family. Blood means something, and is particularly precious once it's gone. What you two share is far more special. He is your brother, lass. Better or worse, and all infighting included. This anger between you will pass. Don't trade the solid foundations of the past with him for a future with me that is likely to destroy us both. I have nothing to offer you, but your brother is a good man. He has a home and a business waiting for you in Williamsburg. I have nothing but the ragged clothes on me back and the hammock below, where I sleep."

And with those words spoken, he let go and walked away.

Tears swam in her eyes and choked her as she watched him go. Part of her begged her to run after him and to tell him that none of that mattered. She'd been raised with nothing more than a cold tick mattress in the drafty attic room of the Black Swan Inn in Williamsburg. She wasn't used to finery or better things.

Yet "used to" something didn't mean that she liked it. While she *could* live that way, she didn't *want* to live like that. Not anymore. And she damn sure didn't want to raise her children the way she and Paden had been raised.

Hand to mouth. Watching every farthing. Saving every rag. Praying to hold on for one more day. And to live in fear of dying and leaving her babes as orphans the way she'd been left with Paden.

Nay, she wanted to ensure her children had a decent life. A happy home and full bellies. With someone who could watch over them should something happen to her and their da. Give them plenty to sup on, and an actual wardrobe of clothes—at least three dresses for the girls, and three suits for the boys. Proper clothes that weren't frayed and patched at the knees and elbows. Coats not made of old blankets or donated rags.

Two pairs of shoes, and two pairs of stockings. One of cotton for daily wear, and one of fine silk for church.

That was her dream.

She saw it all so clearly. In fine details that were etched along in her mind, cast from years of bitter misery and hunger. Mockery and abuse. Of aching for things she couldn't have, and of doing without.

As the ship's striker, Kalder didn't make the kind of money she needed for that life. And he was right, this was no place to raise a family. Constant danger. Unpredictable weather.

She wanted solid ground beneath her feet, and he was a creature of the sea. It would be unfair to ask him to give up what he was.

A mermaid.

He had to have water in order to live and stay healthy. It was required for his species that he have water the way she needed air to breathe. Which made her wonder, what kind of children would they produce?

Tadpoles?

Minnows?

The very thought chilled her as she realized just how little she understood about him and his people.

You are a fool, Cameron Jack. There is no hope for anything with Mr. Dupree.

"Cameron?"

The sound of her brother's voice rattled her to her bones and set her fury off to an even higher level. "Don't even start, Paden. Mood I'm in, I'm likely to deck you where you stand." She raked him with a hostile glare. "Or worse . . . gut you with me rusted spoon. So I warn you now not to tempt the beast within me that's salivating to use you for the scapegoat of me current distemper. Best you run, big brother . . . run fast. Run hard. Run long."

*P*rince Kalderan?"

Coming out of a sound sleep while he lay curled in his swaying hammock, Kalder froze at the whispered voice in his head. At first he thought it a dream. Or a noise conjured by the creaking sounds of the ship.

Until he heard it again. Only louder this time.

Clearer.

A voice from the past he hadn't heard in so long that it took him several heartbeats to realize it wasn't his imagination. Or some strangeness coughed up from the bowels of his mind.

It was real.

His heart picked up its pace as he threw his covers back from his body, and checked to see that his brother was still slumbering in the bunk beside him. As were most of the crew. Equally asleep, they lay in their bunks and hammocks while the ship swayed quietly on the waves in the wee hours of the night. Only a handful of them were up and about. On watch duty at this hour, they would be scattered about the ship, doing various chores.

Yet he knew he wasn't alone in the darkness of this cramped space. The presence was there and it was demanding.

Licking his lips, Kalder slid out of his hammock and snuck up to the deck to follow . . . well, honestly he wasn't sure what was pulling him toward the port stern. Just a strange sensation in his gut that wouldn't be denied.

One that lured him toward that presence he kept telling himself couldn't be real.

It just couldn't be.

That was his thought until he reached the wooden railing and peered over the side into the dark waters that sloshed against the boat. There in the bright moonlight he saw that which stunned him most of all. A shining glimmer of a form bobbing about that he'd never thought to see again.

"Chthamalus?"

Barely discernible in the inky night waves, the old sea demon grinned up with golden fangs. The color of cold, dark seawater blue, he was a peculiar sight to any who didn't know his breed. Part squid, part barnacle, part humanoid, the Barnaks could shapeshift to blend in with humanity. At least temporarily. Longer if they "preyed" on humans. The only way to tell one of their breed, even in human form, was by the unholy light blue luminescence in their eyes that would shine whenever something bright reflected against their pupils. Otherwise, they were beautiful perfection.

But in this form . . .

Hideous fishlike ghouls not even their mothers could stand to look upon. And yet Kalder had never seen a more beautiful vision—except for Cameron.

Aye, Chthamalus Morro was a sight for sore eyes. Even if his face did look like a dried puffer fish's head stretched tight over a shrunken skull and his ears had more in common with a starfish than a human. He'd take it.

"What are you doing here?"

With his mouth twisted down into a perpetual grimace, Chthamalus breathed from the gills in his neck. "I heard that you had been reborn and were back alive. My place is at your side, my lord. As I vowed to you once. So here I am to serve you as I should and as you need."

That solemn oath of loyalty touched him a lot deeper than it should have. Leave it to his old friend to track him down, even all these centuries later. "I can't accept your oath, Tally. I freed you from the service me father demanded of you. You know that." All of Chthamalus's species had been held in bondage as guardians for their royal family. It'd been something his father had decreed after he'd conquered them.

But Kalder had never believed in holding any species as slaves.

Not that it'd mattered. Within moments of Kalder's birth, Chthamalus had been impressed to serve as his guardian and teacher. A task the lunatic had taken to with zeal—like an old mother hen possessed by the devil. He'd all but sat upon him to hatch.

So the two of them had spent years tussling back and forth for some form of freedom. Tussles Kalder had lost more times than he'd ever won.

"And I have missed you, my lord. Wyñeria isn't the same without you. Indeed, it's terribly boring. Oppressive. Depressive. Disgusting, truly."

He scoffed at those words. "Given that it failed as a civilization centuries ago and me people are all dead, I can well imagine that."

"Nay, Highness. Not dead . . . *Hidden*."

Kalder scowled. "What?"

"'Tis true. King Varice veiled the kingdom after you and Prince Muerig were slain." Tally rose from the waves to slither up the side of the ship so that he could be nearer Kalder's position. He cupped the edges of the railing with his webbed hands so that he could peer around the deck. Then, he looked to the waters below as if fearful of being overheard by something more than the earless water.

Peculiar actions for a fearless creature.

"He's put a price upon your life, Your Highness. He fears you'll return and take the kingdom from him."

Stunned over such ludicrous paranoia, Kalder stared at the demon for several seconds. When he could finally gather his ability to answer that, it was a resounding "What?"

He nodded. "On your return to the living, the veil opened. The king believes you're the one who did it, so that you can invade your homeland and take his power as he did yours. He's gathering his army for it. That's how sure he is that you're returning to take it back."

Kalder's head reeled with this new information. Honestly, he wasn't sure which part of it shocked him most. That his brother had called in dogs to hunt him down, that his brother had killed him, or that they still lived.

It was all too much to handle.

"Has he lost all reason?"

"A good bit of it. Aye. Did you not hear what I said?"

Leave it to Chthamalus to not understand his sarcasm. "And my mother? Does she live? What has she to say?"

"She drives him to it. Feeds his madness with a frightful frenzy."

You should have guessed that. "Well, that's awesome."

"Nay, Highness. 'Tis most foul."

Kalder rolled his eyes as he remembered that sarcasm was often lost on his old friend.

"Hey, Kal? You all right?"

Kalder turned at the sound of Bart's deep voice as the man approached suddenly from below the deck.

Tally dropped down under the railing, out of sight. "Friend or foe? Should I kill him for you, my lord?"

Kalder took a moment to consider that. While Bart could be a surly bastard, he had no desire to clean his guts from the ship tonight. "Friendly foe."

Tally grimaced in confusion.

"Don't kill him." Best to always clarify these things when dealing with a Barnak. While mostly unpredictable, the one thing anyone could trust in was their loyalty. A friend's friend was always a friend.

A friend's enemy was quickly annihilated.

And if anyone killed Bart, then Kalder wanted that privilege. He'd earned it for tolerating him this long.

Sighing, he turned toward Bart. "Just visiting."

Bart scowled. "What? The privy? Please tell me you're not pissing off the side of the boat. Captain will have an apoplexy if he catches *that*."

Kalder growled low in warning before he leaned down and offered Tally his hand. "It appears another friend of mine has washed up unexpectedly." He didn't bother to glance at his old mentor before he hauled him up easily so that Bart could catch sight of him. "Bartholomew Meers, meet Tally."

It wasn't until he saw the gaping hunger in Bart's eyes that a bad feeling went through him.

Shite! Please tell me he didn't . . .

But he already knew to dread this. His stomach cramped with fear, he turned to find Chthamalus not in his Barnak form or that of a man.

Nay, *that* would have been kind and merciful.

Rather, Tally wore the skin of a beautiful mermaid. One as naked as the night was long. Worse?

The instant Tally cleared the deck, Cameron drew up short behind Bart as she caught sight of the same nightmare that was currently scarring *and* scaring Kalder.

And that was the fact that he was holding a butt-naked woman in his arms and it wasn't Cameron.

8

Momentarily confused, Cameron stood in utter shock at the sight of the unbelievably beautiful, *completely* naked woman with Kalder. Long curly red hair coiled around a body that was about as perfect as any ever formed, and it left her feeling hideous in comparison. Truth be told, she wanted to slither down a hole and die rather than risk comparison and be found so lacking.

Aye, there was no way for her to compete with a

woman such as *this*. Or most any woman, for that matter. Even Aphrodite would have lost the apple to this woman!

Especially given the fact that Kalder had yet to move away from the wench.

I picked a perfect time to visit the privy. . . .

Sputtering, Kalder gestured at the woman Bart was currently leering over. "It's not what you be thinking, woman!"

Obviously it was *exactly* what she be thinking, otherwise he wouldn't be acting all so peculiar right this minute at having been caught in the midst of his inappropriate behavior, whatever said behavior was, and she had a mite good idea of what all that would have entailed had nature not come a-calling on her just then, and had she not ventured out here at this unholy time of night.

The blighter had guilt written all over his handsome face and nervous twitterings and stammerings! Dang it to perdition that all men had to go and tell on themselves the way they did, what with their roving male eyes and protruding body parts! Faithless, every one of the bilge rats! She wanted to choke him for it!

Disgusted with both of the cock-toting crew, Cameron did what they should have done with the poor wee bit of a lass when they'd fished her out of the cold, frigid sea. She whipped her own coat off and quickly wrapped it around the shivering girl.

Rotten, lousy blighters! She should have known that at the end of the day, they were all alike! Selfish, lecherous little bastubles!

"Don't you be telling me what to think, Mr. Dupree. As I've had quite enough of that here lately, what with me brother on board, and all that rot." She raked a furious glare over his body, which thankfully wasn't protruding at the moment. No doubt only because of his guilt over having been caught. "And what I'm thinking is that the fair lot of you ought to be ashamed of yourselves, taking advantage of the wee one here, which you ought, so I've got every right to be thinking it, and I resent you telling me not to!"

Growling at them both, she hugged the poor woman. "Come along, dearie. I'll get you below with the others and we'll take good and proper care of you, and get you warm and cozy before you catch a death chill. Men! I cannot believe they'd leave you out to freeze in your birthday britches what with no cares but for their own personal lechery. For shame to them! Hope they both catch a cold for it!"

She continued to chide them as she escorted the woman as far away from them as fast as she could.

Laughing out loud, Bart clapped Kalder on the back. "Be damned, mermaid! I haven't heard the lass go off like that since her first night in our company. Thought we'd quelled her tongue, what with our wild and woolly ways. Leave it to you to find it again, and get it working in such a comical manner."

"Ah, shut it, Meers. I'm in no mood for you. Not now and not while *this* is going on. This is a terrible fix, truly!"

Bart glanced about the deck in confusion. "This? What this is *this* you be talking about?"

Kalder gestured after them. "That be a demon, and a general at that, she just took below with her to sleep in the women's quarters."

All the humor fled from Bart's face. "Demon?" He started toward Cameron's path with a dark intent.

Kalder cursed himself as he realized he'd only made it that

much worse, as the man would no doubt kill Chthamalus if he caught up to him. He took him by the arm and held him fast to his side. "Nay, Bart. Still not what you're thinking, mate! Stand fast, would you! Avast! You're jumpier than a virgin in a whorehouse!"

That at least caused him to stop and arch a brow. "And you are never so chatty either. What the hell has possessed *your* tongue to give it such flight?"

The demon known as stupidity, apparently.

And in spades.

Honestly, he didn't know where to begin unsorting this mess. It was gnarled beyond redemption and all common sense. Even *un*-common sense, for that matter. His head ached just trying to begin to start sorting through it all.

Which left Bart glaring after him, waiting for him to explain.

So he sighed as he released Bart, and raked his hand through his hair. He might as well just jump in and start somewhere with the explanation, though this was never going to go well for any of them. "Tally's an old friend of mine. . . . From before."

"Tells me nothing, mate. Especially given *your* reputation from your old life. If anything, that says we shouldn't trust the beast at all."

Like he didn't know that. Kalder grimaced, hating Bart all the more for the truth of it, and aggravated at himself that he was having such a hard time of this. So he began again. "Aye. But he was my mentor."

"Of what? Dumb-assery?" Bart screwed his face up. "Are you daft, man? I just saw the totality of that *wo*man. Ain't no male parts hanging off *that* tree. Trust me. I'd have noticed any such dangling fruits in her amply visible and desirable nether regions."

Aye, but . . .

Kalder held his hand up in testimony. "And I swear on me rotted-out soul that I've seen him as a man as sure as he was a woman just now. It's part of who and what they are. They're both sexes, and they're neither."

That didn't help Bart's expression any, or the need inside Kalder to want to wipe that look off his face with both fists.

"You've lost me completely, son."

Pushing down the base urge to beat the bloke, Kalder ground his teeth and attempted to explain it better. "I know. It's a peculiarity among their kind. They're neither male nor female. They function as both and neither. At times, such as when they're in battle, they don't have the sex organs of either gender. They just are battle drones. And then when they're around others, they choose what they want to be, depending on their moods and the environment. Believe me, it was the most confusing thing for me as a lad . . . until I got used to them, and their breed. Me father thought it hilarious to use them as his primary scouting force. It was actually ingenious, if you think about it. 'Cause they could move about freely, and shift forms at whim with none the wiser, as humans knew nothing about who and what they were. Unless you're of the sea, like us, you've never heard of their species before and so you know naught of their abilities or whimsical ways."

"And what are they?"

"Barnak demons."

He gaped at Kalder. "*That's* a Barnak?"

Now it was his turn to be stunned. "You've heard of them?"

"Well, of course. I am a Simeon Mage. I've just never actually *seen* one."

"Wait, wait, wait. How do you know of them?"

"Simeon Mage," Bart repeated slowly as if Kalder were as daft as Kalder had accused him of being, and that by the very mention of the term for Bart's abilities Kalder should have instant clarity of Bart's unheard-of knowledge about Tally's species. "What part of *that* do you not understand?"

"Mostly all. I've never met a land-walker who knew of them before. At least none what didn't fight against them in battle and come up the short for it."

Bart flashed him a taunting grin. "There's a reason me brothers and I were kept secret from the world, and why Bane brought me and Will onboard this ship as part of his crew, and placed us as his seconds-in-command."

And Kalder *still* wondered why, given their sorry temperaments, but he knew from experience that Bart wouldn't answer. Neither would Will. They were as cryptic and private as he was about their kind. Bloody bastards both.

But that was neither here nor there at the moment. They were welcome to their secrets.

He had a much more pressing issue at stake. "Anyway, Mr. Meers," he reminded Bart in his most sarcastic tone, "the point of this most illuminating discussion is that said demon just took off with the lass toward the others, and none's the wiser for it."

"Is he harmful to them?"

He supposed that depended on the definition one used for "harm."

"Well, speak up, man!" Bart snapped. "Does he intend to hurt our crew?"

"I don't think so."

"You don't think, or you don't know?"

Kalder shrugged in total frustration. In all honesty, he didn't know what Chthamalus had planned in that squiddy little mind of his. While he didn't think Chthamalus was a direct threat per se, he still wasn't completely sure why the demon was here and trying to protect him. "You interrupted us before I could finish my interrogation and find out what's going on. If he was sent by someone else to spy here, or what for."

Grumbling, Bart took him by the arm and headed after them.

Normally Kalder would have had the bastard's bullocks for daring to manhandle him in such a high-handed manner, but his curiosity was too great at the moment for him to protest it too much. Especially since he had a bad, bad feeling in his gut.

More than that, he felt as if something or someone was watching him. The sensation crept over his skin like a living, breathing creature.

Unnerved, he hesitated and glanced about, half expecting the very air to be spying upon him.

While that might be a bit unorthodox, he wouldn't put anything past his older brother's abilities, especially with Chthamalus here. Varice had always been a treacherous bastard that way.

Worse than all his other brothers combined.

All Kalder knew for certain was that something was wrong, and

Chthamalus being here was just the beginning of it. Something was definitely rotten in the ocean, and it wasn't just the bilge water, dead fish. . . .

Or Bart's smelly shoes.

Cameron patted her new friend's hand comfortingly as she led her into the cabin and shut the door. Sancha was asleep in her bunk with her long white hair spilled out over her pillow.

For once Belle was resting in the bunk beside her, snoring softly. Even Valynda was asleep, and she rarely rested. Only Janice was awake, and she, their resident Dark-Huntress, was reading by candlelight.

She looked up from her book to pin a peculiar frown on Cameron. "What the devil?" Suspicion hung heavy in her dark eyes as she swept a gimlet frown over their dripping, shivering guest.

Cameron pulled the girl into the light so that Janice could better see her, then wondered why she bothered since Janice's Dark-Hunter sight didn't need any light whatsoever to focus with. In fact, she saw better without it, but it was easy to forget that since the woman acted more human than most humans Cameron knew, which was probably why Janice used the candlelight to read by when she didn't really need it. It was more for their benefit than hers, as it kept up the appearance that Janice was still human and not a soulless Dark-Hunter demon slayer living amongst them.

Unlike the Deadmen on the ship, Dark-Hunters didn't answer to Thorn or Captain Bane. They were well-trained warriors who'd sold their souls to the Greek goddess Artemis for a single Act of Vengeance against the person who'd betrayed them by wrongfully killing them and their loved ones. After they were given a single day to fulfill their pact, they were then conscripted for eternity to fight in Artemis's immortal army against the Daimons who preyed on human souls for sustenance, as well as to help others, such as Thorn and his Deadmen, police any preternatural predators out to make meals off mankind.

Janice had come to their crew after a group of Daimons had set her adrift at sea in an open dinghy, hoping she'd die under the burning rays of the sun—something as lethal to a Dark-Hunter as it was to their special breed of demon. Luckily, the Deadmen had seen her first and known her for what she was, thus saving her life and giving her a new post as part of their motley band of sailors.

Grateful for her friendship and nocturnal Dark-Hunter ways that prevented her from living the normal hours of a daylight creature, Cameron presented their latest guest to Janice. "Would you believe Bart and Kalder had her cornered on the deck and weren't rendering aid to the wee thing? Rather, they were gawking at her undressed state?"

Janice laughed at her obvious ire. "'Course they were. She's naked."

Why was she so amused while Cameron was beside herself over their obnoxious and scandalous behavior? "Are you not horrified?"

"Only be shocked if they weren't, given the rather impressive proportions of her curves." She winked at Cameron. "Or the fact she be a demon, love."

Cameron went cold at those words. "Pardon?"

Janice laughed at her startled expression. "She be a demon, love," she repeated. "Surely you knew that. Right?"

Um . . . nay. She'd had *no* idea.

Her stomach fell straight to her feet as she turned to gape at the "girl" who blinked innocently at her. "*You're* a demon?"

"You won't be holding that against me, now, will you? I like you. You seem very nice . . . and sweet. Are you sweet?" She blinked innocently at Cameron.

Her heart pounded in her chest. *Sweet?* As in "to eat" sweet?

That would be the natural assumption, especially when dealing with a demon that like as not would want a bite of her flesh!

Squeaking, Cameron jumped away from the wet demon, ready to fight.

Yet for all that, Cameron's hair remained dark and she stayed in her human body. Which only confused her more, as that didn't normally happen around creatures of this ilk. Especially not if they meant harm to her or another.

"What are you?"

The demon shrugged. "Naked and wet. Bit cold and getting colder. You said you'd take care of me? Is there some mead about? I rather like mead for drink. It usually warms me when I'm cold like this."

Disarmed by the oddly charming beastie, Cameron gaped at Janice, who seemed to be as equally perplexed by their guest. The creature appeared about as guileless as an infant. So either she was harmless . . .

Or the most treacherous creature ever born.

No wonder men were terrified of women, if this was a sample of how they appeared duplicitous in their eyes. She finally understood how her brother felt whenever he dealt with her when she was in one of her more contrary moods. It was, indeed, quite confusing.

All of a sudden, there was a knock on the door. "Miss Jack? You there?"

Never had she been happier to hear Kalder's deep, resonant voice. She went to open it and allow him and Bart to enter their small, cramped space. But to her instant dismay, their entrance, as quiet as it was, also disturbed her sleeping companions. And while Valynda woke up in a relatively polite mood, given the unholy hour of it all, the same couldn't be said for Belle.

She hated to be disturbed when she slept.

And Sancha came awake downright hostile and ready for war. "What the bloody hell is this, mates? Ship better be on fire and demons best be at the gate! Or else your bullocks are about to be in me fists!" She glared at Bart, then Kalder, with fury in her eyes and hell's wrath twisting her lips.

Smirking, he crossed his arms over his chest. "Half that statement be right."

Sancha growled fiercely as she righted herself in her bunk. "Ship on fire or I'm about to take a testicle from you both?"

"Demon at the gate." Kalder crossed the small cabin to grab said demon by the arm. "Why, Chthamalus? Just why?"

"Why what, my lord?"

He let out a frustrated growl. "Why did you choose to be a woman just now?"

"So as not to scare the humans. It's what you always said, is it not? Kill none without direct orders. And even with orders they must be armed, and at least over four and a half feet high, or we have to let them go . . . per your namby-pamby dictates."

Bart laughed.

Kalder raked him with an irritated grimace. "You laugh, but his kind once ate an entire nursery of children."

"Not what I'm laughing at. What I find amusing is that he thinks *you're* the namby-pamby."

Cameron bit back a laugh at the thought herself. Bart had a point. Kalder was the last person she would use those words to define, as he was a bit surly most days, and quicker to brawl than most.

"Any rate," Kalder said, turning back toward the demon, "I think it best that—"

Something struck the ship hard and spun them about. The impact was so abrupt that it knocked Kalder, Bart, Cameron, and Chthamalus to the floor. Janice barely managed to stay in her bunk while Sancha fell from hers and let out a curse so foul even Bane would have been impressed with its color. Belle was thrown into Valynda's bed, and then the two of them landed in a sprawled heap on the floor.

This time, Cameron's body did react to whatever was out there. Her wings sprang from her back and unfurled. Iridescent in the faint light, they appeared to breathe. Pushing herself to her feet, she turned around, slowly, looking for the threat, and half expecting said threat to come at them through the very boards of the ship. After all, it wouldn't be the first time such a thing had happened.

Indeed, threats such as that had become rather common for them since the gate had fallen.

But there was nothing evident.

The ship quieted and righted itself with an eeriness that was even more frightening than that unexpected attack.

Still, something was here. Creeping through the shadows and air. Every part of her being felt an insidious chill that defied explanation. It skipped up her spine and caused the hairs on her neck to stand up.

The silence was deafening. Listless. Wandering.

Whispering.

Whatever had come aboard was searching for them. . . .

Slithering and seeking.

Kalder lifted his head and tensed as he felt a presence he hadn't felt in a long, long time.

Nay . . . can't be.

Those have been dispatched. None should be left anywhere in this realm.

You're dreaming. Imagining things . . .

He met Cameron's wary gaze, then Bart's. "Keep them here." He turned his attention to his old friend. "Tally . . . guard them with your life." He had to go and check to see if he were correct with his assumption. To see if his gut were lying.

His heart hammering while they straightened themselves, Kalder wrenched open the door and ran for the deck, where he prayed he was wrong about the premonitions torturing him. But with every step, he was more and more certain that hell had frozen over, and that his nightmare was reality.

Shite . . .

Outside, the smell of the acid and sulphur was unmistakable. It hung in his throat and burned on his tongue.

The sea around the ship appeared to boil. This was a specific kind of attack that his brother had once led for his father against ancient navies. One from which their enemies had never survived.

They couldn't.

Suddenly, Mara appeared as an apparition on the deck beside him. "What are those, Mr. Dupree? Why can't I outrun them?"

Because those creatures weren't fed by the wind or sails.

They ran on the emotions of the crew they frightened. Negative emotions such as fear, dread, even anger made them stronger. Faster.

Invincible.

"In short, my lady, utter destruction."

There was a reason why his father had dubbed them "Dread Waters." It was how they functioned and what made them work.

What made them lethal.

And right now, those Dread Waters began to percolate and dance harder against their hull. Higher. A rhythmic, hypnotizing beat. He could hear them in his head like a second heartbeat that caused his own to synch up to it. Louder and more demanding. They struck against the ship more insistently, causing Mara to solidify and stumble on deck beside him.

Devyl materialized out of thin air to catch her in his arms before she fell. He cast a furious glower to Kalder that said he knew exactly who and what they were facing, and that he was no more thrilled by the threat than Kalder was.

"Mr. Death!" he shouted. "Ready the mages! Strixa, if you're hungry, lass, I won't stop your buffet."

A happy screech sounded, quickly followed by the blurred sight of their resident water witch in the form of a black owl taking flight so that she could attack this newest threat. It wasn't often Bane allowed her to feed unimpeded.

And still Kalder felt the threat growing more lethal as every second passed.

This was different from all the other times they'd been attacked. The Dread Waters were a lot stronger than they'd ever been before. Something had roused them up to a rare form tonight, and made them even more powerful than they'd been at the height of his father's reign.

What could cause such a transformation . . . he had no idea. His people had been on the brink of dying out when his mother had killed him. Their forces, like their numbers, should have dwindled and weakened over the centuries, not grown. And definitely not increased into something of *this* magnitude.

This made no sense whatsoever.

How was it even possible?

Closing his eyes, Kalder summoned his powers and listened to the voices in the aether, seeking some form of rational explanation.

Yet only agonized screams filled his ears. The voices of a million souls in torment . . .

Then in a single instant he understood what was happening.

And why.

"Swing her about!" he shouted. "Fire to the wind!"

Bane arched a brow at his unexpected and shocking orders.

Orders Kalder knew ran contrary to everything Bane stood for, and normally, so did he. "You'd have us retreat? Are you insane?"

He pointed at the water. "That's the Malachai rising beneath those waves. It's what's giving them such power and why they're surging like this. We can't fight *him*."

Only a fool would try when that malevolent beast was *this* strong.

For the first time ever, he saw hesitation in Bane's eyes. Not out of cowardice.

Respect. The Malachai wasn't like any other creature or demon alive. He was a force unto himself and he carried with him the knowledge and powers of all the Malachai who'd been born before, throughout time itself. Each generation growing deadlier.

More destructive.

None more powerful, vengeful, and hate-filled than the one they claimed had been driven mad by his captivity.

Adarian Malachai.

Created by the dark gods so that he could free them and they could finally rule over all of the earth and put down their enemies. Only Adarian had never agreed to be anyone's flunky. Not even that of the ancient gods who'd bred him.

Now Adarian was out for blood.

Everyone's.

And especially the gods who had sought to rule and use him. Those who had fed from him and weakened him for their own selfish purpose.

For centuries, Adarian had been doing his best to find his way out—to escape his captors and rain down his wrath upon them for the punishments they'd doled to the beast.

That insolent, insatiable anger and hunger was what had finally caused the Maystresse Gates that held the Malachai prisoner from the human world to buckle and fracture.

Long before mankind had begun to record history, the ancient gods had fought a vile and vicious war.

In those days, the Malachai wasn't a single demon, but many, and he and his army had fought for the Cimmerians or Mavromino—the darkest of the gods. Those who'd wanted to burn the world down. To make it a sinister place of fear and pain where they ruled with total brutality, and held supremacy over the siblings they viewed as weak and kind-hearted. Those who thought the Nine Worlds should be shared and protected.

That protection was something Kalder agreed with. Even at his worst, he'd never been the type to tread on anyone's freedom. Not for any reason. That was where he differed most from his brothers.

And it was something he shared with Cameron and Paden Jack. They were remnants of the Sephirii—the Kalosum army that had once protected the weaker species against their darker brethren. Those who'd wanted balance and light over all the lands—both enchanted and not. Gods of peace and prosperity, who believed the worlds could, and should, be shared, and that hatred and intolerance should be banished from them forever.

Unable to come to terms with one another or find common ground, those two great armies had almost destroyed everyone and everything in their quest to put each other down.

Including the gods they fought for.

For centuries, their war had torn the worlds apart and laid waste to countless lives. Led to utter destruction.

And had ended only after a mutual act of supreme betrayal had caused the two main leaders of the dominant armies to be put down, and the last Malachai to be cursed and enslaved by the six Source gods who had created them all.

To be the last of his kind.

Forever alone. No friend. No family. Always betrayed and bereft. Unable to trust anyone.

Even himself.

Doomed to an eternal cycle of living a cold, brutal life without happiness or friendship of any kind that would ultimately end when his own son came of age and ruthlessly slaughtered him to take his place and begin the reign of terror all over again.

That was his legacy.

Hatred. Murder. Pain.

Conceived in violence to do violence and to die violently.

For no other reason than the gods were shits, and because the original firstborn Malachai had had the grave misfortune of being born to their queen of destruction who'd had the audacity to fall in love with her own Sephirii warrior.

Misery takes pity on none. She serves her dishes up without regard to a person's life or their accomplishments.

Now, this latest Malachai warlord had found a way to cast off his chains of bondage and escape the hell they'd banished him to, and Adarian was taking his chance for freedom. More than that, he was furious over their latest attempt to overthrow him with a child he'd been duped into fathering.

And *this* was the result. The gates were open and he was coming for the world to take it back as his own, starting with the sacrifice of that child he'd fathered.

Vengeance is mine. . . .

Be careful what you do, for with every action taken there is a corresponding overreaction. It was easy to cast out the devil you feared. But the true monster wasn't the one you saw . . .

It was the devil unknown. *For that beast who came next was oft far worse than the one you originally threw down. And the one to fear the most was the one who came up quietly while you were distracted fighting the monster you thought you knew.*

Fear that beast unseen. The one who snuck from the total darkness within. Unheard and unknown until it struck with fatal accuracy.

Kalder's mind whirled as he remembered his father's prophetic words.

They're coming for me, boy. And one day, they'll come for you . . . watch your throat and your bullocks. For they'll strike where you're weakest, and at the thing you're paying the least attention to.

And still the turgid waters rose up, boiling in their anger, seeking to overturn the *Sea Witch* and drown them all. They pounded against the sides in a primal rhythm, demanding the lives of everyone onboard.

Over and over.

The war was no longer coming. It'd arrived and this was ground zero.

Mara cried out as the ship began to splinter apart. The boards under their feet were giving way.

"Divide yourself from the ship! Pull out before they destroy you!"

He barely heard Devyl's orders for his wife to remove her nerve endings from the ship's structure before they ripped her asunder. All Kalder could do was stare in disbelief at what was coming for them out of the dark depths below. Paralyzed in shock by an attack from the past that he'd thought was gone, stirred up by the wrath of a monster that had been released by treachery. These were creatures that shouldn't exist anymore. They were supposed to have been banned after his father's reign.

The Dread Waters are no more.

Kalder had rounded them all up and destroyed them. Unlike his father, he hadn't wanted them as part of his army.

Yet here they were. Back like some invincible nightmare phantom that wouldn't be denied. How had they resurfaced after all these centuries?

Hatred is never ending.

Fear always endures.

Dread will out. There's nowhere to hide that it won't find you.

He should have known that an enemy so insidious could never be truly defeated. Only held at bay for a bit.

"The ship's coming apart!" That cry went up in unison from the crew.

"Drop the dinghies! Abandon ship!"

It wouldn't do any good. The swell of the waves would overturn the tiny lifeboats in a heartbeat and drag them all to the bottom of the ocean, where they wouldn't stand a chance against the riptides that would trap them. Again, that was why his father had gone undefeated during his entire reign. Why no army or navy could touch their people.

Not until the Myrcians had destroyed themselves with infighting.

More orders followed all around him, but Kalder barely heard them. Mostly because he knew what the Deadmen did. This far out at sea, there was no help for them. They were alone. If the ship went down, they would be stranded without food or shelter. And while Deadmen couldn't die, there were plenty of things worse than death.

Having been tortured in hell more than once, he could testify to that.

I can't leave them here to suffer.

To be lost at sea . . .

He wasn't his mother. He didn't glory in the pain and suffering of others. Not even in that of his enemies. Never mind what would happen to those he considered his real and true family.

"Chthamalus!" Kalder watched as the Dread Waters rose ever higher and pounded harder and harder against the sides of the ship, stripping more planks from the hull and sending them to the sea below.

The demon appeared by his side in his warrior form. "My lord?"

"Can you open a portal back to Wyñeria?"

He actually turned green with the thought of it. "Why? I just came from that place. . . . You don't want to go there. Trust me. It's not the home you once knew."

"We have no choice." It was the only place where the crew would have any semblance of dry land this far out.

His eyes bugged even more. "My prince . . ."

The ship whined and lurched as more of the hull fractured and came free. Lightning flashed in the dark skies above. Howling screams echoed around them.

And that was just the crew.

They wouldn't have much longer. Any second and they were done for.

Kalder braced himself against the railing and held tight against the bucking ship. He ducked as a mast came free and swung wide, narrowly missing his head. "I won't run, Tally. It's not in me to do so. Ever. You say me brothers want me. Fine, then. I'll take the fight to them, and if I have to dig me own grave, I'll make sure to plant the shovel up their arses before I go. Now open that portal and make sure Muerig goes with us through it."

In the midst of scrambling to see Mara and the crew safe, Devyl caught sight of Chthamalus by Kalder's side. The furious glower on his face would have terrified a lesser man. But as noted, Kalder backed down from no one.

Not even Devyl Bane.

"What's *that* doing here?"

The fact that Devyl was familiar with Tally's breed surprised him more than his captain's anger. "You know his species?"

The captain gave him a droll stare. "Aye. I've pulled the gills off a large number of them."

Chthamalus shrank away with a squeak at the thought of being maimed in such a manner.

Unwilling to see him harmed, Kalder put himself between them. "This one is counted among me family, Captain. More so than those I share blood with."

"Du?" Mara's voice was even weaker.

The captain turned as pale as Cameron's Necrodemian hair, and for the first time ever, Kalder saw fear in the captain's eyes as he glanced down at the woman in his arms. There was no missing the love in Devyl's heart for her. She and his sister were the one true weakness he had. The only thing that could defeat their invincible leader. And that right there was what Kalder would sell his soul to have.

A woman whose destiny was forged with his. A partner who would fight by his side through all of hell itself.

That one kind hand that touched him with comfort when he needed it, and gave him strength when he was weak. Someone who would mourn for him when he was dead and gone.

Devyl grabbed him by the shirtfront in one meaty fist and jerked him forward. "Save the crew, Mr. Dupree. Do whatever you must! I will trust you."

Knowing that those words weren't spoken lightly, Kalder inclined his head to him, then turned to Chthamalus. "Open the portal."

Reluctance flared in the demon's eyes before he nodded. "Aye, my prince. Your doom is my command."

And it seemed to be his ever quest. At least that was what everyone had always said of him. Self-destructive from the moment he'd taken his first breath to his last.

Kalder felt the primordial surge in the aether the moment

Chthamalus opened the portal to the deep ocean floor where their home lay. It was forbidden for any of them to bring outsiders in. Their father used to gut anyone who dared such.

And your mother gutted you for less.

Or perhaps more, given that his failure to arrive on time had resulted in Muerig's brutal death. Kalder tried never to think of that day, when he'd made the mistake of going home to seek solace over what he'd caused to happen.

Instead, his mother had buried a dagger in his heart. Literally.

I hope you go to hell and rot for all you've done.

Those words still rang in his ears. But then what had he really expected? He'd never had any memories of her tender embrace. Why had he believed for even a single delusional moment that she might welcome him home?

Because I'm an idiot.

No doubt, today he'd be an even bigger one.

As the portal opened, the ship began taking on water. Kalder started to lead the way into his homeland for the others, but Bane stopped him.

"I'll go through first . . . with your brother in tow to clear the way and make sure it's safe on arrival for everyone."

Having just joined them on deck, Muerig widened his eyes at that comment. He was also confused to find them all scrambling about to evacuate. "Beg pardon? Where are we going?" He glanced out at the dark seas that were attacking them. "There's no land out there! No safe place to go!"

Bane glanced to Kalder before he answered Muerig's question. "Wyñeria."

Muerig's jaw dropped. "It still stands?"

The captain ignored the shocked question. His features grim, he clapped Kalder on the shoulder. "Make sure everyone clears the ship, Mr. Dupree."

"I will."

Bane grabbed Muerig and began the departures, with Muerig protesting every step of the way into the darkness.

The rest of the crew proved to be easy until Cameron planted herself firmly in front of him and refused to follow after the others, into the portal. "I'll wait until you go. You need someone at your back, watching for treachery."

Kalder arched a brow at her stubbornness. And her loyalty as he began to rethink his ideas about having someone who would be by his side.

Of course, that wouldn't last long. Especially given where they were headed. Experience had taught him better. Friends today made for enemies tomorrow.

He only prayed that she wouldn't learn to hate him, too. He couldn't stand the thought of seeing hatred in her eyes.

For that matter, he couldn't stand the thought of what would most likely be waiting for him on the other side of that greenish-blue light.

"Cameron . . . should I be a different man where we're heading, I want you to remember me as you've known me, and not as they see me."

"I don't understand."

He glanced past her shoulder toward the sea beasts that were quickly tearing their ship apart. "I know. Just remember that we don't always get to be who we want to be. Sometimes others force us to act against our natures. And survival is the harshest master of all. It's easy to praise a man in good times and condemn him in the bad ones. But never should we be judged for the totality of our lives during that erratic pendulum swing. For fate is a fickle bitch who slaps us on one cheek, while she caresses us on the other. Rather it's who we are most of the time, when no one's around to force our hands. That's the man I want you to remember when you think of me. For that is the truth of who I really am. And that's the memory of the man I want you to hold to in your heart."

"You're scaring me, Mr. Dupree."

Honestly, he scared himself more. And they were out of time. Kissing her lips, he forced her through the portal. Then he turned toward the creatures who'd been sent after him.

The Dread Waters preyed on fear and used that power to build and swell until they swallowed their victims whole. No one could escape their clutches. For that was always the thing about dread, it only grew in size. The more you feared, the more power you gave the beast.

There was only one way to defeat this nightmare.

Face-to-face confrontation. In the light of day, they were never as insurmountable as they seemed. Never as tough as they let you think they were.

Rather, they were made up of shadows of fluff. Bluster and taunts. Bullies who relied on the willingness of others to believe their perpetrated lies to give them strength.

Hold them up to the light and they fled like the cowards they were.

"Fuck what you think of me!" Kalder shouted at the darkness that tried to drag him down. "If you want to fight, then I'll see you in me brother's palace. At the foot of his throne."

He swept a taunting sneer at the lot of them as they continued to tear the ship out from under his feet. "You might want to take a moment to seek reinforcements, me bitches. 'Cause it's going to get bloody and I'm going to fight you with everything I am."

And with that, he jumped into the midst of the troubled waters that had been sent to end him.

9

"He's going to kill you, you know."

Vine froze at that deep, resonate voice that sent shivers over her. It was so rich and masculine that the sound of it alone was practically enough to make a woman climax. Never mind what the sight of the man who held it could do to one's senses.

Aye, he was gorgeous. Perfect. Delectable in every way. From the top of that long, wavy dark hair to the tips of those black leather boots.

Even more so than her ex-husband, and Duel was the epitome of masculinity.

But then he wasn't a god.

Jaden, however, was. Or at least he had been once upon a time ago. Before he'd fallen from grace by his own volition, and became enslaved to the Dark Ones.

Now he was nothing more than a servant. Like her.

Only there was nothing subservient about this magnificent beast. He still walked with the deadly lope of a predator. With the full knowledge of a creature well aware of the powers he commanded, and his original place in the universe.

Of the damage he could wreak and the lives he could take.

Al-Baraka. The broker who bartered between demons and the darker powers. He held the ultimate power over life and death. There was nothing he couldn't do. No realm he couldn't venture to, or soul he couldn't claim.

Yet for all that, he was a houseboy nowadays, really.

But an incredibly sexy one. Tall and muscular with eerie mismatched eyes that beguiled and reviled simultaneously. One a vibrant deep green and the other a dark, earthy brown. Haunting in their contrasting shades, and set in a face of utter male perfection.

She paused in the dismal corridor of Noir's palace, where the screams of the damned echoed as a constant reminder of why she didn't want to fail in her mission. "What are you talking about?"

"Noir . . . or Kadar, rather. I really hate that mundane name Azura gave him. Never thought it quite fitting for such a treacherous bastard. He's not going to let you live through this, you know. Once he's done with you, he's done with you. He'll toss you aside like the garbage you are."

"And I should trust you . . . why?"

"You shouldn't. At all. I've betrayed everyone around me. Have no love of *you,* whatsoever. But there's no one I hate more than my evil brother and sister. So you can trust in that hatred that will allow me to help you by screwing them."

"That makes no sense."

He smiled coldly. "It makes all the sense in our nonsensical universe. Trust me." Then he stepped closer to her. "The Malachai is the one creature who can destroy Kadar. Yes?"

"It's what I've been told."

Jaden paused as one of the screams crescendoed. He flinched at the same time she cringed from the horrendous sound of pain.

"That comes from Rezar's son, the demigod Seth. Imagine what they'd do to *you* if they held you in his place."

Those words sent a chill down her spine. "They torture their own nephew?"

"That surprises you? I'm their brother. They've never shown me any mercy, at any time. Why do you think Braith is in hiding? And she's their beloved missing piece they need to overpower the Malachai. She, alone, can bring him down or bring him to heel. Yet she knows better than to show her face around them. So she keeps herself hidden from them and their schemes."

That Vine hadn't known.

He leaned forward so that he could whisper in her ear. "Why do you think I brought you back from the void, Vine?"

She shrugged. "You had no choice."

"I always have choices. Even while held in bondage. Never mistake that. They only control me because I let them." He smiled coldly in her face before he spoke again. "Nay, my dearest harpy. I want my freedom. We have one shot at Kadar. If we strike together, we can bring the beast down. The only question you have to answer is if you want to live out your life again, or do you want to spend eternity in a dark, vacuumless void, or worse, like Seth in screaming agony while they rip out your entrails and have sex to the sounds of *your* screams?"

Cameron pulled up short in the glistening throne room that shone so brightly it made her eyes water. What the bleeding blue devil was this underwater amazement? How was it even possible? It made no sense whatsoever!

And she wasn't the only one to be taken aback by its unexpected splendor. Every member of the Deadmen stood in stunned silence as they took in the glittering underwater palace that shouldn't be physically possible.

"Blimey." Will finally spoke under his breath while he held his hand up to shield his eyes against the sharp glare of lights that seemed to have no natural source.

"Fuck me." Leave it to Bart to be the most colorful with his verbal expression. "How is it that we're able to breathe under the ocean?"

Simon Dewing, their stalwart, stoic, and ever-amusing former priest of the African spirit Exú, flashed a taunting grin in Bart's direction. "It's magick, mate. Have you learned nothing in all our travels?"

Screwing his face up in pain, Bart tossed a dagger at Simon's head that Simon caught and flipped back at him to lighten their somber mood.

But not by much, as they were all very aware of how tenuous their lives were in this mysterious and unknown place.

Valynda stepped beside Belle for cover, while Janice held both her hands up to study them closely in the light that danced like living water around them.

"Why am I not bursting into flames?" Janice scowled at the captain. "This is daylight, isn't it?"

Cameron would have said aye. It appeared to be such, and yet Janice was right. Sunlight normally made the Dark-Huntress blister and burn, and it should prove most fatal to her unique species.

Yet fortunately for them all, it did none of those things and left her appearing as normal as any of their crew.

William turned toward Bane. "Captain? Where are we?"

Paden stepped closer to Cameron while he turned a slow circle, inspecting every inch of the elegant room with walls that seemed to be made of sparkling amber crystals. "What is this place we've come to?"

"My home." That deep, melodic voice that was filled with suspicious malice answered before the captain had a chance to explain it to them. "But the real questions are, what are you doing in it? And how the hell did you get here?"

Turning into the body of a thin squidlike male, Chthamalus slithered behind Cameron, then shifted into a small, thin line so as not to be seen. He clutched at her arm and trembled.

The grimace on Paden's face said that her brother was about to denounce the demon and offer him up to the newcomers as a sacrifice, but she quickly shook her head to keep him from speaking. Best to let the captain tend these things without their interference. Besides, the one thing she'd learned growing up in a tavern—most intelligence came from knowing when to keep one's mouth shut, especially during tense moments and conflicts. And this seemed like a prime time to heed that sage advice and ride herd on her wandering tongue, and leave it to the captain to take the lead through these turbulent waters.

Especially given the size of the man asking the question. Equal in height to Captain Bane, he was a massive beast. Well muscled, with black hair that hung in braids to the middle of his back. He reminded her of their mate Rosenkranz, who wore his dark blond hair in braids and dreads. Unorthodox in all things, that was their fun-loving Rosie. But while Rosie was forever good-natured and jovial, this man showed only the most somber of manner and humor. He also lacked Rosie's wildly mixed, flamboyant Caribbean dress.

Instead, he was robed in a rich fabric of gold unlike anything she'd ever seen before. The cloth flowed over his muscular body, reminiscent of molten lava. And he held himself with the regal carriage of a king—proud and arrogant—flanked by two equally sullen watchmen. In matching uniforms of a gunmetal gray. And both eyed their entire group as if the Deadmen were asps who'd slithered across their favorite pair of expensive shoes and had decided to rest there for a spell.

And take a dump.

Something the captain tolerated about as well as she did.

He set Mara down on her feet and tucked her in behind him

before he moved toward the newcomer to address him as an equal ruler who wasn't intimidated at all by their dour faces and soured moods.

William and Bart, along with Simon, Rosie, Kat, and several others, stepped forward to form a barrier between them that said they weren't in the mood for none of their shite, but if they wanted to persist in a brawl, they'd be happy to meet it.

Yet they didn't get a chance to say anything.

The moment they neared the one in charge, a bright light flashed in the room and Kalder appeared. Still in his mermaid form that left his skin a shimmering silver, his tattoos were extended out as gills that vibrated with every breath he took. Something that made him appear even fiercer and deadlier than normal. Truly an impressive feat that was altogether spellbinding.

His clothes clung tight to his well-muscled body, but that wasn't what made Cameron's jaw go slack at the sight of him. It was the raw, unmitigated rage on his face. Not that she hadn't seen him looking angry and lethal in the past.

He rather lived in that state.

Yet never quite to this extent. There was a special ferocity to him now that said he wanted to taste blood in the worst sort of manner, and that he was salivating for a taste of theirs. More than that, he held a malformed demon by its throat in his left hand.

Curling his lip, he tossed it at the three men in front of them.

"Greetings, me brothers. I thank you for the welcoming party you sent for me homecoming."

The tossed demon screeched as their leader kicked at him, then it skittered off into the shadows and vanished.

If Cameron had thought their leader cold and stern before, he'd been downright grandmotherly and warm in his affections compared to the hatred that flared in his eyes at the sight of Kalder now.

But it was only there for a moment until it was replaced by disbelief. "I thought you dead! How could I send you a welcoming party when I had no idea you were still about?"

"Not dead enough for your sanity, eh?"

The watchman on the left gaped. "Prince Kalderan?"

That title was met with audible gasps from the Deadmen. Especially Cameron, who turned to stare at him over something he'd failed—in all their conversations—to mention.

And how could he, given it shouldn't have slipped his mind?

Hi, mate, I have dark hair, a gimpy leg . . .

And *a royal title.*

"Prince?"

Before he could answer, the watchman on the right snarled. "He's no prince of this empire! Just a piece of whore slag!"

Kalder ignored Cameron's shocked question so that he could smirk at his idiot brother, who was dressed as a watchman. If he wasn't in so foul a mood, he'd be amused at the fact that Perrin was insulting his own mother, too, with that slight.

As it was . . . "Better to sell the flesh than the soul. At least I can look at meself in the mirror and not flinch."

"Can you?"

Kalder ground his teeth and steeled himself so that he didn't let his brother know he'd hit the mark with those words. The one thing when dealing with his oh-so-lovely family was that one could never show them weakness of any sort. Not unless you wanted them to pick it deeper and leave you a bleeding, rotting corpse at their feet.

Stay on the offensive and keep them on the defensive. It was the only way to deal with them. The minute you retreated to lick your wounds, they'd set in on you like a pack of vultures to pick your bones clean.

It was a hard lesson learned from his youth and one he hadn't forgotten even these many years later.

How could he?

He was still bleeding in places from their last encounter, and that had been centuries ago. Their level of cruelty tended to linger.

"Me beauty is so great, I seek every mirror I can find, brother." Kalder moved to stand right in front of Perrin, who looked so much like their father that it was hard to be this close to him and not slap him for it.

It was bad enough that Kalder had all the years of hatred for what his brother had done to him to deal with, but that was compounded now by the added anguish of unresolved pain left in the wake of his father's neglect and abuse. They were the same size. Same build and sculpted features.

Same dark curly hair and amber eyes.

Smug expression. As if the gods themselves had sought some sort of sick satisfaction in wringing as much misery on their people as possible by reincarnating their prior king's visage in that of his son.

Or maybe they just hated Kalder so much that this was some sort of personal grudge-fuck against him.

It definitely felt that way.

But Varice wasn't as merciless as he stepped between them. "Enough, Perrin! Mind your manners, boy!"

Perrin's jaw went slack as he stared at the one who was obviously now the Myrcian king. "You can't be serious! Surely you plan to execute him slowly for the death of our true brother?"

Kalder tsked. "What's that foul taste in your mouth, Perrin? Besides your foot?" He paused to arch a taunting brow. "You should know, brother dearest, you've feasted on it enough in your life. It's called disappointment."

He stepped aside to gesture at Muerig, who was easily hidden behind Devyl's massive form. Although he appeared more to be cowering, if the truth were told—though why Muerig would be doing such, Kalder couldn't imagine. Unlike him, their brothers had always favored Muerig. Protected him, even. "I didn't come back from the dead alone. I brought dearest family with me."

Kalder savored that priceless look of shock on their faces. It was better than the expression they'd worn when they'd first seen him in the room.

Muerig finally rushed forward to embrace their brothers. "Varice! Perrin!"

Kalder didn't miss the tense awkwardness in their brothers' stances. But whether that came from not wanting to see Muerig or because they couldn't legally execute *him* anymore for Muerig's murder, he wasn't sure. Either way, he knew the joy they exuded was feigned.

"Great to be reunited, eh?" Kalder couldn't help throwing kerosene onto the fire and nettling their agitated states.

Varice's eyes narrowed, but he quickly recovered to clap Muerig on the back and smile. "We shall feast this day, dearest Muerig! Let everyone revel at the miracle that's returned you home to us."

Perrin gestured at Kalder. "And arrest him!"

Devyl's eyes flared to red. "What for?"

Perrin went rigid at the confrontation. He'd never been able to contend with anyone questioning him on any matter. "He's broken a sacred law, and well he knows it. Outsiders are forbidden in to our city and yet here he's brought all of you!"

Kalder didn't flinch, as he'd expected nothing else from his brothers. It wasn't as if they were about to suddenly find love for him after all these centuries. That only happened in bad books, kids' fables, and fairy tales. "It's fine, Captain. Under the laws of me people, they can't harm you. They're required to see you all released back to your world safely in exchange for your word that you'll never return to their lands, or reveal how it is you came to be here."

Cameron, with Bart of all creatures, stepped forward to defend him. "No one's arresting Mr. Dupree." She did that adorable stubborn stance where she planted herself right before his brother, legs braced wide and arms crossed as if she'd take on the whole Myrcian army alone.

Perrin blinked slowly as he glanced from Cameron to Kalder and back again. "I see your tastes have taken a peculiar bend, brother."

Those words heated his fury to a dangerous level. "Careful, Perrin. You insult me lady *phearse* and I will take that sword from Varice's side and shove it into an orifice that will require a great deal of skill to extract it from." And with that he stepped forward and placed an arm around Cameron's waist to pull her against him so that there would be no mistaking his affections for her.

This wasn't the human world where such things were frowned upon. Here they were necessary.

However, her brother didn't appreciate it.

Paden started forward in protest.

Devyl caught him and, with a warning glare, forced him to stand down before he was caught in the cross fire.

Kalder felt her nervousness, but she gave no outer sign of it, and for that he respected her immensely.

Debate hovered in both his brothers' eyes, and in particular Perrin's as he weighed the option of pressing this issue. While it wasn't in his nature to back down, they both knew that Kalder could kick his arse. That he'd done it plenty of times when they were boys and Perrin had tried to overpower him. Hence why his brother had learned to resort to treachery where he was concerned.

Perrin had never held the same degree of fighting skill. Or perhaps that wasn't the exact truth. When it came to skill they were about even. What Perrin lacked was Kalder's fury. His willingness to suffer a blow and not give in to the pain of it.

That was where Kalder reigned supreme. He didn't mind getting bloody or hurt. Rather, he reveled in physical pain and the distraction it gave from the unseen ache in his soul. A never-ending misery that Perrin, as a favored son, knew nothing about, and so he was unwilling to suffer the other.

Varice placed a comforting hand to Perrin's shoulder and held him next to him. "Let us see about returning the humans to their world. And Muerig to ours."

"You would forgive him for this trespass?"

"Let us focus on our brother's return and the happiness it'll bring our mother. 'Tis a day for celebrating. Not one of war."

Kalder didn't miss the underlying strain in Varice's voice, nor the fact that he glossed over his fate. Those two things put him on notice and on edge.

So be it. They'd never been friends, or even friendly, and he hadn't expected mercy anyway.

Kalder didn't move as Varice snapped his fingers for their servants.

Four of them ran into the room in a nervous manner that said Varice ruled with the same iron fist and volatile temperament as their father. Especially when they hit their knees in a groveling act of submission that turned Kalder's stomach.

Varice, however, thought nothing of it. "Take Prince Muerig to his chambers and see to his needs. Make sure he's given clothing appropriate to his station."

They hastened to obey him.

As soon as they were gone, Varice turned his attention to the watchmen. "Have our sacerdos prepare the portal for the humans. I'm sure they've no wish to be here a moment longer than is necessary."

"And Kalder?" Only a fool would miss the challenge in Devyl's voice.

Varice swept a suspicious grimace over the captain as if finally seeing him for the first time. "Do I know you?"

Kalder answered for him with the title he knew the captain wouldn't use, but that his brother would recognize, and shit his breeches over. "Dón-Dueli of the Dumnonii. Once known as the king of Tintagel. You know, brother dearest. The Dark World-King."

That took the last bit of color from Varice's skin. He swallowed audibly. Aye, that was a name he knew well. They all did. Devyl had been their father's ally and the only land-walker their people had ever feared. Back in the day, he hadn't just been the king of Tintagel, he'd been dubbed the World-King and the Dark One. Not because of dark looks, but rather for his brutal, bloodthirsty reputation that had made even the bravest warrior wet himself at the mere mention of Devyl's name. Entire armies had thrown down their weapons at the sight of his warhorse on the horizon.

Aye, he'd been just that bad-ass, alone.

"What concern is Kalderan to you?"

"He's a most valued member of me crew. Any harm done him and I'll be taking it personally." Devyl pinned a pointed stare on Perrin. "And seeking vengeance for it."

Varice gave him a forced smile that didn't reach his eyes. It was cold and sterile. "Have no fear, my lord. As noted, he's a member of our royal family, and shall be treated as such."

When had that ever made any difference?

Kalder barely restrained himself from rolling his eyes. "Does this mean me inheritance will be reinstated?" He couldn't resist digging at a wound when he knew it would rub against everything his brothers held dearest.

Their mutual greed.

Ah, the beauty of being a younger sibling. There were some things that one couldn't resist. And being a barnacle bitch was definitely one of them.

Forget Tally and his Barnak demon status, right now, Kalder could give even his old mentor a good run for his money, and do the old blighter proud.

Before Varice could answer, a sudden loud scream rang out from the hallway.

The watchman ran for the door to check on who was being murdered—a likely assumption given the volume and hysterics of it. Kalder stood back while the crew rushed outside, along with Cameron.

Recognizing that shrill, ear-splintering voice, he knew there was no need to rush out and see about the cause of it. Mostly because he wasn't in the mood to heave and lose his lunch. He'd seen enough sickening things for one night.

Perrin's face, for one thing.

He was in no mood to be nauseated further. And sure enough, he was right.

Outside in the elegant, gilded hallway that was lit with bioluminescent plankton buried deep within the walls, stood their mother, latched onto Muerig while she rained kisses all over his face. She wept and shouted in turn with ecstatic welcome. Muerig returned her happiness with his own hugs and kisses.

Aye, it was all Kalder could do not to unload his stomach all over the lot of them. Disgusting public display, really.

"My precious baby! I can't believe I have you back!" His mother held his head to her bosom as if she were attempting to breastfeed him again. Gah! How could his brother stand it?

Cameron frowned as she saw the reunion and it dawned on her

who the elegant older woman had to be. Not that it wasn't plainly evident by her regal bearing and dark hair and pale eyes. Coloring very similar to someone else she knew well . . .

Confused, she glanced back to Kalder, who made no move whatsoever to approach the queen or get her attention in any way.

Had Cameron not already known that his mother had killed him on their previous encounter, their mutual actions here and now would have clued her in that their relationship had a bit of a strain to it.

And while this wasn't quite as bloody and cruel as Kalder's thorough gutting during their last meeting, Cameron was, however, quite certain that in his mind this session ranked right up there behind it.

How could it not?

You bloody bitching-troll . . .

Cameron wanted to slap the woman for her unnecessary cruelty as she showed such blatant favoritism between her children. Especially when she saw the way Kalder's pewter gaze remained guarded and emotionless, as if he were afraid to let any part of his façade slip for fear of what they'd do to him should he display any sort of weakness.

It infuriated her on his behalf. Family shouldn't be like this. They were supposed to support each other. Bolster you when you stumbled. Hold your hand when you were afraid.

Embrace you whenever you came home, and hold you as if they were afraid of letting you go again.

Instead, Kalder stayed in the doorway while his brothers went to their mother and Muerig. Like an outsider who didn't belong with his family.

And that made her ache for him. He should be welcomed with the same happy fervor.

Yet they turned their backs and treated him with less regard than they gave her and the rest of the crew.

He meant nothing to his family, and it showed. The fact that they displayed this so openly was all the meaner.

But the real rub to her was the fact that Kalder didn't expect better. He didn't bother to reach out.

Because this, to him, was normal.

And *this* should never be normal to anyone.

"Why didn't you tell me Muery was back!" their mother chided as she reached for Varice's hand to rub it tenderly.

"He just arrived."

"How is this possible?" She glanced around and then her happiness faded as she finally spotted Kalder in their group.

In one instant her expression became the epitome of cold and ruthless.

Kalder inclined his head to her respectfully. "Greetings, Mother."

That made her eyes go as dead as the grave. "What are *you* doing here?" Her tone dripped with a coldness that even the Arctic would envy.

"Returning your son to your loving arms. I knew how much you missed him." And with those emotionless words spoken, he headed off in the opposite direction, away from them.

No one stopped him.

No one.

Cameron couldn't breathe as she realized that not a single

member of his family cared for him. They went right back to his brother without a single second glance at his retreating form.

He didn't matter to them at all. He was forgotten the moment he vanished from their sight.

Unable to bear the callous way they treated him, and aching in sympathetic pain, she rushed after him. No one deserved to be treated this way. To be so disregarded.

She couldn't imagine a worse cut.

By the time she caught up to his long strides, he was outside the building, in a peculiar marketplace. She paused at the strangeness of it all. There were many more creatures here similar to Chthamalus who walked about on tentacled legs, alongside "humans" and other entities she couldn't even begin to identify. Some as beautiful as angels and others . . .

Hideous would be a kind description.

But the buildings were the oddest things of all. Iridescent and shiny, they were made of a material the likes of which she'd never beheld before. It reminded her of the skin of a pearl, yet the texture was closer to that of steel. And just as inside the palace, there was a light here akin to sunlight, yet no obvious source for it.

What magick made this place possible? How could this exist and her world know nothing of it?

Incredible!

"Mr. Dupree?"

He slowed at her call to look back over his shoulder. Then he paused, too. "You shouldn't have followed me, Cameron."

Biting her lip, she closed the distance between them. "I couldn't leave you be. Not after *that* cruelty."

A tic started in his cheek. That was the only sign he gave as to how much their actions hurt him.

Aye, he was a strong one. Always. He kept his pain locked in and spoke nothing of it. Only those stormy eyes betrayed what was locked inside his heart.

And it made her burn for him that he'd been so neglected. Yearned to hold and soothe him until the pain was gone from those stormy eyes. To keep him close and give him what they'd so obviously failed to.

Before she could stop herself, she reached up and placed her hand to his cheek. The roughness of his whiskers teased her palm and contrasted sharply with the softness of his lips. "You're a good man, Kalder Dupree. Never let them, or anyone else, tell you otherwise."

He crushed her against him and gave her the hottest kiss of her life. One that left her breathless and aching. It was raw and hungry and whetted her appetite for things she knew better than to even think about.

Yet she couldn't help it. Every time she neared him, she hungered in a way that was sheer madness.

When he finally released her, he cupped her face in his hands and ground his teeth as if he were fighting with himself. "You don't know what you're saying, lass. A good man would walk away from you."

"Why? Because your brother's an arseling? You've met mine. Trust me. Few is the family what doesn't have a stockpile of them. So what if some have a few more than others. It's more about the size of the one above the overall quantity of them, anyway."

Kalder laughed, amazed that she could amuse him when he felt so low and hurt. Yet that was the beauty of her. She always made him feel better. And he didn't know how. Others annoyed the very shite out of him. He couldn't stand to be near most people. They tried his patience with nothing more than the sound of their breathing. In and out. The sheer monotony of it made him want to choke them till they stopped.

Cameron . . .

She, he craved with a madness indescribable. When others would ride his nerves into the ground, with barbed spurs on, and make him crave their hearts for it, her mere presence amused him. Soothed him. He could spend forever listening to her most inane prattle. And he didn't know why.

The sound of her voice alone brought him peace.

Unaware of how she affected him, she glanced around the city. "What is this place?"

"Wyñeria."

"Your homeland." Her smile made him instantly hard and wanton. "Now I see what you meant when you tried to describe where it was located, you tricky man. Though you could have told me about some of these incredible marvels." She tsked at him. "We're under the sea, aren't we?"

"Aye. Very observant you are, lass," he teased lightly. "Truly astute."

Without taking offense, she turned around, trying to take it all in. "It's so beautiful. Wondrous! Unlike anything I've ever seen. So where does the light come from? Surely the sun cannot reach this far down, can it?"

"Nay. Bioluminescent plankton that only grows down here. We call it surilah."

She sucked her breath in sharply. "That's a lovely name! It just rolls off the tongue, doesn't it? So then, how is it dry here, anyway, if we're under the ocean? Shouldn't we be wet? How do you bathe? Can you bathe? Can it rain? How do you grow food? Do you have seasons?"

Kalder laughed as she rattled off on a roll, asking more questions before he had a chance to answer any.

Cameron was always so full of questions. Always rambling them off, one after another, usually in rapid-fire succession.

And he didn't mind a bit. "Our legends say that it was placed on the ocean floor by the first king after his Myrcian wife told him that she would only birth him a son when she could lie comfortably on a dry bed of silk. But since he insisted his son be ocean born, as was the way of our people, this city was his compromise with her."

"And the portal that brought us here?"

"Only the Barnaks and our versions of priests control them. They can come and go as they please. And they can bring humans down from the surface. Getting you back to your world without killing you is trickier for them for some reason—that requires one with special skills—a sacerdos. They are able to bend the laws of magick enough that they can prevent the human body from becoming ill and dying. As for us . . . we have to swim back and forth between the two. Our bodies don't survive the portals well."

So that was why he'd arrived wet while the rest of them weren't. And why his gills had been exposed. Now she understood.

"Is it a long way?"

"Not the way we swim. But you wouldn't survive it. The human body can't adapt to the water like ours does. We're made for it. You're not."

She moved to touch the wall of the nearest building. "It's so pretty the way it shimmers so."

Its beauty couldn't touch hers. Especially not the way the light played against her skin and in her eyes.

In either of her forms. He'd never seen a more beautiful woman in all his life.

She looked up at him with an adorable smile. "I can't imagine you as a boy here."

He jerked his chin toward a group of them who were playing nearby. "I wasn't as carefree and happy as they. Me brothers and father saw to that. Rather, I spent the majority of me time skulking about the ruins."

"The ruins?"

He nodded. "Aye. Would you like to see them?"

"Sure."

Kalder took her hand and led her out of the city, far away from the bustle of the Myrcians he'd thought were long dead. How weird to be back when he'd been fully convinced that the entire city was gone. It was surreal to find it so eerily the same and yet very different from the place of his childhood memories.

He recognized much, and at the same time it was like being in a foreign land he'd never seen before. Familiar and lost, at the same time.

I should be used to being an outsider. He'd always felt that way here. Never quite fitting in. Never feeling wanted by anyone.

It was what had driven him to find solace in his own solitude where he didn't see disappointment or irritation in the faces of others. Where he didn't hear open agitation in a strained voice as it barked at him for being in the way when all he was trying to do was become invisible. Here, he didn't have to guard his words or actions.

He could just be.

That precious and ever-elusive peace he'd savored and clung to every moment he could. Because he knew how fleeting it was. And that all too soon they'd be on his back again. That the insults would return, a relentless soundtrack in his head, and from their angry mouths that never gave him any reprieve.

Only Cameron silenced that wave of endless criticisms that constantly flogged his sanity. The inner hatred that threatened to drown him. He didn't know how, but her presence made him want to be a better person. Made him want to be the man she saw him as.

She allowed him to breathe for the first time in his life. And he wanted to share things with her that he'd never shared with anyone else. Most of all, he wanted to keep her laughter ringing in his life.

In his heart.

Cameron slowed her steps as they came to an edge opening that looked out over the tumbled stones where bright fluorescent coral had grown. Like the walls, it glowed, only this was a vibrant coral as opposed to green and blue. The water over it made it appear to move and breathe.

As far as she could see, there were the remains of shattered buildings in the dark water, covered by the glowing plankton. A vibrant and yet dead and crumbling city underneath the water that lay outside the city's walls. "What is this?"

"The remains of a war my people fought against Poseidon, long ago."

"Who won?"

"We did. But at a great cost, and loss of life. It's what really happened to the Pharos of Alexandria. It wasn't destroyed by an earthquake. Rather, a group of our warriors went after it in retaliation for the destruction they did to us here."

He gave her a sheepish smile that lit the shadows of his handsome face. "Would you like a closer look at it?"

"I would love one." Cameron glanced out the window that was covered by a membrane where the sunken city lay asleep beneath treacherous dark ocean waters. "But how?"

"Do you trust me?"

How could he ask her such a thing? "Of course."

Cameron froze as he began to slowly unbutton her heavy woolen jacket. "Mr. Dupree?"

"It'll weigh you down in the water."

She would ask about that, but his hands were directly over her breasts now, and it was all she could do to maintain her composure. Especially when one accidentally brushed across her hardened nipple, causing her stomach to involuntarily contract. Worse, it sent a sharp stab through the center of her body, giving her a sudden ache and hunger the likes of which she could barely understand.

It took everything she had not to rise up on her tiptoes and kiss him. Or, more to the point, grab him and start tearing at his own clothes.

Her breathing turned ragged.

And when he dropped her jacket to the ground behind her, she'd never felt more exposed in her life. Honestly, her white linen shirt might as well be bare skin the way she felt.

By the devilish grin on his face, she suspected he knew as much. Rather than apologize, he pulled her body against his and fell back into the water, through the membrane, with her in his arms.

She gasped as they plunged into the lagoon and the ice-cold water enveloped her whole body and invaded her every sense. But this was unlike anything she'd ever experienced before. The pressure of the water was heavy and thick.

Invasive and dark. She held her breath and still they went deeper into the blackness with no end in sight. Not that she could *see* anything.

Worse, the salt stung at her eyes when she opened them. Her lungs began to burn as the pressure against her chest built even more.

Panicking, she started to flail in an attempt to save her life.

Until Kalder kissed her.

Nay, not kissed . . .

He breathed air into her lungs. Air that alleviated that pressure and made her feel instantly lighter.

Startled, she pulled back to stare aghast at him and those mesmerizing eyes that glowed mercury silver in the midnight depths.

" 'Tis the Adum." Somehow, she heard him plainly through the water, as if he were speaking normally.

Cupping her face in both of his hands that were now webbed and clawed, he again breathed air into her so that she could live beneath the waves. His tanned skin turned to a peculiar luminescence that made his tattoos stand out even more. "Underwater, my people exhale pure oxygen, so I can breathe for us both . . . if you let me."

Stunned, she stared at him in his Myrcian body, which was even more handsome than his human one. "Can you understand me?"

"Perfectly." He kissed her hand while she hovered in the water by his side. "Are you scared?"

A little, but she kept that to herself. "Not when I'm with you."

His smile warmed her more than anything could. He breathed into her a gentle kiss, then pulled her through the crushing weight of the water so that he could show her a dark, cavernous world unlike anything she'd ever seen before.

But the best part, bar none, were his breaths of life that he stopped to give her every few seconds.

His gaze turned warm and teasing. "I'm right here, Cameron. Grab a nip whenever you feel short of breath."

Yet as they went on, all the light vanished. It became an endless, oppressive night that began to terrify her with visions of a painful, watery death. "It's so dark here . . . how can you see to know where we're going?"

She'd barely finished those words before the entire area lit up. Gasping, she turned to see that the source of the light was Kalder, himself.

He glowed from the inside out.

Her jaw went slack. Never had she seen anything like this.

"How are you doing that?"

He winked at her. "One of me many talents, me lady *phearse*. We're able to secrete light in the water. I can do it on land, too. But tend not to, as it makes the humans lose all semblance of reason whenever they see it. Damn near scared one bugger to death when he caught me lighting up once in the woods. Next thing I knew, he'd written a whole series of stories about a will-o'-the-wisp ghoul over it and turned me into a major villain. Sadly, I was only out to take care of me business in private. Truth be told, I was the one who should have been horrified by the whole, personal encounter, more so than he."

Laughing, she allowed him to pull her through the heavy water that caressed every part of her body. All around her, the aquatic life seemed to dance to some song only it could hear. Schools of beautifully colored fish swam by them, and some that were so ugly she couldn't even describe their forms. They twisted out of shape and contorted.

Like the skeletons of fallen Titans, the crumbled buildings spread out as far as she could see. But what amazed her were the creatures who made them their homes. Both plant and animal gave new life to the destruction left behind by war.

Out of devastation comes hope.

Out of death, there is life.

Cameron paused as she remembered something her parents had taught them when they were young. Something she'd hadn't thought about in years.

Out of tragedy comes strength.

Out of pain comes wisdom.

Out of sorrow comes insight.

You will never know how high you can soar until you've learned to fly with wings that were broken by enemies and reforged by your own determination to succeed and let no one hold you down ever again. To show them all that their cruelty will not define you. That you will not live by their rules or dictates. You are your own master and they will never have power over you again.

Let nothing hold you back. Let nothing hem you in. You set your course and you fly to the heavens. A beautiful, imperfect creature, capable of love and trust, even after betrayal. Capable of mustering courage in the midst of utter terror. And capable of delivering mercy even after all you've ever been shown was cruelty.

You will rise above the ashes of the future they attempted to burn to the ground, a stronger creature, steadfast and more determined than ever to see this through. For there is nothing more terrifying in this universe than the Soul Determinatus. For it will not be stopped and it will not be daunted.

So go on and bring to me your worst if you must, and I will deliver unto you my very best.

That was Kalder in every way. Like her father and her brother. Life and enemies had done their best to tear him down and leave him heartless.

Instead, he'd chosen to soldier on past the pain, and while withdrawn from others so as to protect himself, he didn't lash out at the world. Lash out at strangers who were innocent.

He was a good man. In spite of it all.

Nay, in spite of *them* all, he'd risen above their cruelty.

And as he kissed her so that she could breathe she knew just how much she wanted him. Even though it was foolish. Even though there was no hope of any future with him.

She wanted to share with him what she'd never shared with anyone else.

Don't be stupid, girl!

Her thoughts were scandalous!

More than that, they were sinful. And yet she'd never felt like this about anyone else. She didn't know if she ever would again. Of all the men she'd known over the years, not a single one had ever made her blood quicken with nothing more than a coy look. Nothing more than the brush of his hand.

And Kalder did so much more than that.

Especially when he paused next to an old column where a section had been hollowed out. With a gentle hand, he pulled her down below and into a glorious room that must have been a grand hall at one time.

"What is this?"

"The remains of the first palace." He put his hands at her waist so that he could guide her into a cubbyhole that was cushioned by a spongy type of vegetation. "This is where I used to come to read."

Surprised, she turned to study his luminescent eyes. They were silver in color now, with a dark, stormy blue outline. Unbelievably beautiful. "You look so different like this."

"Hideous, you mean."

"Nay. Like an angel." She kissed him for a breath of air.

Kalder savored the feeling of her lips on his. Of her tongue brushing lightly against his teeth. Just as he reveled in the sensation of her in his arms. And the one thing he loved most about being underwater—her male clothing clung to her soft feminine curves and became completely sheer. The white linen was so fine that it revealed more than it covered and allowed him to see every bit of her charms. She'd be horrified if she knew how bare she was to his gaze.

How hungry and rock hard it made him that he could see the perfect outline of her areolae. Of the dark triangle of hair at the juncture of her thighs that kept drawing his attention to fantasies he really shouldn't be thinking about.

This was a terrible idea.

And at the same time he wanted nothing more than to peel her clothes off and run his hands over every inch of her lush, supple skin. Indeed, her dark chestnut hair looked sublime fanning out in the water. Like a dark halo that framed her beautiful face.

He couldn't think straight as he stared at her. She looked like some watery fey creature come to capture him, body and soul, and at the moment, he couldn't imagine anything better than being ensnared by her. Indeed, he'd gladly consign himself over to her for all eternity.

Body and soul.

Kalder watched as she slowly explored the room with bold fingers, while learning to swim. Her every movement a seductive dance of someone not quite at home in the water. Yet even so, she rolled her hips and moved her arms with the art of a practiced courtesan.

She was all fluid grace as she spun about in the water. The linen of her tunic flared out, showing him a bit of her stomach, while the white linen of her breeches continued to show him the darker hairs at the juncture of her thighs. And all he could think about was unbuttoning them and sliding his hand down so that he could stroke her. Watching her writhe to the rhythm of his fingers . . .

His body erupted into fire as he watched her. He needed her in a way that made him burn from the inside out.

She paused as she caught his gaze. Her face fell instantly. "Am I doing something wrong?"

He struggled for control. "Nay, lass. I like it. A lot more than I should."

Her gaze darted down to the part of his body that the water made it impossible for him to hide. While his breeches were dark and therefore kept him covered better than hers did, there was no missing the size of the bulge that betrayed his hunger for her.

Even in the darkness, her cheeks glowed, and the enhanced color only made her eyes glisten. Worse, it made his cock jerk with a need he couldn't control.

Kalder's throat went dry. He fully expected her to stop or pull away.

Or slap him. Which he deserved.

Though he knew she couldn't go far, given that she needed his breath to survive here.

But to his utter shock, she reached for him and pulled him closer.

She stopped just short of touching his mouth to hers. They hovered in the water barely a hand's breadth apart.

Damn, how she looked wild and wonton there. Like some manifestation of his fantasies. Not real, but a fey creation sent to torment him worse than any of the horrors Vine had used against him.

He wanted her more than he'd ever wanted anything. And he knew all the reasons why he shouldn't. All the reasons why he had to keep away from her.

She deserves better than you. She's a creature of light and air. You're born of watery darkness.

And none of that mattered to him.

Cameron pulled his lips down for another breath. He moaned at the taste of her as every piece of him screamed out for more. She was unlike anyone else on this earth.

Above or below. Never had he met her equal.

Drunk with her sweet taste and unable to rein himself back from the edge of this, he dragged his lips from hers to her throat, half expecting her to protest or shove him away.

Praying she would slap him.

She didn't. Instead, she cradled him with her body. Held him there as she sucked her breath in sharply. His head spinning, he buried his head between the deep valley of her breasts so that he could taste the creamy skin that tormented him. The salt of her skin blended with that of the ocean and burned his tongue. More than that, it whetted his appetite, making him demand more of her.

Cameron closed her eyes, savoring the sensation of Kalder's tongue on her flesh. She knew she shouldn't allow this—in her world, her reputation and purity were everything—but she didn't want to stop him.

Not now. She was long past the age of childhood. Had her parents not died and had she not been forced into the role of playing a lad, she'd have married long ago and been settled with a husband. Most likely to a loveless match.

And while she wasn't sure exactly what she felt for Kalder, she knew that she cared for him. Deeply.

Most of all, she knew in her heart that she wanted this moment. With him, and no one else.

She couldn't even imagine being with another man. She'd wanted him almost from the first moment they'd met and he'd scared her in the dark with his saucy walk and mysterious ways.

Determined to see it through, she pulled at his shirt until he shrugged it off. Her breath caught at the sight of his scarred chest. Of those sculpted muscles that teased and flexed as she ran her hands over his shoulders and down his arms to his clawed hands that were scarred from the countless fights he'd been in.

Her merman was a brawler, through and through.

"You're beautiful."

He shook his head in wonderment of her. "I'm not the one who's beautiful, me *phearse*."

"Aye, you are. More handsome than any ever born. In the sea or on the land." She laced her hands through his hair and nibbled his lips.

Kalder groaned at the passion he tasted, amazed by it and by her. How he loved the way this woman kissed him. The way she looked at him as if he were the only man in the world where she was concerned. No one had ever made him feel the way she did.

As if he were special.

Like he mattered.

She wrapped her legs about his waist. "Tell me how to please you."

Her boldness startled and pleased him. He loved the fact that she was so brazen and unabashed. "You do that just by being with me."

She smiled. "Do I?"

He nodded.

Her smile widened as she rubbed herself against his swollen

groin. He groaned at the feel of her there and imagined how much better she would feel if he'd had a chance to remove their breeches.

"Is there anything else I can do?"

"That's a good start, me *phearse*." He reached up and unlaced her tunic until her breasts were free.

Kalder held her close, while his heart raced madly with hunger.

How strange that the only place he'd ever felt at home was in her arms. And he knew in that moment that he'd follow her anywhere. Even to hell itself. She made him feel so warm and welcomed.

No one else had ever offered him so much by doing nothing more than smiling.

You're free now. No longer bound to Thorn. You could take a wife and start over.

Marry her.

But he knew better than that. It wasn't so simple.

Starting over was for other people. People who didn't have a brutal past like his. Those who were normal. Those who lived on the land.

Besides, he knew nothing about Cameron. Not really.

Does it matter?

It could. Better than anyone, he knew that alliances played a large part of his family's life—that they impacted the ship and her crew—and any decision he made would affect all of them. He had too many enemies gunning for him.

Not to mention that Cameron held the blood of Michael in her veins. Her brother was a Necrodemian. And that blood would pass to any child Cameron might have.

Any child that might be born to them. A creature of the land and sea.

Those children would have a higher calling that would give them no peace, whatsoever, from the worst creations the gods had ever spat out of hell. It would cause all of them to be hunted forever.

Generation after generation.

How could he think to pass on such a cursed legacy? It would be the worst sort of selfishness.

And yet even though he knew that about her, he couldn't bring himself to let go and leave her. She was like some missing part of himself.

A vital part.

The *best* part.

Cameron watched Kalder's features as he pulled back from their kiss to look down at her. He stared at her as if trying to memorize her face.

There was a dark, deep sadness in his glowing eyes. One even more intense than it'd been before.

"What is on your mind that you look as if the Second Coming is upon you?"

"Wishing that I was a simple human peasant who'd stumbled into your tavern for an ale. Do you think you'd have found me as alluring then?"

Her eyes twinkled with humor. "If I said nay, would you toss me aside?"

"Nay?"

She wrinkled her nose playfully. "Given that I would have assumed you were after me as a lad? I'd be a bit offended."

Laughing, he ran his forefinger over the arch of her brow and studied her face as if he were trying to discern the truth. "And if I made sure you knew that I knew the truth of your gender?"

"Then the truth is that it wouldn't have mattered. Peasant or king matters naught to me. All I see is the heart of the man."

"And if I said that I had no heart?"

"I'd never believe that. I know you better, Mr. Dupree. I've seen your heart. Felt it the night you fought so hard and determined to save me from the demons what were determined to drag me to me doom."

Kalder trembled at her words. He trembled at the warmth of her soft body contoured to the hardness of his own. Her stomach was feather soft against his erection. Her hands tender on his shoulders.

He stared into her ever-curious gaze and lost himself there. What would it be like to spend the rest of his life staring into those light, sea hazel eyes?

To hold her like this for decades?

And in this moment, he could imagine her plump with his child. See her warm and welcoming in his bed forever.

The thought both terrified and thrilled him.

How could he even think of allowing himself such a weakness? To curse their children so? Her brother would forbid such a thing. And what could he offer her really?

I'm nothing.

Everything he touched, he ruined.

Even now, he could see the day Muerig had died. Because of his neglect.

Even worse than his brother's fate, he could see her being swept over the ship and ripped from his hands by their enemies, and all because he'd started to care for her. Because of his curse . . .

He wasn't allowed to love. He knew that.

Yet how could he live without her?

You have to. Otherwise she'll pay for your folly. And so will your children.

Kalder couldn't bear to lose her again. Even now he could feel that day deep inside his soul. The winds had been fierce and cold. The water dark and choppy. He'd looked out across the waves, his heart sickened as he saw her vanish beneath the water, while he was helpless to stop it. Taken by enemies he couldn't fight.

His soul was forever burdened by the unending grief and self-hatred that came from knowing the fault of it all was solely his own.

Just as it'd been the day Muerig had died because he'd failed to meet his brother on time.

"I will never again take any pleasure in me life. I will spend the rest of eternity paying penance for me stupidity."

Cameron cupped his face with her hands, and her touch brought him back from his maudlin thoughts. Back to the only pleasure he'd known since the day his mother had killed him.

Her arms.

"Have I lost you? You look as if you're far away, lost in your thoughts. Should I go and leave you to them?"

"Stay with me, Cameron."

Stay with me forever. . . .

How he wished for the courage to say that last bit out loud. For the courage to keep her by his side.

But he couldn't.

He didn't dare. It wouldn't be fair to her, and he couldn't bear to be the reason for anything else bad happening to her.

May the gods help him, but if Vine did force him to choose between Cameron and his brother, Muerig's goat was the guinea. He'd offer the bastard up without hesitation—he knew that now without a doubt—and that would be ruinous for them all.

She tightened her legs around his hips, then leaned up to kiss him blind with bliss.

Kalder let her taste roll over his senses as he lost himself to her completely. Forcing his thoughts away from anything except the need he had to sample her fully, he swam with her into a cavern where he pulled her from the water to a small sandy cove so that she could breathe on her own.

Amazed, she took a second to look around the darkened underwater cave while he gently peeled his remaining clothes off.

Until he returned to her side and laid her back against the moss-covered sand. But she didn't pull away. Instead, she ran her hands over his body, timidly exploring every inch of him. Her innocent touch reached deep inside him, setting him free of his past and soothing him in a way nothing ever had. Especially when she bit her lip and touched the most private part of him for the first time.

Cameron felt her cheeks turn red hot as she cupped him in her hand and explored his cock with her fingers. He was so velvety hard. So different from her own body. And she delighted in the look of pleasure on his face.

Feeling more powerful than ever, she ran her hands through Kalder's short, wet hair and down his whiskered cheeks. How she loved the manly feel of him lying atop her. It was such a peculiar thing. This pressure of his body pressing against hers. Of his arms surrounding her.

She ran her feet down his legs, feeling the crisp hairs that dusted them, and reveled in the differences between their bodies. And it was then she realized just how much she did love this man. How much she treasured his rare smiles, and peculiar ways. Human or not, he was everything to her.

He was what she needed most.

This man whose kisses set her afire. Whose strong touch made her weak.

He was her heart. Her soul.

But what good was it? Really? This was all kinds of folly and she knew it.

She couldn't stay with him.

Forgetting the fact that they were two different species, Paden would never allow it. He couldn't stand Kalder. Or any man who came near her, for that matter.

It was hopeless, this love.

Aching with the thought and wanting him regardless, Cameron wrapped her arms around Kalder's neck and held him tight as pain wracked her body.

"Cameron," he rasped. "You're strangling me."

She loosened her grip, then buried her face against his chest and closed her eyes, wishing for things she knew could never be. She didn't want to let him go.

You'll have to.

But, it wasn't fair. Not when all she wanted was to love him. Be with him.

He's another species. And she was completely fine with it. Indeed, she was about to make love with him. . . .

Under the waters he called home. Her life had become the strangest of strange.

Kalder nibbled her lips.

Pushing away all thoughts of reality, Cameron sighed contentedly. She would think no more about that. For now, she was where she wanted to be and with the man she wanted to be with. That was all that mattered.

She closed her eyes as he trailed kisses over her body, down to her breasts, where he teased and played. Arching her back, she melted under the onslaught of his tender care, and trembled as he loosened her breeches, then slid them from her body.

Kalder moaned aloud at the taste of her salty skin. If he lived forever, he would remember this moment. The way she felt beneath him.

The way her hands played in his hair while he licked and teased her.

It was heaven.

Growling deep in his throat, he left her right breast and made his way over to the left so that he could draw that taut peak into his mouth and let his tongue sample it.

He slid his hand down her body, through the moist tangle of curls, until he could touch the part of her he craved. She gasped and moaned, then opened her legs even wider for his exploration.

"Tell me what you want me to do to you, Cam?"

"I want you to kiss me."

"Where?"

She touched his lips with her fingers. "On my lips."

He obliged her until he could scarce breathe for the fire inside him. "Where else would you have me kiss you?"

"Here," she said, turning her head so that she bared her neck to him.

Again, he licked and teased her neck. He felt the chills spread over her body, felt her nipples harden even more against his chest.

She made little noises in the back of her throat as he nipped her skin with his teeth.

"Is there any place else you would have me?"

Her face pinkened and she looked away sheepishly.

"Here now," he said, capturing her chin in his hand and turning her face until she looked up at him. "'Tis not like me lady Cameron to be timid. You've never shirked away from talking before."

Her eyes softened.

Kalder turned serious as he leaned on his arms and met her gaze. "Never be afraid or embarrassed over telling me what you want. So, I ask again. Where would you have me, me love?"

She bit her lip and slowly trailed her hand down her body. Kalder watched the path of it, his breath rattling in his chest. It was the most sensuous thing he'd ever seen.

She braced one leg up, spreading herself open to his hungry gaze, and touched herself between her legs.

Cameron shivered at the hot look Kalder gave her. She still couldn't believe what she was doing, but there was no shame in her heart.

Only love for the man who was with her.

He kissed his way down her body, slowly, languidly. The touch of his lips on her skin made her burn with fiery need. Who could have imagined a man's touch could be so pleasurable?

When he took her into his mouth, she cried out in total abandon.

His hot tongue licked and teased, around and around, stroking and delving. The watery room spun out of control while she lay there, weak and panting from the ribbons of pleasure that shredded her. Now she understood Sancha's bawdy talk completely! Gracious! The woman hadn't been jesting at all.

She reached down and took his large, masculine hand into hers.

Kalder laced his fingers with hers and gave a light squeeze. Cameron smiled as her love washed over her. There was truly nothing more sublime than having him like this. Feeling him with her body, holding on to his strong hand that was now human again in appearance.

Cameron looked down to see their entwined hands. Her skin was so pale compared to his. Scars marred his knuckles, and stood out against the darkness of his skin.

Content and thrilled, she sighed as his thumb stroked her palm in time to his tongue stroking her body. Then, she lifted his hand up to her lips so that she could kiss his scars.

But she didn't stop there. She opened her mouth and suckled his fingers one by one, tasting them. Nibbling them.

Kalder looked up, startled by her actions. No woman had ever kissed his hands, let alone given them so much consideration. But he had to admit that her tongue felt heavenly sliding over his skin, between his fingers, and for that alone he was glad he'd found dry land and allowed his skin to return and the webbing to recede so that she could do this.

He crawled up her body and then stared down at her, warm and open beneath him. The sight tore through him.

How he craved her. Needed her.

Her hands released his. Then she trailed them over his chest, his hips, ran them down until she could cradle his hot, rigid shaft in her hands.

His body jerked in response.

Kalder moaned at the sensation of her hands sliding down his cock, of her reaching down lower so that she could cup him in her hands.

"Tell me what you want, Mr. Dupree," she breathed.

You.

The word hung in his throat. Unlike her, words were strangers to his tongue.

But he couldn't say that out loud. He'd been rejected by everyone else, and while he was used to it, the thought of her turning him away . . .

It would finally destroy him. She, alone, had the ultimate power over him.

So, he did what he did best and held his feelings in.

"First, I want you to call me Kalder," he teased. "No need in such formalities while we're so intimate, *Miss Jack,* and I would rather show you." Dipping his head down, he claimed her lips, then slid himself deep inside her body.

He growled at her warm, sweet wetness that surrounded him. At the feeling of her body welcoming his intrusion.

For the briefest moment, she tensed and dug her nails against his back.

Kalder froze. "Are you all right?"

She nodded against his shoulder as she panted ever so slightly. "It's a rather shocking sensation, isn't it?"

He wouldn't really know. "Am I hurting you?" He glanced down at her.

Looking up, she met his gaze, and he didn't know but there was something far more intimate about this than any other encounter he'd ever had. It was as if his very soul were bared to her and not just his body. Never had he felt closer to anyone.

"It's subsiding now."

Cameron swallowed with the realization that she'd just crossed a threshold from which there was no going back.

Ever.

One for which there could be extreme and dire consequences for both of them. For all she knew, she could conceive a child out of this. And that thought terrified her. Not because it would be a baby, but because of the responsibility it would bring. The scandal.

If I do conceive a child, I shall love it forever. Just as I do Kalder.

How could she not?

The look on his face as he made love to her was, and would be, forever seared into her memory. He'd been hurt by so many. The fact that he could be tender at all mystified her. God knew that he hadn't learned it at home. No one had shown him kindness. The scars on his body bore testimony to that.

All he knew was violence. Strife.

War.

Yet he made love to her slowly, and with the tenderest of care, making sure not to hurt or harm her. Ever careful of how much weight he placed against her body. It was such a wickedly sweet sensation of his hips sliding against hers. Of him kissing her while giving her unbelievable pleasure.

Never would she have imagined anything more glorious than this. More incredible than him.

How could she?

Kalder closed his eyes and savored the way Cameron held him. The sensation of her running her hands over his back while he lost himself deep inside her. If only this moment could last.

You have to let her go.

But letting her go would be the hardest thing he'd ever done.

It's for her own good.

Everything you love, you kill. He knew that. Without fail. The gods would never allow him to have something and keep it. They took too much pleasure in giving him pain.

I can't watch her die, too.

Kalder kissed her lips as he thrust against her hips. He had no idea how long they'd have together, but fate and circumstance would separate them. One way or another. Of that he had no doubt.

Fight for her. You have to.

Did he dare?

Do you dare not?

He tried to imagine going back to his life without her. Tried to imagine making it through one day without her smile warming his heart.

He couldn't.

The pain of the thought was too much. *I have to find some way to keep her with me.* No matter the consequences.

She was the only thing that was good in his life. The only thing that made him happy, and no one would take that away from him.

Not without a fight.

Cameron saw the determined set of Kalder's jaw as he quickened his strokes.

"Are you all right?" she asked, wondering what caused the sudden change in him.

"Aye, love," he said, punctuating his words with his thrusts. "When I'm with you, it's the only time I'm right."

She melted at that. Wrapping her arms around his shoulders, she held him close and reveled in his hot, naked skin sliding against hers. There was nothing more erotic than to hold him against her like this.

She teased his jaw with her lips and tongue and trailed her hands over the smooth plane of his back to his hips. She splayed her hands over his delectable rear and closed her eyes as she urged him on.

Her body quivered and tightened until she could stand no more.

Moaning deep, she let her orgasm take her and held him close until the last tremor had shuddered through her.

He cupped her face with his hand and kissed her deep.

Then she felt it. He growled into her mouth as his own release took him.

He buried himself deep and froze.

"Oh, me lady *phearse*," he breathed in her ear. "There is truly nothing better than the feel of you in me bed."

"There is nothing better than the feel of you in me body." Heat exploded across her face as she realized what she'd said.

But her embarrassment faded the instant she saw the warm, satisfied look on his face.

He gave her a light kiss, then withdrew. He rolled over onto his back and gathered her into his arms.

Cameron draped herself over his chest and listened to his heart pounding under her cheek. The deep thud was so incredibly soothing. How she wished she could lie like this forever.

She traced circles around his chest and toyed idly with his nipples.

"You keep doing that," he said huskily, "and neither of us will leave this place."

Cameron was beginning to think that she wouldn't mind spending eternity here with him. And that thought terrified her. He made it so easy to forget herself.

To forget everything.

If only she could.

But all too soon they hunted down their clothes and dressed, then swam back to the palace, where Kalder retrieved her dry jacket to wrap around her before they immediately ran into a section of the crew that had been searching for her since she'd followed after Kalder.

Rosie let out a relieved breath at the sight of them before he called out for the others. "Cameron's not dead yet!"

She scowled at him. "I beg your pardon?"

He shrugged unrepentantly. "Our natural assumption was that something here had eaten you, given that all we found of you was your coat."

"Oh." Cameron prayed there was no color in her cheeks over *that* remark, especially as she remembered some of what Kalder had done with her. Harder still was resisting the sudden urge to not look at Kalder and see his reaction to those words.

Yet luckily she managed not to give in to her temptation and betray their tryst.

Until Paden stormed toward her and took her roughly by the arm. "Where the devil have you been? We've searched everywhere for you! Have you any idea how scared I've been?"

Grimacing, she jerked her arm free of his tight grasp and pushed him back. "Kalder was touring me around the city."

"Why are you sopping wet, then?"

"We went for a swim."

"You can't swim! You don't know how." Paden glared at Kalder.

That set off Kalder's anger in turn. "If you're questioning the lady's honor, then I'll be taking it from your hide, man. And your teeth! Now, you apologize to your sister!"

"Me? I'm not the one what took her out alone. Unchaperoned, I might add. If you care so much for her sterling reputation, then you needs be minding it, you bloody wanker bastard, and not blighting it every chance you get by dragging it through the mud like you've gone and done every tart and whore-slag you've come across!!"

"Here now! 'Nough of that what with the both of you, or I'll be playing conkers with your bullocks!" Devyl stepped between them, then faced Paden first. "For the record, mate, his people can share air with us, and allow us to breathe beneath the seas as if we were born to it, same as they. I've seen them do it. If he says they swam, then 'tis so. There's no reason to doubt it, and you've even less reason to doubt someone as honest and forthright as your sister. I trust Kalder, Captain Jack. Completely. And of all people alive, you ought to be putting faith in Miss Jack."

A tic started in Paden's jaw. "Cammy, I trust implicitly. Him's another matter entirely, and then some. I don't like him keeping company with me baby sister. At all. Especially not alone when no one's around what to be watching him, and his wandering male body parts, as if *I* don't know well enough what they're capable of when left unsupervised by a third party. And not after all the stories what I've heard about him, while we've searched."

Cameron gaped at her brother.

Bart stepped forward quickly. "Well, there's been no harm, aside from the time we've slaughtered. So, now that we've located the lass, and proven false Paden's cannibalism allegations about the Myrcians, I say we join the party, as we *were* invited to it, and play nice with the merpeople until they decide to throw us out. Aye? Who's with me?"

Devyl nodded in agreement. "Why not? We might as well go and give them more reasons to dislike and mistrust us."

Mara scoffed at her husband's dour tone and dire prediction. "You're all incorrigible."

"But notice the lady doesn't discount what we say," William said loudly to Bart.

"That's 'cause the Lady Marcelina knows it's truth we be speaking, and what not."

As they headed away, Cameron caught a brief unguarded expression on Kalder's face before he shielded it.

Concerned about what was causing it, she went to him.

"What's wrong?"

At first, he smiled and started to discount it, then he grimaced and decided to confide in her. "I have a feeling of disquiet."

"About?"

His countenance said "everything," but his lips contradicted what her instinct was telling her about his mood. "Not sure."

Belle came up to stand beside Cameron, and passed a knowing glance to each of them. "So, Miss Jack, did you find the—" She cleared her throat meaningfully. "—*fruit* to be suited to your tastes, after all?"

Kalder scowled at the veiled question that Cameron more than understood, as it pertained to an earlier discussion she'd had with Belle and the other ladies upon her first arrival to their ship. One that stemmed from their initial discovery of her most virginal state.

This time, Cameron felt the heat of embarrassment scalding her cheeks, as she knew that Belle's powers allowed her to know well enough what had transpired between them. There was never any hiding from the Lady Belle.

"It was most succulent, indeed, Miss Morte. And yes, definitely to me tastes. Thank you very much for asking."

"Lucky you, me lady. For there are many who'd give much to sample a bite of it. 'Specially here in this land. Guard yourself, as they'll be most unhappy should they learn that you were the fortunate one who plucked it for her own."

Kalder scowled. "What are you two talking about?"

Belle patted him on the cheek. "Pretty sure you know, love. As I've never seen you more tranquil than what you are right now."

Kalder snorted before he cornered one of the watchmen who was trying to slink past them. "You there! See to the Lady Cameron's needs, posthaste. She needs dry clothing and something suitable for whatever event my brother has seen fit to put together for our guests."

"I'll have to—"

"Am I not still a prince of this empire?"

That ferocious tone of power even managed to send a wave of apprehension, and a tremor of fear, down Cameron's spine.

The watchman's eyes bulged. "Aye, Highness."

"Then you will do as I command and see to the lady's needs. Avast!"

Cameron's eyes widened at a tone she'd never heard Kalder use before. He sounded more akin to the captain than her tender mermaid.

Kalder turned toward the shimmering wall. "Chthamalus?"

The Barnak demon appeared instantly in the glassy depths, where he stared out at them with a blank, curious expression. Then he blinked at Kalder before his eyes widened and he leapt from the wall to stand by Kalder's side. "You summoned me, my lord?"

"Make sure he"—Kalder jerked his chin toward the watchman—"sees that me orders are carried out and that the lady is attended to in chambers worthy of a royal consort and that she isn't shunted off to a closet fit only for a scullery maid."

"Aye, my lord."

"Good demon, Tally. Thank you."

Cameron hesitated. While she was grateful for his concern and courtesy, she wasn't quite so sure about the thought of being alone in this place. Kalder's orders made her a bit uncomfortable since she barely knew his demon. Not that she didn't trust Chthamalus per se, she just had a bad feeling in general.

"Want me to come with you?"

More than the Caribbean sorceress could imagine. Grateful beyond measure, Cameron hugged Belle for her perceptive powers, and kindness. Every day she loved her dear friend more. "Aye! Thank you!"

Kalder didn't move until the ladies, with Chthamalus in tow, were completely out of sight. And still that feeling that something was amiss persisted deep in his gullet.

Trying not to think about it, he took a few minutes to tend to other pressing matters with another servant, before he started on his way.

And no matter how much he tried to ignore it, he couldn't shake that uneasiness. It walked over his flesh like a living, breathing creature. Someone was definitely watching him. He turned around to scan the walls and corridor with both his eyes and his "other" senses.

Nothing. Everything appeared normal. There was nothing on this plane or in the aether. Yet the feeling persisted.

Uneasy and spooked, Kalder headed for his old rooms and wondered what he'd find there. Most likely one of his brothers had taken them over as soon as his mother had dumped his body for the sharks to feast on. Darcel or Eyson would be his first guess as to the current occupant. Out of the eleven of them, they had hated him most.

He doubted if any had given more than a passing thought to his death. Or a single thought about him since. They'd probably been relieved to see the deaths of their mother's favorite and most hated sons within days of each other, as Muerig's death would have made more room in her cold heart for them, and his death would have chilled her more caustic moods.

But as he turned the corner of the hall that led to their bedrooms, he stopped dead in his tracks.

Right before him stood his older brother Marcel, Darcel's fraternal twin.

The only saving grace was that unlike Perrin, he looked nothing like their father. However, his striking resemblance to their mother wasn't much better. In fact, it made him want to punch him all the more.

Or better yet, hack him to pieces.

Damn, I really did hate my parents.

"So it's true. You *are* alive."

Kalder smirked at the caustic, bitter tone that was a deeper version of their mother's voice. "Nay, brother. I'm merely a figment of your lack of imagination."

Awkward silence fell between them as Marcel struggled to ignore his sarcasm. Which was nothing new. They'd never had much to say to one another. Kalder had spent most of his time here alone and without speaking, as he'd learned early in life that anything he said would only be used against him, and always at the worst possible time. Every one of his brothers, and in particular his mother, had a nasty tendency to take whatever he said out of context, twist it around, then relay it to a third party so as to paint him in the darkest light imaginable.

Ergo, he spoke never. It just made it easier.

Fewer bodies to hide.

Fewer punches to throw later. Verbally and physically.

Which he prepared himself to do now as Marcel raked him with a sneer that cut almost as deeply as a razor. "You shouldn't have come back here."

"Didn't plan for it. Rather, happened unexpectedly."

"Then why are you heading for private quarters when you don't have a room anymore?"

"Am I not still part of the family?" Kalder dared him to declare his enmity the way Perrin had done earlier.

Marcel didn't answer. Instead, his gaze went past Kalder's shoulder to something behind his back.

Turning his head, Kalder saw Rosie and Simon approaching them with their unorthodox manners and clothing. As a former priest of the African trickster spirit Exú, Simon Dewing, who was larger than most and therefore off-putting on his best day, could be a fierce protector or one hell of a vengeful enemy, depending on his mood. It was something Kalder respected most about him. That and the fact that you always knew where you stood with him. Unlike Kalder's siblings.

Simon didn't play games with people. If he hated you, he walked up, tapped you on the shoulder, and announced it plainly. In your face.

Then he punched your jaw while he laughed.

He and Justinian Rosenkranz, or Rosie, as they called their ever-jovial crewmate, were a motley, unsettling pair who didn't appear at first glance to have anything in common other than the fact that neither gave two shits what anyone thought about them.

That, too, Kalder respected.

And it was something Rosie proved as he planted his long, lanky form on Kalder's right side and perched his ornate, twisted iron staff that was decorated with feathers and braided leather cords over his muscular shoulders. With a quirky grin that made his golden whisky-colored eyes shine, he pushed his flamboyant burgundy tricorne back on his head so that he could scratch at his dreads. "In a bit of a snit, Princeling?"

Kalder frowned. "Pardon?"

Rosie answered the question with a charming grin. "You look like you need rescuing, Princess. So your knights in shining armor are here to render aid. Shall I slap your annoyance and challenge him to a duel on your behalf? Or would you rather do it yourself and save me wrist the pain of it all?"

"Something is profoundly wrong with you. Isn't it? Tell me truthfully, did your mother drop you on your head as an infant? Or suffocate you while you were breastfeeding?"

"Given me fashion sense and wardrobe, you're going to ask me that with a straight face?" Rosie snorted and slid a smirk toward Simon. "And he thinks *I'm* the one with a problem? Seriously?"

Simon let out a gruff, noncommittal "Heh."

But while Kalder and Rosie knew they were teasing each other, as was their nature, Marcel gaped. "You're allowing him to speak to you in such a manner?" he asked Rosie.

Dropping the staff down to his side, Rosie braced his arm on Kalder's shoulder and leaned against him. "We're brothers, Kal and I. But I guess you can't understand that, can you, now? What it means to bleed for someone and have them bleed for you. His words to me aren't barbed to bite. They're good-natured sport meant to poke fun and make him laugh at the absurd bitch that we call life. As are mine to him, and he well knows I would never hurt his tenderlings, as I value them far above me own."

"That is why I brought them here when we were being attacked," Kalder said. "Their lives mean more to me than me own does, and I'd rather die than see any of them harmed."

Simon took a step forward. "And it's why if anyone or anything comes at our fish-brother, here, we'll be taking it personally."

Rosie nodded. "And be taking it out of the throat of the fool what does it."

Yet even as they said those words, Kalder's bad feeling tripled. The skin on the back of his neck crawled with a sense of hostile foreboding.

Aye, there was something sinister here. Something foul.

And it was coming for all of them. . . .

Coming for their blood and their bones.

The threat was real and it was imminent.

You will have to choose. No one gets to eat their cake and have it. . . .

10

Cameron stared in shock at the image of herself in the mirror. "Is this really me?"

Belle smiled at her from over her shoulder, while Chthamalus grinned in approval. "Aye, love. Who else would it be? You act as if you've never seen yourself in a gown before."

She hadn't. At least not since the death of her parents, when Paden had burned every girlie item she'd possessed in order to protect her as best he could. To keep her from being separated from him by others, and to make sure that she didn't fall prey to some drunken randy male while they were forced to work menial jobs for their sustenance and survival. Because of his paranoia for her safety, Paden had forced her to dress and act the part of a boy for most of her life.

Truth, she could scarce remember being a girl, never mind a woman.

"I can't believe he sent this to me."

"Aye, my lady." Chthamalus settled the hem around her feet, which were bedecked in the prettiest shoes she'd ever seen in all her life. Dark blue velvet shoes that sparkled with pearl and crystal buckles. Peeking out from just below the delicate lace hemline, they caught the light every time she moved. "His Highness was emphatic about it, and the colors. Said he'd seen the way you admired the gowns of other ladies and he didn't want to see that hunger in your eyes go unsated for another hour. You mean a lot to him. Admittedly, I haven't been with him in quite a while, but never have I seen him care for any person the way he cares for you. And in spite of all the centuries we've been parted, I know that he isn't the type to have changed much, if any, from the man I knew so long ago. 'Tis not in his nature to let others close to him. So you can trust when I say that you are very special to his heart."

Cameron felt giddy with joy over Tally's words and Kalder's thoughtful gift. The beautiful white dress was softer than anything she'd ever owned. Modest and fashionable, it contrasted sharply against the vibrant peacock blue silk jacket that hugged curves she hadn't known she possessed.

She really was a woman!

Tears of gratitude choked her as she fingered the curls that Belle had styled for her into a proper chignon. She looked so posh and fine that if she hadn't known it was she herself, she'd have never guessed it.

"Do you think Mr. Dupree will like what he sees?" she asked them.

"Mr. Dupree?" Belle teased.

Heat stung her cheeks as she realized how silly she was being with her insistence on something so formal given what they'd shared, especially since Belle was more than aware of it. Still . . . "Can't help it. It's foolish of me, isn't it?"

Belle hugged her. "Nay, love. Not foolish. *Precious*. Your unassuming sweetness is what I adore best about you." She gave her one fierce squeeze before she let go and stepped away. "Come, me dear. Let's go find him so that you can thank him properly for his gift, and make your brother go off into a right apoplexy over it. Want to take bets on what manner of colors that man'll be turning when he sees how fair and lovely you are dressed like that?"

Cameron laughed, even as she clearly envisioned Paden's tantrum well in her mind. Paden would indeed explode into a fit over this. Not just because Kalder had given it to her, but because she did indeed look like a woman, and Paden refused to see her as such. Ever. And God have mercy on any should they ever catch even a modest glimpse of anything even remotely resembling the teensiest bit of a breast bump on her body. She could only imagine the conniption he'd have over the whole swell of her tender bits showing on her décolleté like this.

If he'd had his way, he'd have cut off entire parts of her anatomy long ago and turned her into one of those Amazon warrior maids like he'd read to her about when she was a wee lass.

But she supposed that was fair enough, since most days she, in turn, wanted to cut off his cod-dangle.

"You're an evil one, Lady Belle."

She winked at Cameron. "That I am, me love, but your brother . . . he makes it easy to harass and mock him for his boorish ways, he does."

Cameron wouldn't argue that. And she looked forward to seeing her Myrcian lord, and thanking him most personally for his sweetness in giving her such a fine and lovely thing as this dress to prance about in and feel like a fairy princess. It was the sweetest thing he could have done for her.

At least that was what she thought. But as they entered the ballroom where the others were gathered alongside Kalder's people, she quickly rethought her gratitude and felt her confidence dwindle into absolutely nothing.

Less than nothing, if such a thing were possible.

Along with every last shred of her happiness.

While she'd known Kalder was more beautiful and sexier than anyone ever had a right to be, and that it should be criminal for a man to tempt everyone who saw him to want to take a bite of that luscious caramel skin, she hadn't realized his unique charisma and charms were innate to the whole of his people!

In fact, every single male in this room was quite a fine specimen of male perfection . . . though, granted, none were equal to Kalder, in her opinion. Her Myrcian could still tie knots around all the others and leave them hanging in want of more.

However, as she scanned the great multitude that was gathered about to socialize in their snoot and pomp, it was plainly evident that the Myrcian females outshone her looks and lineage, by leaps, bounds, *and* cartwheels. They were so beautiful as to make even a sainted angel weep with envy.

I'm a hideous troll.

Nay, to call *her* a troll in comparison to these blooming falderals was an insult to trolls the world over. She was the mangy flea on top of the troll's wart compared to the great beauties in this room.

Why on earth Kalder would ever want her when he could have his pick of these elegant beauties, she couldn't imagine.

The man was daft.

Or blind.

Mayhap both.

And she wasn't the only one to think it. Indeed, the moment she entered the room, heads came together and tongues began to wag madly with their speculations as to what binding spell she'd used upon him.

"You think it's blackmail?"

"It'd have to be. Look at her! And she's human to boot! She must have sold her soul to her devil to turn his head."

"You sure *she's* the one? Could be one of the other ladies in the crew. What of that tall skinny one?"

"Maybe it's a prank or a ruse?"

On and on it went until she was ready to run and hide in the deepest, darkest pit she could find. Anything to get them to find a new topic.

And a new target for their mean speculation.

Only her pride kept her in place. But it was the most difficult of actions, and her heart was pounding for all it was worth, and more, as she leaned closer to Belle. "Did we step in something foul like Cookie's three-rotted pie? I'm beginning to think I might have some dog feces on me shoe, what with the way they be staring, and gossiping, and all. Could have sworn I took me bath and everything."

Just as Belle started to answer, a posh brunette lady approached them. Perfectly formed in her elegance and stuffed into her lacings so tightly 'twas a wonder she hadn't harmed herself with the bindings, she was grace incarnate. Tall and lithe, she only worsened Cameron's low opinion of herself, and left her wanting to cringe that she didn't hold even a candle's wick to the lass.

But rather than let the woman, *and* the room, know it, Cameron forced herself to stiffen her spine and keep her head up high. Though she didn't feel it, she could at least pretend to have some self-esteem.

The lady quickly looked past Cameron to sweep a less-than-flattering stare over Belle. "Are you the one my Kalderan fancies?"

Her Kalder?

The fish-bitch had some nerve there . . .

Cameron arched a brow over that possessive tone that flew up on her about as well as someone messing with Sallie's soul bottle.

Belle looked aghast. "Beg pardon?"

"You can beg all you want, commoner, but the prince is mine. Now that he's returned home, I suggest you both slither back to your respective holes and remember that you don't belong here and that you cannot compete with one of *us* in looks, grace, intelligence, or abilities."

But apparently they could in manners and decorum.

And good old-fashioned common sense!

Not to mention decency and compassion!

How dare this whore-slag confront her friend or anyone else about Kalder given the way they'd all treated him while he called this place his home! Had he meant so much to her, and them, they should have stood up for him when his mother had assaulted him back in the day.

Had they?

Nay! The bloody wankers had never once been there! Rather, they'd piled on. Blamed *him* and been absolute turds, one and all! Now she stood here and dared to try and claim him? Really?

That, she refused to allow!

Furious, Cameron moved to stand in front of Belle, and backed the woman up two steps. "For the record, gal, I be the one what you be having your issues with, not the proper Lady Belle here. Make no mistakes about that! And the last time I checked that man's manifest, Mr. Dupree be having a mind of his own. A very capable and strong one, point of fact, and the last thing he be needing is some scheming little cock-snottle farthingale like you a-thinking she can come in here after all this time and put a ring on his finger because she wills it so. Well, Miss Lacy Cotton Wig, you needs be loosening up that over-cinched corset of yours so that some oxygen can get up to your poor air-starved brains and think with them. 'Cause if you knew anything about that man at all, then you'd be a-knowing that Mr. Dupree's more than quite clear and adamant that he be dancing on to no man's tune save his own. And no woman's neither. Nor the devil's himself. So he don't be needing you, nor anyone else, putting any words in his mouth for him. I assure you, the man can speak quite plainly for himself, and he don't be mincing no words whenever he does it, neither!"

The woman laughed at Cameron's hot outburst. "*What? You? You* would dare to lecture me? A milkmaid who fell off her stool and must have knocked her head or been kicked by her cow? Please! As if you knew the minds and whims of your betters, even if they have used you for their pleasure. Not that a man of the prince's caliber would ever deign to touch something as plain as *you*."

Cameron flinched as if she'd been slapped. And she had. Just with words, not with a palm. Though honestly, it felt about the same. Nay, it stung twice as deep as a physical blow.

And that certainly withered up her confidence and turned it into a teensy little ball of nothing. She could actually feel herself growing smaller on the spot.

Worse, she felt tears stinging her throat. But Cameron refused to have them fall. She wouldn't let this poor excuse of a sentient being see them. She wouldn't give her that satisfaction.

Rather, Cameron would like to give her a swift kick to the derriere. Especially as there was now a crowd gathering around to hear every cruel syllable of it.

A crowd that made a collective gasp at their conversation.

That was disconcerting and demoralizing on a cellular level, and stung to the very inner depths of her soul, where it left a blister she was quite certain would never heal.

But as bad as that was, it was nothing compared to a moment later when the crowd parted to leave them at the full attention of everyone.

It took her a moment to realize why.

What she thought was the loud staccato droning beat of her heart in her ears wasn't. That was the sound of Kalder's boot heels clicking across the polished marble floor.

He'd finally joined them.

And all eyes were fastened to him as the crowd held their collective breath in expectation of his reaction to their untoward drama.

Cameron had always despised being the center of attention. She'd hated being involved in petty cattiness even more. This was her worst nightmare come to life, and she had no idea how it would end.

Even more painful, she didn't know what this woman really meant to Kalder. They could be great lovers and he could fall into her arms or bed for all Cameron knew.

That thought chilled her. Mostly because she wouldn't blame him for it. The lady was lovely. The kind of attractive bitchington a man like Kalder should be with.

Why did the beautiful, glorious men always go off with soulless snakes like her?

But Kalder didn't give the posh bird a second or even a first glance.

His gaze stayed locked on Cameron. As did his smile and unfaltering gait.

"There you are, me precious *phearse*."

Ignoring the crowd, Kalder gave Cameron a courtly bow and kissed her gloved hand. "So sorry to have kept you waiting. There was something I had to see to before I joined you. I pray you can forgive me for me thoughtless ways. But hopefully this will make some amends for it." He straightened and stepped behind her to lay a heavy necklace against her décolleté.

His hands tickled her skin as he fastened it there then leaned down to kiss her cheek. "I knew the color would be the perfect match for your eyes. And I was right."

The woman in front of them turned as red as a beet as she glared with murderous intent at Cameron's throat. Aye, there was no doubt the tart wanted to tear it off, or strangle her with it.

And as Cameron glanced down to see what Kalder had so gallantly given her, she understood why.

Holy mother and then some!

She sucked her breath in sharply at what had to be the most incredible piece of jewelry she'd ever beheld in her entire life. Truly this exceptional brilliance was fit only for a grand empress, and never meant for the likes of *her*.

The ethereal, fey stones were surrounded by flawless diamonds; a majestic peacock blue, they seemed to glow from some inner supernatural light. And those glowing blue teardrops formed an intricate lace collar that shimmered around her throat like delicate lace, capturing the light and sparkling with every breath she drew.

She lifted the largest grand blue stone that was so massive it filled her entire palm to capacity so that she could study the magnificent, deep, unholy color of it. "What is this?"

"They're called tourmalines, me love, and are exceptionally rare. That particular shade is only found in the Brazilian colony, and are brought out at great sacrifice by the bravest of the brave and most skilled miners who have to be highly trained to spot them in the raw. The stones were given as a gift to me father as part of a peace treaty long ago. When I came of age, he passed them to me as part of me inheritance. They're worth a king's treasure."

Bron shot to her feet in outrage as she realized what it was Kalder had done. "And I forbid you to give those to a human being! And a lowborn one at that! Have you lost all shred of your intelligence?" That screech cut across the room at a decibel level that turned truly deafening.

And it silenced every last bit of revelry. What few handful of folks hadn't been staring at them before suddenly became acutely aware that a royal scandal was unfolding in the midst of their soiree. As any reasonable being would expect, it held their rapt attention, as they quickly focused on them with an embarrassing amount of intensity.

"Those were to be mine on our marriage! They were promised to me!" the brunette who'd been attacking Cameron on Kalder's arrival added.

Raking the woman with a cool stare, Kalder laughed bitterly at her words. "Stop stirring shite with me lady, Hafren, when you know well enough that I told you long ago you and I were never to be. Your charms have never enticed me. They never will. Don't you dare try and take the shine from me lady's gift this day when I want nothing more than for Cameron to enjoy this moment. Shame on the lot of you for tainting it with your pettiness when you've had so many moments of gloating before others that you'd begrudge her this single one where she could feel beautiful and special. You should hold your heads down and slink off to the corners like the mange-ridden bitches you are."

He tucked Cameron's hand into the crook of his elbow and slowly led her forward to where his mother stood on a dais at the front of the room.

With a sneer, he tsked at her. "As for your wants and desires, dearest Bron, they stopped mattering to me the moment you buried a dagger in me gullet. I'm not here to please you. Or ask your permission on any matter, as I passed the age of needing your consent long ago. You've taken everything else from me, including me life, but I won't let you take this necklace that is mine by all rights and laws to give to whomever I see fit. Not when it can give Cameron the future she wants and has worked hard to have. For that, I will fight you. Claw and fin. And everyone here has borne witness to the bitter truth of it. This necklace is the only piece of me father's property what was given to me by way of inheritance before he died, and you can't steal it from me. It was given freely and all know it."

Stunned, Cameron felt her jaw drop at what he was doing. "Kalder . . ."

He faced her with a grim twist to his lips. "I've no use for it, me lady. It's always clashed with me dark wardrobe and callous taste. Does nothing for me eyes, either. Trust me. Looks much more fetching on you. And with it, you won't be needing your brother's money to buy that tavern you've worked so hard for, and dreamed of owning. You can have it outright and be beholden to none."

"Except you."

"No worries there, love. That piece had already been confiscated from me, so I wrote it off long ago as stolen and in the hands of someone else. Never did I think to see it again, and I'd much rather it go to someone I choose and care about than someone I despise, who's gone out of his way to do me harm. Besides, I like the thought of it easing your life and giving you pretty things. You deserve them and I like seeing them on you."

He winked at her. "As you've seen, I'm a mermaid of meager needs. Give me a hammock free of Rosie's snoring, or a quiet cubby, and I'm a happy fish. You take that necklace and do some good with it, and make me mother miserable with your happiness, and I'm more than thrilled. It's what I want."

Cameron didn't know what to say. She was used to selfish arselings. No one, not even Paden, had ever been this generous where she was concerned.

Tears welled in her eyes. "I won't accept this unless you agree to be a partner in me tavern, Mr. Dupree. It wouldn't be right to take your money and offer you nothing in return for it."

Kalder's throat tightened as he stared into those sea blue eyes and saw the depth of her tender heart. That was why he loved her so much.

Fair in all things. That was his Cameron. He'd never met anyone else like her. She wasn't out to use others to get what she wanted. She didn't lie or manipulate. Ever. Cameron just was. Honest as the day was long. Brash at times. Blunt at others. But in a world where others used words for deception, he appreciated that.

"Fine, then. A silent partner. I'd never interfere with your business. You run it how you see fit. Deal?"

She nodded.

What do you fear most?

Kalder froze as an unknown voice whispered through his mind. He tensed. Had anyone else heard it?

If they had, they didn't react as if anything unusual had happened—like a ghost whisper had tickled their ear.

"Kalder?"

He blinked as Cameron's voice thankfully intruded over the nightmare of that unwanted invasion. "Aye?"

"Are you all right? You went pale for a moment as if Rosie were standing upwind after eating a particularly large portion of Cookie's pot of pork bellies and beans."

He forced himself to smile to allay her discomfort. "I'm fine."

"There's something here. Like a fetch. . . ." Belle moved to stand at his side. "I feel it. Do you?"

"I *heard* it."

Cameron's eyes widened at the mention of a type of demon known to taunt others so that it could feed on fear and discord. She glanced around the room. "I haven't changed forms. Perhaps it's not a fetch or its ilk. Mayhap something benevolent for once?"

Kalder laughed. "When are we ever *that* lucky, lass?"

She popped him playfully on his stomach. "Can I not pretend? Will you not let me have a single moment of delusion, please?"

Devyl's eyes began to glow red—something as reliable as the shifting of her hair turning white when it came to denouncing the presence of evil. "I smell the stench of a daeve."

Paden shook his head in denial. "If one were near I'd be changing already to combat it." He pulled his sword out. "Show me the beast and I'll finish it off."

Belle scoffed. "Don't count on that, Lord Arrogance. They're not the same as other demons. They are a particular breed of demonic super-assassin nastiness. Highly trained to fight your kind and to sneak up on you to cut your throats long before you ever know they've left their astral plane and ventured to this one."

Devyl concurred. "Miss Morte's right about that. I've seen a single one of their kind take down an entire army of Hell-Hunters *and* Hellchasers, then afterwards pick his teeth clean with the bones of their horses before going after a dragon Were-Hunter for no other reason than he was in a particularly shitty mood and thought its hide would make a pretty pair of boots. But hey, mate, if you're feeling particularly suicidal, door's in the wall. Make sure you give me regards to the sharks you pass on your way to the surface, and remember to hold your breath in the water no matter how much it burns."

Quelled by those words, Paden swallowed hard and slid his sword back into his sheath.

Amused by her brother's uncommon and sudden reserve, Cameron turned toward Captain Bane. "Could one of those beasts have found us here?"

"Our luck? Anything's highly probable."

William snorted. "For that matter, the more preposterous, the more likely."

Bart nodded in agreement. "Aye to that."

Perrin growled in outrage as he faced Varice. "I told you to kill him, brother. You see the danger you've exposed all of us to by allowing him to bring strangers into our city?" He started forward to attack Kalder.

Cameron's eyes widened as Kalder summoned a ball of fire to his fist. She hadn't known he possessed those kinds of powers. Yet as shocking as that was, it paled in comparison to the next words out of the captain's mouth.

"Bron? Care to tell your sons who Kalder's real mother is and why the lot of them should be shitting their britches right about now, and running for the door? Better still, 'tis long past time me boy here stops torturing himself with the thoughts that his own mother hated him so much that she killed him."

She arched a regal brow. "What? You think knowing the bitch hated him so much that she couldn't bear the sight of him so she abandoned him at birth is better? Fine." She pinned a cold stare on Kalder. "I'm not your mother, Kalderan. You're a bastard piece of shit. Unwanted and abandoned on our doorstep the moment you were whelped by the real whore who brought you into this world."

Cameron gasped at the cruelty of those words as the fire went out on Kalder's hand.

He took the news without flinching or showing any emotion whatsoever. She had no idea how he managed it. But he did. Indeed, it was as if something inside him died with those words and left him as cold and lifeless as a statue.

Yet she knew that it had to be shredding him inside and bleeding out every part of him. How could it not? That was such a low, cruel thing to do.

And for it to be so public, no less . . .

Damn Bron for this! Did she have no soul whatsoever? She was worse than even the demons they were after.

The only clue Kalder gave of the pain he must be feeling was the subtle tensing at the corners of his lips. "I suppose one whore's as good as another, then. Makes no difference which one birthed me and which one killed me, in the grand scheme of things."

Her nostrils flared at his insult.

The captain let out an evil laugh at that. "There, me boyo, you'd be most wrong."

"How so?"

He jerked his chin toward the coat of arms on the wall above the queen's head. "I defy you to ask Bron for the name of your real and proper mother. Go on, I dare you."

Kalder hesitated as he caught the sudden look of fear on Bron's face. More than that, he saw the panic in Varice's eyes.

A fissure of foreboding went through him as he considered what about his birth would scare them so. Shite . . . who would his father have shagged to scare them like that? Knowing his father, it could have been anyone.

"Who's me mother, Bron?"

No sooner had Kalder asked that question than a horrid realization of what, or more to the point *who*, Devyl was looking at hit him, along with why they'd be so trepidacious for it.

That wasn't an animal or symbol on the royal Myrcian coat of arms, and well he knew it.

Oh no . . . It was a person they held in such regard that she was emblazoned on their arms and flags. A woman they all worshiped and paid homage to.

And not just any woman, at that.

Nay, leave it to his father to have nailed a goddess, who possessed the upper body of a beautiful female and the lower body of a mermaid. Winged like a dragon. In one hand, she held the world in her palm, and in the other, a key that balanced two rings above it.

And this particular goddess wasn't known for her kindness or gentility. Rather, she was a vengeful devil said to have slaughtered her own father when she was nothing more than a girl. One who'd been cursed by her mother for said slaughter . . .

His jaw dropped. "Are you saying that me mada was the goddess Melusine?"

Devyl nodded grimly. "And contrary to what the bitch said, your mother didn't abandon you by choice. She wanted to keep and raise you as she did her daughters, but merewyns aren't allowed to raise their sons. They're a matriarchal race. Had she kept you near her, her sisters would have killed and devoured you. A harsh lesson she learned after they murdered her other two sons when she returned home with them. So against her tenderest wishes, she left you here with your father. It was with the bitterest of tears. Tears you can still hear echoing in the wailing chambers of this land."

A chill went down Kalder's spine at that. He knew the sound the captain referenced.

All their people did. It was a shrieking scream of ultimate heartbreak in the cavern where no one ventured. Because the sound was so unbearable to hear. No one could take it for long. His father had used it for torture against his enemies and to interrogate his prisoners.

If exposed to it for too long, the intensity of it could drive even the sanest of mind mad.

Kalder couldn't believe it was a sound someone made over him. Devyl pointed to Kalder's biceps. "Tears don't come naturally to merewyns. They are creatures of war. Women of action and extreme violence, who strike out in bitter fury and with alacrity. They have no tolerance for weakness of any kind and can't abide it. The scars you bear across your left shoulder and arm? Those are mementoes from the tears your mother shed at her parting while she clutched you to her breast. Merewyns secrete bitter tears of acid that burn deep. The sadder their heart, the more potent the acid, the deeper it burns and the more it scars. As you can see by the depth and scarring of yours, she didn't easily let you go, and I can assure you, she didn't want to scar her own son, and taint your beauty in any way, as that isn't their nature either. Had there been any way for her to keep you, she would have. Believe you me. She would have defied them all for a single day at your side, and it's why Chthamalus was so attentive to you while you lived here. She charged him with your care and upbringing, and told him if he didn't guard you like the most precious and sacred object you were to her, she'd have his heart for her war chest so that she could torture him eternally."

With two tentacles wrapped around his "chest" and "abdomen" for protection, Chthamalus nodded eagerly and bobbed away on his other five tentacles with a look of absolute terror on his face.

Until Kalder pinned him with an arch stare.

He froze and gulped audibly. "What he says is true, Highness. She threatened me with more than that." He flashed his fanged teeth. "Not that she needed to. I'd have watched you anyway. Mostly because your father threatened me with worse and more should I ever breathe a word about your real and true origin. But still . . . After a while I got used to you, I did. Grew to like you, even. You're actually not so bad. Death threats notwithstanding, I rather do like you. You're not a terrible sort for only having four and one-quarter mismatched tentacles."

Ignoring his outburst, Devyl continued. "Your mother also left two rings as gifts in parting. One your father could use to summon her should he ever be in peril and need the aid of her and her sisters in battle, and one for you so that if you were deprived of his throne, you would have her army to command to reclaim it. Because that was their deal. You were to inherit everything here at his death."

His gaze went to Bron. "And that is what the Myrcian *phearse* has always feared most. Why she's hated you from the moment of your first breath. Because as the son of their king—*your* father—and that sole son of a sea goddess, by all Myrcian law, you are the right-ful heir of this kingdom, above all her sons. Your birth supersedes whatever bastard she whelps, and well she knows it."

Kalder went cold as memories flared deep and slapped him hard. But the one that stood out most was the day his father had died. While he'd never felt particularly close to the man, the news had hit him hard.

More than that, he'd respected his father as a warrior. So, the reality that such a fierce fighter had gone down in battle had rat-tled him to the core of his being. Mostly because he'd believed his father to be invincible and immortal.

The fact that Daven hadn't been . . .

It'd taken the wind out of Kalder's youthful idealism. Left him adrift and stunned. Especially since he hadn't known his place in his family without his father's iron hand there to guide him, keep him in line, and hold the other jackals at bay.

It was strange to him how that day seemed so close and yet so very far away. How he could be numb to it and still raw over it.

But then, his father had always left him conflicted and confused.

Kalder had been training with Chthamalus when the news had arrived. Not by a friend or family member.

By the common shouts of the town criers as they'd swum through the city, delivering the news to all.

No one had sent word to break it to him gently. Rather, he'd been in the middle of sparring, his shield held high as they went through their daily maneuvers.

"King Daven is dead! Felled in battle! Long live King Varice!"

Stunned by the callous words and unexpected pain of it, Kalder had lost his grip on the shield at the same time Chthamalus had struck a blow. The impact had sent the edge of the shield slicing through his mock armor and into his skin, leaving him with a gash and a scar that still marked him. Yet it was nothing compared to the pain in his soul.

"Highness? Did I kill you? Oh dear gods! Highness! Speak to me and let me know I didn't kill you!"

On his ass and tangled in seaweed, he'd barely registered Chthamalus's concern. All he could hear were the crier's echoing words that repeated his news as he'd swum farther away to tell others. "King Daven is dead! Felled in battle! Long live King Varice!"

Chthamalus had stroked his cheek with one tentacle while he tended Kalder's wound with two more and rubbed his back with a fourth. It was only then that Kalder had realized he was sobbing in the seawater.

"Me father's dead, Tally." He hadn't even recognized the hollow tone of his voice.

"Aye, my lord. I'm so sorry. He was a good . . ." Tally had paused as if searching for a word that wouldn't offend him or be a blatant lie. ". . . warrior."

Kalder had nodded, knowing that was about all one could say in honesty. Yet even so, he'd loved him. Brash and brutal though he was, he'd been his father. All he'd known as such. Daven had been the one who'd taught him to hold a sword. Taught him to drink and prank.

Taught him how to take a blow and not cry from the pain of it.

Except for today. His father would be furious to see him blubbering like this over something as natural as death. He'd be the first to backhand him for giving in to grief, and letting others know that he had a weakness.

Are you a man or a child needing a tit to suckle for comfort? Should I be sending for a wet nurse to burp you?

Kalder swore he could hear his father's angry roar even now. Feel his fist striking his chest as he shoved him back in fury that he'd dare show anything other than utter and complete strength at all times.

Never let anyone see weakness, boy! Ever!

Sucking his sobs in with a ragged breath, he'd forced his tears away as he disentangled himself from the weeds, and stood in spite of the pain. Physical and mental. That was what Duprees did. No matter the maelstrom. No matter the turmoil and pain.

Strength through adversity.

Then he'd taken the sticky cloth from Chthamalus's tentacle and pressed it to his neck to stanch the flow of blood. Be damned if he'd shame his father, even in death.

Or himself, even in grief.

"That'll need stitching, Highness. It barely missed your jugular."

Knowing his mentor was right, Kalder had gone to have it done, before he sought out his mother and brother. His thoughts being to pay respect to his mother and swear loyalty to his brother for his new regime. Standard Myrcian practice. It would be expected of a prince of their empire.

Nothing more. At least that was what he'd told himself.

Yet the moment they saw him in the palace throne room, they'd gone on the attack like sharks after freshly chummed water.

"What do you want?" His mother had raked him with a glare so foul that it'd practically seared his flesh with its causticity. No concern or question whatsoever about the stitched wound on his neck, or the blood on his clothes. For all they knew, he'd been under attack. Yet not an ounce of concern for his well-being.

And all he'd really wanted had been a hug. Someone to hold him and tell him that everything would be all right.

A single word of kindness in his hour of grief.

But it was apparent *that* wouldn't be found here. Not with *his* family. And why should he expect it from *them*? They'd never given him any such kindness before. He should have known better than to ever start expecting anything comforting from them now.

Perhaps Chthamalus had given him a head injury during their training. It would explain his stupidity for thinking even for an instant that they might actually give a shit where he was concerned.

"I came to pay me respects and wish Varice the best for his reign."

"Or are you here to challenge his right for kingship?"

Those words had struck him like a blow. "Why would I do such?"

She'd scoffed in his face. "Are you telling me that you have no desire to be king of your people?"

Was she serious? He barely felt weaned most days. While they considered him a man, it wasn't a label he embraced willingly, and he certainly didn't feel ready to cross that full threshold yet. There were still a lot of "manly" things he had yet to experience. His first beheading.

His first child.

He barely wanted to get out of bed most days. He damn sure didn't feel ready to take on the responsibilities of governing his people.

Honestly, he wasn't sure what madness possessed his idiot brother that Varice thought himself able to take on that role given that he wasn't much older, and especially since their people had been known to rebel and randomly cut the heads off rulers who angered them or made laws they didn't agree with. But then, Varice had always been an arrogant prick with more stupidity than caution.

"Nay, Mada." He was aghast at her accusation. "I'm here only to support you both."

"Then prove it."

Hurt and confused, he'd blinked and blinked again, trying to think of some way he could convince them of his sincerity. But nothing had come to mind. "How?"

"Give up your signet ring. You say you've no eye for the throne. Then you've no use for it. You have eight older brothers anyway, so it's not as if you need the ring for succession. So hand it over and then we'll know that what you say is true and that you've no desire for your father's throne."

And like a fool, Kalder had complied. After all, the small gold signet ring had been of little monetary value. It was so old that even the crest was barely discernible anymore. He'd assumed the only reason his father had given it to him was because it was so ancient that none of his brothers had wanted it.

Not once had his father ever bothered to explain its importance. He'd merely passed it over to him on the day he'd turned one-and-three by gruffly shoving it in his face and saying, "Guess you're old enough now to have it. Don't lose it, or else."

Then his father had walked off and left Tally to tell him it was a family signet ring. No other explanation beyond that. So, little wonder he'd put no other significance to the piece.

He'd assumed the only reason his father had given it to him had been because he'd forgotten to buy him anything else to mark his birth.

How stupid am I?

But then, it was more an indictment of their carelessness with him than anything else. Because they placed so little significance on him, he would never have dreamed that he'd have been given something *this* important.

And *never* at that age.

Kalder winced as his gut tightened and he relived that moment when he'd pulled off his father's ring. . . .

Nay, not his father's ring—his *mother's* ring from his pinkie and had handed it over to this treacherous slag without a second thought.

To prove his loyalty to a viper.

Sick to his stomach, he glared at Bron now and shook his head. "You knew what the ring was when you demanded it from me! How could you?"

His anger mounted as he turned toward Chthamalus. "And *you* . . . why didn't you ever tell me?"

"He didn't know anything more than it was a signet ring with the royal crest." Devyl placed his hand on Kalder's shoulder. "I only know what the rings are because I know your aunts and their treachery, and magick. And I promised your father that I'd watch over you for him. As you know, your father trusted no one." He turned his red eyes toward Bron. "For good reason. He didn't dare let anyone know what the ring was, for fear they'd take it from you and use it against you."

Which they'd done.

"How did Bron find out, then?"

"That is the question, isn't it?"

Bron lifted her chin. "You're not the only one who can cast a spell, Druid."

Kalder laughed at her words, drawing her attention back toward him. "Nay, he isn't. And I'm not the only one in this family who can bleed." Summoning his fire, he threw it at her.

She screamed as it hit her. But before it could engulf her, Varice whipped his cloak off and put it out. He ordered the watchmen to attack Kalder.

Bring it, you bitches.

For the whole of his life, he'd fought against the unreasoning rage inside him. Had tamped it down and tried to ride herd on the darkest parts of his personality that had begged him to lash out at the world that had hated him since the hour of his birth, and destroy everyone and everything he could.

The world was ugly and mad.

Just like him.

Kalder was done with it all. More than that, he was done with them.

If he was bound back to hell, then he planned to chain them to the devil's throne so that he could spend the rest of eternity beating their collective asses.

Cameron gasped as she saw Kalder change forms completely. She stumbled away from him. Her hair and Paden's turned stark white at the same time as Kalder's eyes went from their silvery pewter to something unlike anything she'd ever seen before.

The left one turned an incredible shade of vivid sky blue and the right one turned yellowish-orange. Streaked like the eyes of a hawk and lit as if the fires of hell itself burned within it. Indeed, the colors seemed to flicker from some unholy source she couldn't name.

His hair turned darker and vicious scars appeared over his face like some giant bird had slashed and attacked him, and left them there as a bitter reminder.

"Captain?" Belle drew her sword and prepared to fight their crewmate.

Kalder stalked the queen the way a fierce, hungry lion would go after its prey.

Captain Bane placed his hand over Belle's to stay her attack.

"You asked me once about the fury inside him, Lady Belle. Now you know, and you understand why I wanted him for our crew. He's a Cyphnian."

Paden growled in anger. "He's one of *them*! And you let him out?!"

Cyphnians were rare and most coveted for their abilities to siphon off the powers and emotions of other demons and weaken them. At one time, they'd been rounded up and offered to the god Apollo as part of his menagerie at Delphi. But the downside of their abilities was that since those powers and emotions weren't theirs, they couldn't handle them, and it would ofttimes drive them mad, and cause them to lash out and become more of a threat than the creatures they took the powers from to begin with. Only a tiny handful of their breed could control and master their full destiny, and they were the most coveted of all.

When Paden moved to attack Kalder, Devyl caught him with his powers and slung him high into the opposite wall, where he crashed hard, and slid to the floor. He landed in a painful lump that made Cameron cringe in sympathy.

"Lay one hand to him, Captain Jack, and you'll wish I'd left you in Vine's tender custody."

Kalder turned to hiss, but when he saw that Paden was handled, he resumed his quest for Bron, who was scrambling to escape him.

Cameron debated what to do to stop him.

Her brother pushed himself to his feet and wiped his hand across his bleeding nose. "Those are some of the very demons we've been charged with policing and returning to hell! How could you let one of them out, and serve on your crew?"

Devyl met Mara's gaze, and when he spoke his voice was thick with sincerity. "Kalder cannot help what he was born as." His gaze went to Belle. "There are those of us who chose our path to damnation. We earned what we got and embraced it with both arms, every step of the way. Kalder was born a Cyphnian. As are all the males conceived by merewyns—it's why his mother was forbidden to keep him. They are cursed the moment they fill their mothers' wombs. Every day of his life, Kalder's fought against that rage, even while it's torn him asunder. And you would damn him for that strength and conviction?"

"But he ain't fighting now, Captain. He's made friends and bedded down with that rage. Am thinking they had puppies and are planning a summer palace for it." William jerked his chin toward Kalder, who was tearing through the soldiers dumb enough to get between him and Bron.

Bart started to intervene, but the captain stopped him, too. "He'll kill you."

And if someone didn't do something, he'd kill his own people, *and* the queen.

Terrified, and knowing she couldn't stand by and let this happen, Cameron ran for him. Before her common sense could grab hold and make her do something intelligent, like run for the door and save her own hide, she took his arm.

"Kalder?"

He turned on her with fangs bared and fist raised.

She flinched and held up her arm to protect herself, fully expecting him to attack her, too.

But the moment he saw her there, he froze.

Time hung still.

Her heart broke as she saw his beautiful face that was ravaged by such ugly, vicious scars. In her mind, images played of him in their battles together, and those memories merged with battles he'd fought without her. And as she saw her fierce, handsome warrior, standing bitterly alone for those fights, she knew how he'd gotten those wounds.

The demons who'd put them there while he'd been damned for Bron's actions.

Worse, she saw the very day Muerig had died.

Kalder had been on his way to meet him.

On time.

The tale she knew—that Kalder knew—*was a lie.*

She saw everything as clearly as if it were her memory as much as his. As if she were there that day, living through it with him.

Kalder was in a dingy hovel of a room similar to the ones in some of the taverns where Cameron had worked over the years. The kind they rented to some of their less-than-moral patrons and wenches for things that their owners were forced to pay hefty taxes on or be forced to lose their licenses over.

He'd just finished dressing and was pulling out his money to pay the harlot he'd been with.

Bound up tight in a grimy sheet on the bed, the dark beauty pouted at him. "Must you leave so soon?"

"Aye, love. Have to meet up with me brother. Can't keep him waiting or he'll be kicking me arse and whining all day about it." He'd handed her the coins, then stepped away from the bed and shrugged on his jacket.

As he started for the door, he'd shaken his head, and swayed a bit, before he reached out to the edge of the dresser to catch his balance.

Tucking her chin beneath the sheet, she'd laughed as if daring to play coy after everything they'd done. "Still a little tipsy?"

Kalder rubbed his hand over his forehead and scowled. A dull ache set in, making his ears buzz terribly fierce. He blinked and tried to clear his vision as it continued to blur and make the room spin even more. All the while, the whirring buzz worsened. "Didn't realize I'd drunk so much."

"You have to watch out for Petey's rum. It's more potent than most."

"I guess." Kalder took another step for the door. . . .

And hit the floor near the open window.

Unable to move, he'd lain across worn oak boards while the sunlight reflected off the brass buttons of his coat, and the graying lace of the curtains had lightly brushed against his face.

An instant later, everything had gone black.

No sooner was he out than the woman shot from the bed to check on him to make certain he wasn't about to come to. Once she was assured of it, she'd opened the door to admit three men from the hallway who'd been waiting, hidden in the shadows, for her treacherous cue.

Cameron wanted to curse as she saw them and knew them for the bastard devils they were.

Perrin walked in first, with two of his most worthless brothers at his side. The three of them duplicated the tart's actions of ensuring Kalder was unconscious on the floor . . . and mocked him for the fact that he'd been drugged and duped so easily because, unlike them, he'd been forced to purchase a few moments of the kindness that was so generously lavished upon them for free.

Furious on Kalder's behalf, Cameron watched while they stripped his clothes off and then roughly returned him to bed so that he'd have no idea what they'd done to him.

Laughing, Perrin cleaned out his purse and handed its contents off to the strumpet. And why not? It wasn't as if he'd earned Kalder's coin. Why not be free with it?

"Good work. Did you have any trouble?"

"Nay, me lord. He didn't question it at all. Took the drink and downed every drop without so much as a single comment."

His shortest brother clapped Perrin on the back. "Told you he wouldn't be the wiser. None can taste me brew."

Perrin snorted as he fingered the empty cup Kalder had left on the table beside the bed. "You ever put that shite in me drink, Eyson, and I'll gut you for it. Asshole to appetite."

He laughed. "Don't worry. Unlike Kalderan, Alard and I aren't stupid." He glanced to their other brother. "Are we?"

Alard rose up from placing Kalder's clothes on the floor, where they'd been before Kalder dressed. "Don't know about all that, but crazy's another matter entirely. Of that, I have an abundance, sure enough."

Perrin hesitated as he studied the clothes and then Kalder's unconscious body on the bed. He narrowed his gaze on his brother. "You're quite certain he won't remember that he's been drugged?"

"Nay. He'll think he passed out drunk. His head will ache just the same." Hands on hips, Eyson gave him a satisfied smirk.

Perrin passed a warning look to the strumpet before he turned back toward Alard. "And the others? They've all been paid?"

"Aye." Alard cleared his throat meaningfully. "*Both* sets. It's all taken care of. You've nothing to fear at all. In a sennight, you'll be Varice's right hand in Kalderan's place, and we'll never have to answer to this"—he cut his eyes toward Kalder—"prick again."

Cameron gasped as her mind showed her the truth behind their cryptic meanings.

They'd paid to have Muerig murdered and then the girl killed a day later so that no one would ever know the truth about Kalder's being drugged.

While they'd assumed their mother would be outraged over their youngest brother's murder, and that Kalder would be jailed or banished for it, Kalder's death at her hands had come as a bonus round in their mad scheming that had rid them of two nuisances at once.

And it wasn't until *that* moment that Cameron realized Kalder could see the truth she was learning, too.

Somehow these memories were playing through her mind and his, simultaneously. And she had no idea if it was due to her powers or his. Or why.

She only knew that it was affecting them both. Making them stronger and giving them unvarnished truths. More than that . . . it was feeding his fury and causing the fetid demon inside him to salivate and feed on something she couldn't see.

Yet she could feel it with everything inside her.

Suddenly, he pulled away with a fierce, demanding growl that reverberated deep inside her soul. He was going for their throats.

"Nay, Kalder! Nay!" She grabbed his arm again, and forced him to look at her. To stay by her side and do no harm.

His breathing ragged, she saw the torment inside those mismatched eyes. The anguish that demanded their lives and blood to pay for the brutal pain they'd given him.

Worse? She saw his self-hatred.

The part of him that ached so deep that it didn't appear anything could ever reach it. That it would ever heal or be whole.

It was then that she realized what she saw externally on his face and body was the manifestation of how he truly saw himself. That this twisted demon before her was the beast he envisioned whenever he looked in a mirror.

Not the beautiful man she knew and held close to her heart. A scarred, horrific demonic animal. Unworthy of love or sympathy. One to be hated by all and condemned as despicable.

Disposable.

And in that moment, her parents' words came back to her with a vengeance.

Cupping his scarred face in her hands, she forced him to look into her eyes so that he would see her sincerity and the fact that she didn't see what he did. That she saw past the pain and into the heart of the beast, to the soul of the man inside it.

"Look at me, Kalder," she breathed. "And remember. Out of death, there is life. Out of devastation comes hope. Out of tragedy comes strength. Out of pain comes wisdom. Out of sorrow comes insight. You will never know how high you can soar until you've learned to fly with wings that were broken by enemies and re-forged by your own determination to succeed and let no one hold you down ever again. To show them all that their cruelty will not define you. That you will not live by their rules or dictates."

Cameron swallowed and stroked the scar beneath his eye that ran deepest along his cheek. "You are your own master and they will never have power over you again." Then she placed her hand over the scars at the corner of his lips. "Let nothing hold you back. Let nothing hem you in. You set your course and you fly to the heavens. A beautiful, imperfect creature, capable of love and trust, even after betrayal. Capable of mustering courage in the midst of utter terror. And capable of delivering mercy even after all you've ever been shown was cruelty. You will rise above the ashes of the future they attempted to burn to the ground, a stronger creature, steadfast and more determined than ever to see this through. For there is nothing more terrifying in this universe than the Soul Determinatus. For it will not be stopped and it will not be daunted. So go on and bring to me your worst if you must, and I will deliver unto you me very best. For you will not defeat me. Not now. Not ever. I will not allow you to."

She watched as those scars began to fade beneath her fingertips.

All except for one that lingered faintly over his left cheekbone.

And his eyes remained their new dual colors as he blinked and focused on her face. She knew the moment he saw her. The pain receded from that gaze, and was replaced by a tenderness so deep and profound that it caused her own tears to well up and blur her vision.

"Breathe with me, Kalder. Just as you wouldn't let me drown in the sea, I won't let you drown in your pain." She kissed his lips. "Whenever you need a nip, love. I'm right here, by your side."

Kalder closed his eyes as her touch filled him with a calmness the likes of which he'd never known before. Their world was going crazy around them. He wanted to tear everything apart. To kill every person in this room and he swam in their blood and entrails.

Until she touched him.

She quelled the fury in his heart and made it quiet again. He'd never understand the magic inside her.

Yet he was grateful for it.

"I want me mada's ring, Bron." His voice was thick and grim. Steadfast and determined. And it held the promise of what he'd do to her if she refused him. "It belongs to me, and wasn't yours to take." He cradled Cameron's hand in his and held it against his heart before he looked up and met Bron's terrified gaze. "Be grateful that I only want what's mine. That I don't do to you what you've done to me, and exact on you the punishment you truly deserve for the crimes you've committed. Pray you, that I remain ever so merciful."

"Are you threatening me?"

"Nay. I don't have to. I trust in the Fates to exact me vengeance upon you. In due course. As I know they will. And it'll be far harsher than anything I could ever do. Besides, you have to live amongst your putrid, backbiting, self-serving selves. I can't imagine any worse hell than that—which, considering the fact that I've been to hell and back, says it all."

Curling her lip, Bron pried the ring from her finger then flung it at him. "Take it! I don't want this piece of shite, anyway."

Cameron caught the ring right as it would have struck Kalder's cheek, and clutched it tight in her fist.

For a moment, she was tempted to throw it back at the evil wench. But she didn't want to risk her keeping it. "You are a piece of work, you are. Glad I am to know there's not a bit of you in me Kalder, whatsoever. All the better he is for it. For I can imagine no worse curse than bearing your genes in me bones." She took his hand into hers and slid the ring onto his pinkie.

Kalder felt the strangest sensation go up his arm the moment Cameron's fingers brushed against his flesh. He couldn't explain it really. A peculiar flash of heat that instantly drained his fury. And with it, it brought a warmth in a place where he hadn't realized he'd been cold.

For the first time in his life, he could see past tomorrow and into the future. He could see something he wanted.

Nay, he could see *someone* he wanted. . . .

And it terrified him to the very core of his being.

She's born of Michael's blood. A Necrodemian.

You're a demon of the lowest region.

Heaven and hell.

Two extremes that could only meet and merge in a dark shadowy nether realm of madness where almost everyone lost their way.

Which said it all about their future.

It was insanity to even contemplate the thought of having something to do with a creature such as her. Ever. Her breed sent his back to hell every chance they got. Even after his redeemed themselves.

Yet he could think of nothing else.

Could imagine nothing save being with her. *I'm not the siphon.*

She was.

All his fury was gone now. Buried beneath a tranquility that came every time she neared him. He'd felt it that very first night when he'd seen her on the docks with William. She'd been rambling on about nothing in particular, asking a million and one questions, in rapid-fire staccato drills.

The moonlight had cast shadows against the paleness of her features, making her skin glow like pearlescent cream. Her beauty had drawn him from the sea toward her. A succulent beacon he couldn't resist. In spite of the damp chill he'd had from his late-night swim and her mannish clothes that had obliterated her curves, he'd hardened at the sight of her. At the sound of her soft, lilting accent.

He'd craved the syllables of his name on her lips.

Instead of a sweet greeting at their first meeting, Cameron had given him a startled shriek as she jumped away from him as if he were poisonous.

And yet, she'd faced her fear and refused to give in to it. That had been the moment she'd ensnared him. When their gazes had met on that dock in Port Royal and she'd stood her ground rather than flee.

That night she'd met his questions with questions of her own, and shown a true curiosity about him. There had been no judgment or hostility. No guile or subterfuge. No barbed words or prying for information that she could use against him or to better herself at his expense.

She had been . . .

Cameron.

Honest. Open. Caring. Curious.

Unassuming.

And that he would protect with every breath he drew, and every drop of blood that flowed inside his body.

No sooner had that thought gone through his head than he heard something he hadn't heard in a long, long time. So long that at first, he thought he was imagining it.

It wasn't until Perrin and Varice began scrambling their soldiers that he realized it wasn't his imagination.

The ground beneath their feet buckled and surged, throwing them up toward the ceiling. Devyl grabbed his wife as Kalder lunged for Cameron.

Paden caught her first and hissed at him. "You've caused her enough harm!"

Kalder would argue with the moron about that, but this wasn't the time or place.

William, Bart, and Rosie, along with Sancha and Belle, tried to stand and fight, but none of them could keep their footing as the floor fought against them.

"What is this ungodly madness?" Bart actually stabbed at the buckling floor with his sword. Never let it be said that man ever allowed his common sense get in the way of his violence.

Sick to his stomach, Kalder knew what caused the commotion, but he was praying with everything he had that he was wrong. Whatever doubts he might have had that he could be mistaken only lasted until he met Muerig's gaze across the crowded room, where half their people were fleeing for shelter.

Nay, he wasn't mistaken. At all.

Muerig was doing this. And he was gloating over it.

In fact, his brother sat at the banquet table with an unfounded serenity. The kind only two beings held.

Those relegated to death.

And those who'd orchestrated the requiem.

Kalder swallowed hard. "What have you done, Muery?"

Muerig took a slow, steady drink from his cup before he stood and smiled with a coldness that only added to the chill Kalder felt. "You would be proud of me, brother. I learned from you."

Confused and angry, Kalder couldn't fathom what he meant by that. "Learned what?"

"How to protect me own arse. First and foremost. Damn all the others, as they don't matter, isn't that right?"

Kalder was aghast. He'd never been the kind to throw others to the wolves. That crime was his family's specialty. Not his. "What have you done?" he repeated in a harsher tone.

"Made the decision I knew you wouldn't. Or rather one I wasn't about to risk leaving in your miserable hands. Not after what happened the last time my life was at your disposal, and that was for a bitch whose name you hadn't bothered to learn before you shagged her. You think I don't know what you'd do to me now for a piece of arse you actually favor? As far as I'm concerned, that slag-bitch can have your whore, brother. Be damned if I'll stand idly by and let Vine take *me* again! Whatever blood sacrifice Vine wants from you, she can have with my blessing!" After those words were spoken, Muerig rose up like a tidal wave, changing forms from his Myrcian body into something that resembled Chthamalus's Barnakian race. Only he was much larger, much deadlier.

"Holy mother of God," Rosie breathed as Simon said something a little more colorful while Kat, Valynda, Sancha, and Belle took up positions to attack.

But that wasn't what really concerned Kalder. He saw what they were all missing.

The wall behind them that was buckling to the Malachai's army . . .

The one that was about to trap them squarely between the two opposing forces and end all their lives, once and for all.

11

"Kalderan!"

Kalder jerked awake at the sound of his father's furious tone that carried plainly down the length of their entire massive hall. His heart raced frantically for no apparent reason, and his body was covered with a clammy sweat. The fringes of a peculiar dream hung on in his mind, but he couldn't quite remember it.

"Kal! Damn it, boy, where are you!"

Still not fully alert, he staggered from the bed

and scrambled for his clothes. He had no idea what had his father in such a pique so early, but years of experience had taught him the best course of action was not to keep the beast waiting whenever he was in such a foul temper.

"Kalder?"

He stumbled at the sweet, lilting, melodic timbre of a woman's voice. . . .

A voice so familiar and at the same time foreign. He hesitated in the hallway and turned around to look for her, yet all he saw were the reflections of his own youthful image in the shiny marbled walls.

The instant he became aware of himself, he cringed at the features that were far too similar to his father's for his tastes.

'Course it could be worse. He could take after his hated mother.

Aye, I shouldn't be complaining for the mercy of taking after me father. If I favored the harpy-bitch, I'd be cutting me own throat instead of shaving it each morn.

Renewing his run, Kalder finally skidded to a halt when he reached his father's study. He opened the doors there to find the old barnacle sitting beside a huge beast of a demon lord. Well, perhaps not a *real* demon. Though Kalder wouldn't have been surprised to find horns sprouting out of the dark man's forehead. He had the look of an infernal beast, what with his black, braided hair and fierce demeanor. Not to mention his ruthless aura that said he'd gut anyone who so much as looked askance at him.

Aye, this was one who'd taken many lives in his day and wouldn't shirk at taking more. And for no other reason than he felt like it. Best to stay to the corners of the room, and as far from striking range as he could while this warlord was in their lands. Even the soldiers with him were giving their master a wide berth, and casting nervous glances at their lord every time he so much as moved to scratch his nose.

"Where have you been?" His father glared at Kalder's disheveled clothing.

Kalder tucked his tunic in and decided not to tell him he'd still been abed so late in the morning. His father detested such things and wouldn't hesitate to backhand him even in the presence of guests.

Shrugging, he folded his arms over his chest and moved to stand off to the side while the warlord eyed him with an unnerving interest.

Ah, dear gods, don't tell me, me father's done bartered me like some doxy for this bastard's favor. . . .

For a peace treaty, he wouldn't put anything past his father. Especially not these days of unending war against the Roman bastards who'd been getting the best of their army for months now and decimating it.

"He's a bit scrawny for me, is he not?"

Kalder's eyes widened at an even worse thought. *Ah, gah, Da, are you planning to feed me to the bugger?*

Daven took a deep draught of his mead as he eyed Kalder, as if measuring his worth . . . and finding it lacking, as always. "Wiry . . . and 'tis necessary for what you're asking. Trust me, Duel. There's not a better one among my people for it. Besides, Kalderan knows his place. Holds his tongue. Forsooth, I barely know he's about most days. He's like a phantom shadow. Just what you requested, is it not?"

Duel snorted. "I still haven't figured out why you'd loan me one of your sons to spy for me army, given the battle we're facing."

His father fell silent as a darkness descended behind his tired eyes. Kalder scowled at the expression he didn't quite understand. "He's not worth much. As you noted, he's a scrawny bit of a Myrcian. And these are dark days. If we're to remain independent and strong against our enemies, we need each other. Maybe you can find something salvageable in the little bastard and keep him alive long enough to do some good for us."

Those words had stung Kalder a lot deeper than he'd wanted to acknowledge. He was used to insults. Used to his parents' constant derision. Yet that had burned more than the usual digs they took.

And it'd left a bitter taste in his mouth. One that caused him to lash out in anger the moment Dón-Dueli of the Dumnonii came over to speak to him alone a few minutes later, after his father had left the room so that they could speak in private.

"Don't need your pity!" Kalder snarled churlishly.

"Good, for I have none to offer a sullen child."

Those words caught him off guard. But not nearly as much as the genuine kindness in Duel's dark, deadly eyes. There was more to this unholy warlord than what Kalder had first surmised. And that cowed Kalder's temperament more than any threat or intimidation ever could. And since kindness was the rare beast that he had no experience dealing with, it left him baffled, and ill equipped to counter. Indeed, he didn't know what to say or how to behave before such a thing.

Dón-Dueli narrowed his gaze on him. "Take heed, good Kalder. I don't need a petulant boy in my command. I need a soldier who can pull his weight and follow my orders. One I can rely on in war, and at peace. Give me loyalty and I will return it in full measure. Betray me and I will gut you slowly, so that your screams will echo through the heavens as a testament to all of my displeasure. And I will use your guts to tie my boots and warm my feet. Understood?"

Eyes wide, Kalder nodded.

And gulped audibly.

Duel clapped him so hard on the back that he'd stumbled forward. "Good lad."

As they walked off, Kalder had cleared his throat. "Me lord? Might I ask a question?"

"Sure."

"Have you any children?"

"Why do you want to know?"

Kalder shrugged. "Curiosity, mostly."

Duel arched a dark brow at him that was most chilling. "And again I ask why you'd like to know."

Kalder hesitated before he explained it further. "Well, I know how me father deals with us. I was but wondering how a . . ." He wasn't quite sure what to call Duel, as Kalder still hadn't determined if he were a man or a monster. So he settled for an accurate word that wouldn't offend the creature, or get *him* gutted. ". . . warlord such as yourself copes with his own offspring."

Duel snorted. "Simple. I ate mine upon their arrival from their mother's womb, so as to spare myself any future misery they might bring me."

Well that settled that, then, and Kalder made a note to take care and not offend him in the future. At least not too much. If Duel had no love of his own spawn, it meant he'd have far less for someone else's.

Or at least that had been Kalder's thought until their first battle.

Even now, he remembered well the terror he'd felt when Devyl/Duel's army had annihilated their enemy to the south with the intel Kalder had brought to them.

Drunk on blood lust, Duel's men had been like savage animals as they'd torn through the innocent village that had been caught in the cross fire of the two battling forces. New to the ways of humans, and a virgin in warfare, Kalder had been sickened by the sights and smells of it all. By the wanton slaughter.

Worse, he'd been horrified by the part he'd played in telling Duel's army it was safe to advance on an unprotected population, and had blamed himself for the misery of the victims.

He'd held himself accountable for the countless bodies strewn about and left out on the ground so callously, with no regard for them or how their loved ones would feel once they returned to find them like this.

Until the soldiers had mercilessly cornered him. No longer did they view him as an ally or the one who'd allowed them their victory.

Now he was as hated as the ones they'd slaughtered. Why? Because he had information they wanted, and he wouldn't give them that one piece they didn't need to have.

"Where's the queen, you little rat?"

It'd taken Kalder a moment to understand their language. He was still getting used to their inelegant words and dialect. "I-I-I don't know."

Their largest, beefiest soldier had grabbed and backhanded him so hard that it'd dazed his senses. He could have sworn he'd lost half the teeth in his mouth from that one strike alone.

Doubting he would survive another hit of that magnitude, Kalder had tried to get away, but like a pack of hungry dogs, they'd attacked en masse and brought him low. He'd been certain he was as dead as the innocent villagers around him.

Blow after blow had fallen against his flesh, as well as boot heel after furious boot heel. His body had become numb to the pain of it all. When suddenly, he'd heard Duel's fierce shout in his native Myrcian. He'd looked up to see their commander in his black-ringed armor, astride his huge ebony warhorse.

His armor stained red with blood—along with other unsavory things—Duel had glared at every one of his soldiers. "What is this?"

"He won't tell us where the queen's hiding!" The soldier had kicked at Kalder again, causing him to groan out loud in response. "I know he's hidden her *and* their treasury!"

"He's a mutant!"

"Aye, he's not one of us!"

"Kill him!"

Duel had held his hand up to silence them. "Harm him again, and it's my sword you'll be facing."

That had finally quelled them and sent most of them back to their pillaging. Albeit this time they were less enthusiastic about it.

His expression grim and intense, Duel swung his leg over the back of his massive horse and dismounted. With a feral eye to the bastard who'd started the beating, he dismissed him then knelt beside Kalder on the ground.

Kalder could barely focus on his face through the blood that obscured his vision. He ached so badly that in all honesty, he'd wished himself dead just to stop the pain. And given the amount of fury in his overlord's expression, he'd expected Duel to finish what the men had started. To gut him as he'd done the others who'd gotten in his way.

Indeed, Duel had been just as ruthless in this battle as Kalder had first suspected when they met. He'd spared no man his sword or his fury.

Until now.

With a shocking tenderness, Duel had reached out and gently wiped the blood from his cheek. "Can you stand, lad? Or do you need me to carry you?"

"I can walk on me own."

He cocked a doubting brow.

But Kalder quickly proved that he wouldn't let anyone help him. Especially none of these vile bastards who'd spared no one a second thought or single mercy as they gutted them. Worse, they'd mocked him for the fact that he'd refused to blindly murder or kill.

Duel handed him his skin of wine and waited for him to take a drink. "Did you see where the queen went?"

So that was it, then, was it? He should have known. No real mercy given. Only a ploy to win his favor and use him.

Bloody wanker.

Kalder choked and sealed the skin before he gave it back, wanting no part of it or the man who was using it for no other purpose than to bribe him. "I won't let you or the others rape her or harm the children she took with her. You'll have to kill me first. They took nothing with them, save what supplies they could carry to sustain them. She has no treasure. That I swear to you on me own life."

Duel scowled at him. "You took this beating to protect a woman you know not?"

Kalder looked away as guilt tore through him with fresh talons. "I've killed enough for one day. I won't stand by and see another slain. Not if I can help it."

"I watched you, young Myrcian. You didn't take a single soul in battle."

Kalder swallowed hard against the sour tears that threatened to fall. "I might not have lifted a sword with me arm, me lord, but the information I gave killed more than I could have on me own. I'm just as guilty one way as I would have been the other."

Duel took his chin in one mighty fist and forced him to meet his gaze. "I want you to listen to me this day, Kalderan Murjani Dupree, and you listen well. What happened here today was a tragedy. You're right about that. I take no satisfaction in the deaths of the people slain by this army. Or the part I took in it. But remember this. There's not a man, woman, or child lying upon the ground around you who wouldn't have cheered at the news of the deaths of my own people, and the destruction of my kingdom. Or yours, for that matter. These corpses you pity and cry for are the very ones who would have reveled in the deaths of my own family and all I love and hold sacred, and would have demanded your own life had you been taken by their soldiers. They would have lined the road for a chance to jeer at you, and would have thrown their own stones to carry you to your god as quickly as possible and laugh while you bled out from the wounds they gave you. So while I would not gleefully seek to take their lives when it's not necessary, I will not hesitate to end them when I have to in order to protect the safety of what I hold dearest, and neither should you. For the face of every woman and child you see here this day could very well be the face of your own family at home tomorrow. Remember, while 'tis fine to feel for them and mourn for them, do not let it ever blind you from doing what you must to keep those you love safe. Do you understand?"

Kalder ground his teeth. "Are you saying I should have given up the queen to those monsters?"

"Nay, lad. You followed your conscience. And in that you were true. I will never fault you for that. As you said, she sought only to protect herself and those who posed no risk to us. Just remember that every child she saved today will one day grow up with the memory of what happened here at our hands. And just as you hold yourself accountable for the fate of their families, so, too, will they. They will curse and hate you for your part in their past."

And with that memory, the child would one day come seeking vengeance.

Duel had been right in that prediction.

Kalder bore those scars, as well. Some from later that night, when he'd gone to help the queen escape and she'd cut his throat and had robbed him before they'd left him to bleed out while they used the horses he'd brought for them to run over his body. Had Duel not come searching for him, he'd have paid for his kindness with his own life.

And then, other scars from fourteen years later, when the queen's eldest son had recognized him and, forgetting Kalder was the sole reason they'd survived their ordeal, had buried his dagger deep in Kalder's back while he'd been walking outside a dark tavern in some forgotten town.

That night, drink and fury had gotten the better of Kalder as he assumed his own brother had sent the attacker in for the kill, and before he'd recognized the man behind the vicious ambush that had almost paralyzed him, he'd torn his assailant apart and used the boy's assassin's dagger to cut *his* throat. It'd only been as the prince was taking his final gasps that Kalder had realized why he'd been attacked and who his assailant was.

Not one sent by Varice.

One sent by fate and chance.

In that moment, as the moonlight had revealed the young man's face, even with his own wound throbbing and burning, he'd hated himself again.

War was a vicious cycle of hatred. The past was ever a mounting monster he couldn't escape.

Like the darkness, it swallowed him and he couldn't see past it. He was overwhelmed now. Unable to breathe.

To focus.

Every time he thought himself out of it, and away from it all, it found some way to seep back in and drag him under. An ever-tidal swell he couldn't escape.

Everything has consequence.

Every action taken, and every one not . . .

And now he was lost to the past and he felt even more lost to the future.

Cameron's heart pounded as she struggled to keep their enemies from Kalder's inert form. He was in some strange trance that she couldn't break. Nothing seemed to work to make him realize where he was, or what was going on around him.

His skin was ice cold to the touch. Rigid. He was like a living statue.

Damn his brothers, all! They were a worthless lot to do something like this to him, especially while he was under fire. How could they be so cruel?

While she might not always appreciate her own sibling—wanted to choke the very life from him about half the time he was in a room with her—at least she knew Paden always had her best interests at heart.

Overzealous though he was.

Case in point, he fought by her side in this fight to protect Kalder, even though he couldn't stand him and wanted to send him straight to hell. He fought and he bled for the man, for no other reason than because he knew Kalder was dear to her. His own feelings for Kalder be damned.

That was what family did.

They put the happiness of their loved ones first. Thought of them above themselves. That was what made them family. Not blood or bone.

Their willingness to bleed and die for each other.

To sacrifice.

"We can't hold them back forever." Paden sliced at one demon who came too close and forced the creature back. "I can carry him out for you."

Cameron hesitated as she caught his loophole in those words. And harkened back to some of Paden's more dire childhood pranks that still resonated deep within her soul and psyche. Ofttimes, it wasn't so much what her brother said, but rather what the rascal meant, and wordplay was what this particular devil did best. "Aye, but *will* you, brother?"

He tsked at her serious question. "Tell me the truth, Cammy. Do you love him?"

There was no hesitation in her answer. Just as there was none in her heart. "I do. Scary though it is. And hopeless, even more so. I would never have him harmed."

"Then I'll die before I let them have him. I swear that to you on me life, me precious bit. None shall have him. In that you can trust."

A single tear fell down her cheek as she stared at her big brother in his pale Seraph form. Never had she loved him more. "You better not get hurt, either. I've taken enough trips into hell to spank your rotten arse, Paden Jack. Don't you be making me take another."

He scoffed at her. "You were ever a bossy one, bit. From the moment you came out and first demanded I give up me bed for you."

Smirking, Paden swung Kalder up in his arms and flew off to safety so that she could turn her attention to fighting the demons with the other members of her crew.

All around, her friends battled with everything they had, but it wasn't looking good for the crew. These were some of the fiercest demons they'd ever faced. Never let it be said that the Malachai didn't choose among the best for his army.

Cameron moved to cover the Dark-Huntress, Janice, as one of the nastier beasts came at her back. "Have you ever seen the like?"

"Nay!" Janice hissed as a twisted blue demon caught her wrist with a tentacle and snatched it hard enough to make it snap with a horrendous sound.

Suddenly, Chthamalus Morro was there with a number of his Barnak soldiers. They shot out dozens of small, bright blue gelatinous blobs toward the demons. Blobs that seemed to have the consistency of snot, and when they landed on their targets, they spread out and began to smoke—something that caused the demons to scream and recoil as if they'd been struck by fire.

Or worse.

Flaming snot.

Shocked, she gaped at Chthamalus.

He grinned. "Don't ask how we make them or where they come from. Just be glad we're not shooting them at *you*." He aimed a tentacle at another set of advancing enemies and began lobbing more blobs to stop them.

She clapped him on the shoulder. "Thanks for the cover."

"No worries. My lord prince would have me nethers of both genders if I let anything happen to his lady."

She wasn't so sure about that. While she wanted to believe that Kalder cared, she found it hard to believe at times. Especially right now, when he wasn't here to help when she needed him most. But then she was used to being abandoned whenever she needed someone.

It was something she'd grown used to the moment her parents had orphaned her as a child—that sick feeling whenever she looked around at the worst times of her life only to find that the only thing she had at her back was four solid walls.

If she was lucky.

I came into this world alone and sure as I've lived, 'tis how I shall leave it.

Seldom had any hour in between been any different. In spite of all his good intentions and protestations otherwise, Paden headed out to sea every time she needed a shoulder to lean on, and left her behind to wait for his return.

I'm making a better future for us, Cammy. Those were always Paden's excuses. But she'd have rather had him home, to make a better present, as the future was often too hard to see past the misery and drudgery of what she had to get through minute by minute of every single day. She couldn't stand waiting for that nebulous date that never seemed to arrive, and being forced to stand strong on her own two legs that were getting more and more tired every furlough they carried her.

Truth be told, Cameron again had that desolate hole in her stomach that she'd had most of her life. The first time she'd felt it had been right after the deaths of her parents. When she and Paden had arrived in Williamsburg, among the bustling crowd of noonday people. They'd jostled her about as if she were a piece of driftwood in the ocean with no land in sight, and but for Paden's ever firm hand on hers, she'd have been lost to their tidal, hostile current as they cursed her for being in their way. Rudely, they had elbowed her if she got too close to any.

Oh how she remembered the bright patterned clothes and cloaks coming at her from every direction in an overwhelming sea of color. The stampeding sound of shoes and boot heels striking the cobblestones and boards while her fear welled up that they'd run her over without care or compassion should she fall.

Though she made no external sound whatsoever, inside she'd been screaming in terror. Screaming out for someone to see them and help them.

No one had noticed.

No one cared. Pain was ever invisible to all, except for those poor bastards it eviscerated.

And that day, she and Paden had been the poor bastards torn apart in its wake.

To this day, that emptiness of being alone, even when surrounded by a crowd of people . . . nothing had ever filled it. It'd become as much of her being as another appendage. Granted, a useless one, but nevertheless, always there, and always in the way.

Always hurting.

Since the day her parents had died, she'd never really felt as if she were a part of any group or family. Not really. Perhaps it was because Paden had forced her to live a lie. To pretend to be something she wasn't. To hide herself behind a fake shell of happiness and solitude, in a false guise, that nothing ever really penetrated. Indeed, there was nothing more painful in the world than a false smile pinned over the mask of misery.

Speak as little as possible so as not to betray herself. Make few friends lest someone discover that she wasn't a boy. Keep to herself as much as possible.

No one could be trusted. Not with their secret that could get them both into so much trouble, and cost Paden his commission and her a place to live.

Her job.

If not their very freedom.

While other girls had been learning to dress, and play coy and flirt, and to dance, Cameron had been learning to shoe horses, clean out spittoons, and pour drinks. How to play cards and avoid the notice of drunken men who had a taste for beardless boys.

Paden thought he'd found the perfect way to guard her from the lecherous gazes of randy men, but the truth was, he'd only complicated her already messed-up life. She'd traded slapping one type of male hands for another.

Not to mention the additional pairs of feminine hands she'd been forced to deftly dodge, as they wanted a man they could boss and dominate.

Never mind *their* ever-ready, pouty lips. There were times when she'd swear women seeking husbands were worse predators than men after a tryst.

Her brother would be to bury if he had any idea the number of times she'd been groped and had narrowly escaped a horrid situation with both men *and* women.

But for Lettice's quick thinking and feigned clumsiness in the Black Swan where Cameron lived and worked, she would have been found out long ago.

Even now, she remembered the night when she'd first met Captain Bane and the others in Port Royal. The prostitute who'd sat in her lap, and almost learned her secret with her wandering hands . . .

Aye, Cameron had been groped many times by the wrong people, seeking charms and body parts she lacked.

And that had only saddened her more, as it left her to wonder if anyone had ever seen the real her. If anyone could, when she didn't really feel as if she knew herself. She'd never been allowed to be

Miss Cameron Amelia Maire Jack. To discover what it was that she truly liked about herself and being a woman.

Though, to be honest, as she tripped on her dress and hit the ground hard in the midst of her parry, she cursed the layers of intricate fabric that tangled around her limbs, making it difficult to fight. Mara made this look deceptively easy. As did Valynda and Sancha. They and Elf fought with ease in their gowns and corsets.

Cameron had far too little experience with such. For far too long she'd been Mr. Cameron Jack. *Give me me breeches any day!* At least she had full movement in those.

Demons closed in as she struggled to rise.

Lifting her arm to fight the demons off, Cameron cursed as her wrist tangled in the layers of delicate lace that fell from her elbow. This was fast becoming hopeless. She didn't see any way to escape them. There were too many and they were coming in too fast.

"Take her!" Muerig shouted at them. "We need the bitch for your mistress!"

Cameron's heart sank as more demons turned toward her. There was no hope for her now. Not even Chthamalus and his soldiers could repel them all. Nor could they get near her to lend a hand.

Though they tried, they were fast being overrun. She stood and prepared herself for the next blow.

Determined to remain standing as long as she could, she parried and countered with her sword, turned to kick at a second demon.

Still more came at her back, from the walls and hallways. Chthamalus and his crew were shoved and divided away from her.

She twisted her fist in the skirts, trying to keep them out of the way, but it was so darned distracting.

The captain was pushed away from her position. And still more advanced on her, driving her toward a corner.

Refusing to be backed there, Cameron headed for the dais, hoping the higher ground might give her an advantage. Instead, demons came slithering down the walls and over the furniture. They were everywhere now. Like roaches on a hot summer night vying for a spot on cool tile.

Launching her wings, she tried for flight, but one grabbed her wing and pulled her toward the ground, holding her down. Slashing at the beast, she tried to wrench herself free as pain tore through her back and shoulder.

Nothing worked to free herself.

I'm dead!

She closed her eyes as the death stroke neared her.

But then, just as it would have come, the demons went flying up and around her as if thrown by a hurricane. They screamed out in agony and half of them erupted into a geyser of entrails.

Stunned by the force of this unseen attack, she looked up to stare into dual-colored eyes that reminded her of a demonic hawk. One a glowing celestial blue and the other a fiery burst of orange surrounding vibrant green. A smile curved her lips as she focused on Kalder's handsome, grim expression.

"You're a little late to the party, love."

He quirked a charming grin at her. "Better late than never."

She wouldn't argue that. Especially right now, when she was so incredibly glad to see him.

His breathing heavy, he paused in front of her to lift her up, into his arms. In spite of her wings, he cradled her against his chest, as if daring anyone to try and threaten her.

The demons rose to surround them.

"You can't keep her, Kalderan! Her blood is tainted. Surrender her now, or else I'll take you both."

Kalder glared at Muerig as the scars returned to his face. The flesh around his eyes darkened, making them appear to sink into his skull. "I'll kill whatever fool tries to take her from me. Step up, brother, and you'll be me first sacrifice to the blood gods. Go on. I dare you!"

Muerig rose before them. No longer a Myrcian, he now appeared in the body of a vicious, multi-armed sea serpent. His face was twisted and bore scars similar to Kalder's Cyphnian form.

As Muerig attacked, Cameron felt her powers waning. It took her a moment to realize that Kalder was siphoning off her abilities.

More than that, he was draining energy from everyone around them. Everyone. Including Mara and Devyl.

Her jaw dropped as she became aware of the full extent of Kalder's powers.

Holy mother of God . . .

He was a lightning rod for the paranormal. One that could draw, collect, and then channel all the power for his own use!

Muerig dove at them.

Just as he would have reached them, Kalder raised his hand that had been tucked under her knees, and a great vortex shot up with a blinding intensity that made a mockery of the one that had brought them down to his city. A deafening screech rang out. Cameron felt herself being yanked by an unseen force.

One second they were in Wyñeria, and the next . . .

Sunlight blinded her. The sounds of surf and seagulls filled her ears. Sea salt stung her nose as she smelled the fresh, open, crisp air.

Cameron stumbled about on the sands of a white, secluded beach. And she wasn't the only one.

Their entire crew was there.

Except for Janice. Cameron could hear her calling to them from the depths of a cave not that far away.

"We're here, Mistress Smith!" Captain Bane assured her as he helped his wife and sister sit on a fallen palm tree that strangely bore the shape of a crocodile. "Are you safe, lass?"

"Aye, Captain. I'm away from the daylight."

"Then stay there until nightfall."

Elf held her hand up to her brow as she glanced about the turquoise horizon. It was beautiful here. Perfect.

Except that they had no way to leave it. And they were missing one other vital thing.

Holding her skirts high, Cameron turned around in the sand, looking for Kalder, but there was no sign of him anywhere. "Kalder!"

That being said, Chthamalus and his group were there with them. All of the demons whined as they slid along the sand, and its grains clung to their slimy flesh as if battering them for a deep-fry coating.

"Ew!" Chthamalus slung his tentacles out in distaste, trying to expel the sand from his flesh, which seemed determined to hold on to as many granules as possible. "I've been gritted! Someone! Anyone! Help! This is disgusting! I could polish glass with this!"

Ignoring the demons, Rosie sat near Sallie, helping him cork the rum bottle with his soul, since they were no longer in battle. "There, there. We've got it back in place. No fretting, now."

Sallie held it up toward the sky as if double-checking that status, to make sure his soul was secure.

Belle wrinkled her nose at the lot of them. "I didn't think our Mr. Dupree had the powers to throw us back to dry land."

The captain let out an impressed sigh. "He shouldn't. But apparently the boy has developed a new set of skills unbeknownst to us before now."

Aye to that. And apparently invisibility and disappearing appeared to be two more, since she still saw no sign of the one Deadman she was desperate to find.

Where could he be? Why wasn't he here among them?

I swear, I'm going to thrash you when I find you, for worrying me so!

Cameron ground her teeth in frustration. "Kalder!"

"Do you mind keeping that shrieking down to a small whine? Are you part banshee or Charonte?"

Cameron let out a startled squeak at the unexpected sound of a deep, thunderous male voice.

From the shadows of a large palm tree, a giant man stepped out, making her wonder how he could have ever been concealed by something so paltry.

Indeed, he seemed larger than a mountain at first glance. His powerful aura was closer to that of some ancient, omnipotent god than that of a mere mortal male. And his muscular build would put their large Maasai warrior Zumari's to shame. Never had she seen a man more sculpted. Not that she'd seen all that many in this near-naked state.

In fact, he was barely clothed at all. What with his sole garment being a pair of *very* brief breeches that only just covered his necessaries. They left absolutely *nothing* to the imagination. And she did mean n-o-t-h-i-n-g. Which meant Sancha and Valynda were practically drooling over his wealth of caramel skin, that was decorated by a number of intricate tattoos.

And Kat was drooling, to boot. Something that Simon noted immediately, which caused him to rudely clear his throat then turn his husband around so that Kat couldn't see the man anymore.

The stranger took their ogling in stride. He brushed his long dark hair back from his lavender eyes with one massive paw of a hand before he scratched idly at his small, well-trimmed beard. "Anyone care to tell me what the hell you're doing here on my island? And who it is I'm going to kill for this insensitive intrusion on my midday nap?"

Captain Bane snorted at his question. "Hold your board, Savitar. We didn't intrude by choice, I assure you. As for the how, none of us know the answer to that particular quandary."

Savitar let out a long, exasperated breath. "Thorn put you up to this, didn't he? I knew it. Never could trust that little weasel. I swear I'll rip that little bast—"

"Kalder!" Cameron gasped in relief as she finally saw him over Savitar's tattooed shoulder.

She ran past the large, surly being, toward the beach where Kalder was dragging himself up from the sea.

Her heart stopped as she saw him fall in the waves and be swept back by them. She spread her wings and flew then, rushing to reach him before the tide caught him and returned him to the ocean.

He appeared to be weak or unconscious.

Not knowing which, she was forced to dive for him before he was lost again. For one terrifying heartbeat, she thought she was too late. That the sea had taken custody of him and reclaimed his body.

Then her fingertips touched the flesh of his hand.

Cameron wanted to laugh the instant his webbed claws brushed against her skin in the waves. The moment she had her hand around his wrist, she spread her wings wide. While she might not know how to swim, she did know how to fly.

With all the strength she could muster, she lifted him out of the water and headed toward the shore so that she could lay him gently against the white sand, safe from the surf.

Coughing and sputtering, he rolled over onto his back, where he wheezed, and sought to let his body change over from its sea form to that of an air-dweller.

Relieved beyond belief, Cameron stretched out by his side and cupped his bruised face in her hand. The whiskers of his cheek scraped against her palm while she traced the line of his jaw. His lips were split and one eye swollen. Still, she was so grateful to see that mismatched gaze lock on to hers. "What happened?"

Grimacing, he placed his hand over hers and groaned deep in his throat. "I don't know." He swallowed, then stared hard at her face as if seeking truth in her eyes. "Are *you* all right?"

She nodded and tucked her wings in. "You?"

His gaze went from her to the shadow that was now falling over both of them. "What bugger pissed in your waves, Sav?"

"I'm going to wager his name is Kalder Dupree. What happened to your eyes, man? You look like shit shat you out and left you for dead . . . again."

Before Kalder could answer, the skies above them turned black as thick storm clouds rolled over the sun. Thunder clapped heavily.

"Ah, hell, this can't be good." Savitar cursed. "Duel . . . tell me this is from the gate falling, and that you haven't pissed off something worse."

"I'll say it. Won't make it true. But if it cheers your mood, I'll tell you whatever lie you want me to."

Cameron pulled away from Kalder. They rose slowly to their feet as the sky darkened and growled dangerously. As a black owl with glowing red eyes, Strixa landed near Mara, and transformed into her human body. That single action said it all about how dangerous this storm was, as the water witch hated being human.

And it left her much weaker to fight whatever was coming for them, and that Strixa never did lightly, as her primary motto was to strike fast and fatally.

Whatever was there was bad, indeed.

Savitar curled his lip as he cast a menacing glare at Captain Bane. "Go, raise the dead, I said. Put together a crew of evil to fight evil. What could possibly go wrong with that scenario? Good gets a chance to redeem themselves. Shouldn't the wicked? What the devil was I thinking?"

"That you wanted to save mankind?" Belle asked.

Savitar passed her a droll stare as lightning struck the beach not far from them. "Don't need a lippy minion at the moment. Mess with me, woman, and I'll feed you to the lightning and the beast that's coming with it."

As the weather worsened, the tattoos on Savitar's body began to peel off his skin and transform into winged, colorful demons the likes of which Cameron had never seen before. Muscular and beautiful, they were glorious.

When Paden stepped forward to unsheathe his sword so that he could engage them for battle, the captain stayed his hand. "Those be Charonte, boy. And they belong to Savitar. If you value your life and that of your sister's, you'll cut them all a wide berth and leave them be. Believe me. If Savitar doesn't kill you over glancing askance at them, they'll feast on your bones and entrails, and laugh while they do it."

Cameron scowled at the word she'd never heard before. "What are Charonte?"

The captain grinned. "You're about to find out. And be glad they're not coming for *us*. Their favored menu is varied and non-specific. Basically, anything that's flavored meat over bones. Believe me when I say 'tis best to remain off their menu and out of their predatory sight, if you can."

As the Charonte flew toward the dark, dismal sky, Savitar turned toward them. The moment he did so, a black, cowled cloak appeared over his body, shielding him from head to foot.

Now the only part of him that could be seen were those eerie eyes that glowed an unholy purple hue from beneath the dark depths of his hood. He held his hand out. The sands of the beach swirled up in a small sandstorm to form a long, twisted staff that was about a foot and a half taller than even the massive mountain known as Savitar.

When the parts of the staff finally came together, it was magically topped off by a piece of vibrant round silver that held a golden sun in its center. One that radiated from an inner source Cameron couldn't even fathom.

An echoing shriek rang out.

Muerig, again in the form of a sea serpent, rose from the black, turgid waves. "Chthonian! I know who you are! *What* you are!"

Savitar froze. The shrill winds tore at his cloak, but he made no move whatsoever. Indeed, he was as still as the grave.

"Give me the Cyphnian and I won't tell the Malachai where to find you."

Breaking his stillness, Savitar laughed. "I have no fear of the Malachai."

"Then why do you hide on your island?"

Now it was the captain's turn to laugh. "Who says he's hiding?"

Muerig sent a blast of fire that hit Savitar in the center of his chest.

The moment it did, his cloak disintegrated and Cameron saw why he'd shielded himself so quickly.

Gasping, she met Kalder's gaze, but unlike her, he didn't seem the least bit surprised by their host's alternate body.

"Is he . . . ?"

Kalder arched a brow at her question. "Part demon? Aye. 'Tis the real reason he lives here on this island. Like us, he fears accidental exposure, and what he might do should he be riled to the full extent of his wrath."

The moment Muerig saw Savitar's true form, he vanished beneath the sea, taking his army with him.

Savitar went after him, causing half the ocean to cave in upon itself. A mountain range of water rose up so high that Cameron swore it reached to the heavens and left the ocean floor visible to all.

And when it came crashing down, it soaked every one of them. The only one who wasn't wet was Mara, who'd been shielded by the captain, and Cameron. And Cameron only because Kalder had caught her tight against his body so that his Myrcian skin could prevent her from taking another dousing after her earlier dip into the ocean to save him.

"You can't help protecting me, can you?" She could feel his strong heartbeat against her cheek.

"Nay. But only because I know you've not had enough of it." He brushed her damp hair back from her face.

The humorous light in Kalder's eyes died as he turned toward Savitar.

And Cameron couldn't blame him for it. That was a terrifying sight, indeed.

Savitar's body rippled with flames. What little skin he had exposed was swirled with colors and was covered with an ancient articulated armor. He was even horned.

His expression still furious, he landed on the beach in front of them, and tucked his coal-black wings down. Along with his tail. All that remained of his handsomeness were those vivid purple eyes that swept over their group as if sizing them up for lunch.

After a few seconds, he seemed to calm.

The moment he did, his armor slowly flipped up in a wave to

melt and then vanish inside his flesh as it returned to a normal human hue.

Once it was again its flawless caramel shade, the Charonte flew back, then transformed into small dragons and other beasts so that they could lay themselves over his skin. Cameron's jaw was still slack as Savitar resumed his earlier breechcloth attire and he ran his hand over the Charonte tattoos. That action seemed to calm him and return him to his earlier laid-back lethality.

All that remained of his demon body was the staff and that hellfire stare that dared them to mention what had just happened.

Savitar glared at Kalder. "So . . . that little bastard of fun will be back, won't he?"

"Sad to say, most likely. He never could learn."

"Beautiful. Should I gut you now? Stake you out on the beach as a sacrifice so he'll leave me alone?"

Kalder scratched nervously at his neck. "I'd rather you not."

"And I'd rather be left alone and not be pulled into your little family drama." Savitar growled low in his throat. "Good thing for you that I know it won't placate them. Damn it to the Source! Why'd you have to go and do something so stupid?"

"I didn't mean to land us here. I was trying for Tobago."

"Well, your geography sucks, buddy. You need a new map. Preferably one updated to this century . . . whatever century we're currently in. Not like I give a fuck."

Kalder opened his mouth to speak, but Savitar held his hand up to silence him. "Just don't make this worse." He grimaced at the captain. "And *you* . . ."

"What?"

"Scáthach should have drowned you when you were born."

"Wish she had. Would have saved me endless centuries of trouble."

Cameron bit her lip. "Scáthach?" she whispered to Kalder. "As in the Celtic goddess who trained Cú Chulainn?"

"Not exactly a goddess, but aye. She did train Cú Chulainn and she was the Chthonian in charge of the Dumnonii lands . . . and all of northern Europe when the captain was mortal."

That knowledge stunned her.

"They are the same person?"

Kalder nodded.

"And Kalder trained under her as well."

Cameron's jaw went slack again at Chthamalus's words. "What?"

Chthamalus puffed his chest out proudly. "Was one of her best pupils, he was. And youngest. He fought his way into her fortress in record time with the skills *I* taught him."

"Truth?"

Kalder blushed. "Don't know about record time. But aye. I studied for a year under both her and her daughter."

"In more ways than one." Chthamalus coughed into his hand, making Cameron scowl at what he meant by that.

But her expression was nothing compared to Rosie's deep frown of consternation. "I didn't think Chthonians could have children."

"Her daughters were adopted."

Ignoring their conversation, Savitar struck his staff against the sand. "Leucious!" he roared to the heavens. "Drag your sanctimonious ass here, or so help me, I'm heading into Azmodea and you won't like what happens to you when I get there!"

The dark clouds parted an instant before a fancy dandy materialized on the beach near Savitar. It took Cameron a moment to recognize their illustrious leader, who was even more ornately dressed than normal in a bright pink brocade and an elaborate court wig.

"Keep your shirt off, surf-nut. I sw—" Thorn's words came to an abrupt stop as he realized he wasn't alone on the beach. Lowering his monocle, he straightened. "Oh."

"Oh?" Savitar mocked the word. "Really? That's all you have to say? You dump your misfits off on me and *oh*?"

When Thorn started to speak, Savitar held his hand up. "Just don't. Because I have one important question to ask you before you say something that makes me gut you where you stand, sullying my sand. Out of curiosity . . . whose side were you really on when you cut the throat of a Cyphnian and sent him down to Vine and Noir to keep them company? Huh? 'Cause I keep going over the whole thing in my head, and while I'd like to give you the benefit of the doubt, old man, I just can't make myself believe for one iota of a yactosecond that you'd be that stupid."

Savitar moved to stand in front of Thorn. "You knew exactly what he was when you did it, didn't you?"

A tic started in Thorn's jaw, but he refused to show a bit of remorse or any fear. He met Savitar's gaze levelly and without flinching or faltering. "Aye. I knew."

12

Kalder was stunned by Thorn's unexpected confession. How could the demon bastard have set him free into the world again, if he really knew who and what Kalder was? What he was capable of doing? It made no sense.

"You *knew*?" Savitar accused.

"Of course I knew." Thorn was indignant. "I'm not stupid. I leave that precarious state up to you, surf-for-brains."

Savitar sent a blast of fire straight at Thorn.

Thorn returned it in full measure. "Don't you even start with me, Chthonian. Or I'll wedge your surfboard sideways into a piece of your anatomy you won't ever forget."

"You traitorous bastard!"

That sobered Thorn, who stalked Savitar like a savage predator after the beast who'd wounded it. Rage bled out from every part of his body. "How dare *you* of all creatures accuse *me* of *that*!"

Now it was Savitar's turn to be indignant. "I beg your pardon?"

"Beg all you want, but you won't get it. And you heard me. As if *your* hands are any cleaner in this fight than mine, or that you'd be any less likely to switch sides. If you ever think for one heartbeat that I'd shift loyalties to my father, then you'd best think again, and remember that the day I do, I'd kill my son *and* wife in the process. So fuck you, Chthonian! And your suspicions! You can take them both and shove them up your ass and down your throat! My ties to the right side of this fight are a whole lot stronger than yours will ever be!"

"Wife?" The captain gaped.

Thorn froze instantly. Then took a step back as if suddenly remembering that he and Savitar weren't the only two on the island.

His features paled as he glanced about, and he became acutely aware of just how many had borne witness to his slip of the tongue.

Savitar gave him an evil smirk. "Yes, punkin', we all heard what you said. Want to keep going? What other interesting tidbits are you planning to let out in the midst of your verbal spewage?"

Thorn narrowed his gaze. "Careful, punkin', you know what they say about those who live in glass houses."

"They get a lot of sunshine?"

Thorn sneered at his sarcasm. "I was thinking they get covered in a lot of bug shit, myself. But tomato, tamahto."

Savitar twisted his jaw in a way that said he was barely restraining the urge to punch him. "You really make it hard not to gut you some days."

"Ditto."

"Well, I should have known. . . ."

Cameron gaped as a man appeared next to her and Kalder who was equal in height to Savitar. Which was to say, he was gigantic. Only instead of being muscular, he was lean, yet every bit as lethal and mysterious. There was no mistaking his power that said he could easily match the rest of them.

And then some.

The only difference was that he had exceptionally long black hair and eyes of mercury silver that swirled like the sea during a storm. Aged eyes that said he'd seen more than his fair share of trouble and misery.

And he wore a plain black woolen coat more akin to the captain's than the ornate style favored by Thorn, Bart, or Will.

At his approach, Thorn and Savitar stepped apart like two errant children who'd been caught squabbling by their parents and wanted to hide their misbehavior before a grand spanking ensued.

"He started it." Savitar jerked his chin at Thorn.

"Acheron!" Janice shouted in happiness. "Get me away from these idiots!"

Cameron's eyes widened as she realized that this was the mysterious Acheron Parthenopaeus who led the Dark-Hunters—the group of warriors charged with protecting mankind from the

Daimons who preyed on them and their souls. Unlike Thorn's Hell-chasers, who sent demons back to their dimensions after they escaped or broke whatever rule had allowed them a temporary reprieve, or the Necrodemians such as her brother, who killed the dark demons who refused to go or were too dangerous to be corralled without risking danger to the world or to humanity, the Dark-Hunters were more akin to assassins for the gods.

Pausing in front of Savitar, Acheron arched a quizzical brow. "Question. Who locked my Huntress in a cave?"

Kalder raised his hand. "That would be me, but she's free to leave at any time. I only did it to protect her from the sunlight."

"Then I won't kill you." Acheron made a sharp turn back toward Savitar and Thorn. "And you two idiots . . . Seriously? We have a major demon infestation, buckling gates, *and* a Malachai on the loose, and you two are fighting like infants right in the middle of it all?"

With a perturbed sneer, Savitar crossed his arms over his chest. "You know, you're not so old, or so big, that I can't spank you."

Sancha raised her hand to volunteer. "Might I have the honor of it? Or I could hold him down if you'd like. If he struggles, all the better, I say."

Acheron scoffed at her offer. "Careful, love. My bite is much worse than my bark."

She flashed an inviting grin. "Counting on that, love. Definitely counting on that." She gave him an inviting wink.

Now it was Thorn's turn to smirk. "What can I say, old Ack? They were damned for a reason. And some more so than others."

Acheron shook his head. "Makes me glad I just have to wrangle

Dark-Hunters. And a few stray Dream-Hunters and Were-Hunters."

"And I have to wrangle morons." Savitar gestured at Thorn. "With the lord king of them standing right there in front of us. So I dare you to ask him about the Cyphnian he knowingly sent down to Vine to play with and her friends. Go ahead. I dare you."

Acheron went still for about a heartbeat and a half. His eyes rippled red as his black hair fanned out.

Yet unlike Savitar, he didn't react.

Instead, he pressed one finger to his temple as if suppressing a migraine. "Thorn . . . tell me you had a good reason for what you did."

He gestured toward Kalder. "Have you met said Cyphnian? He's a hard-headed bastard. Reminds me of someone." He glanced pointedly at Savitar. "Only he's a lot more likable. I knew when I sent him there that he wouldn't stay—that I'd be able to get him out without too much of a fight from the others. Since his kind is so rare, I didn't think they'd be able to identify his breed. Worst case, was hoping he'd drain the bitch should she be dumb enough to get near him in the interim. Sadly, I miscalculated how long it'd take me to get to him, and Vine's resourcefulness in finding his brother and using the wanker against us. For that, I apologize." Thorn cleared his throat pointedly. "To you, Ash. Not to surf-bum."

Thorn sighed heavily. "Hindsight, stupid plan. But given that I was in battle at the time, with Michael and Gabriel breathing down my throat and all manner of hell breaking loose, it was the best I could come up with."

Savitar finally calmed down. "Why didn't you say that earlier?"

"You didn't give me a chance, psycho-douche."

Acheron held his hand up. "Knock it off, children! With Adarian running loose in the Caribbean, we have enough problems without you two going at each other. Now play nicely, or I'm feeding you both to *she* who won't be named."

Thorn rolled his eyes, then turned to curse at Kalder. "Of all the islands in all the worlds. You had to land on this one? Really?"

Kalder shrugged. "I've always had bad aim."

Zumari laughed at that. Unlike Kalder, the Maasai warrior was renowned for his skills at throwing knives and spears. "No lie to that. You should see him at a spear toss."

Growling low in the back of his throat, Thorn faced Mara and Devyl. "How long will it take for you to make a new ship?"

Mara bit her lip as she considered it. "From scratch? Months. But I could bond with one quickly." Her amber eyes danced with amusement. "You wouldn't happen to have a spare one just lying about, would you?"

They all turned toward Acheron. At first he appeared irritated by the fact that they deferred to him, but with a sigh, he resigned himself to it.

"Frigate or sloop?" he asked the captain.

Devyl grinned. "First-rate man-o'-war. I've always been partial. Besides, me aeromages need the room to maneuver in battle. And me lady doesn't like to be cramped."

Acheron nodded slowly. "All right. I'll have one docked and ready by dusk." He jerked his chin at Savitar. "Can you manage to be hospitable until then?"

"I'd rather be disemboweled. Or better yet, disembowel *them*."

"Sav . . ."

He sneered at Acheron. "Don't give me no lip, twerp. How'd you come by that *wonderful* pirate coat you're wearing, again?"

Acheron gave him a droll stare. "Moral of the story isn't to draw first blood. It's to draw last."

Savitar rolled his eyes. "Fine. But remember, you owe me. And Thorn owes me twice."

"Me?" Thorn groused. "Why do I owe you?"

"I didn't eat your little Thornkateers when they showed up on my beach without an invitation."

Thorn sputtered in indignation. "Need I remind you that *you* personally recommended about half of them for my crew? Doesn't that make them Saviteers?"

"Or would that be saboteurs?" Belle asked with a wicked gleam in her eye.

In complete synchronicity with each other, Savitar and Thorn turned their heads to glare at her. And with the same exact grimace of disdain.

An impressive feat, indeed.

Bart laughed while William grimaced. "Do those two always argue like an old married couple?"

"They do," Acheron said with a sigh. "Be grateful, you've only had to listen to them for a few minutes. I've had this shite ringing in my ears for thousands of years."

Bart scratched at his beard. "And you're still sane?"

Acheron shrugged. "That's a matter of opinion. Besides, sanity's overrated."

"But silence isn't. So let there be silence on my island. And peace, boys and girls. You can camp in the Omegrion chambers since I doubt the Were-Hunters will be visiting—and they better not be visiting 'cause I can't take any more creatures here today. There's a reason I live in seclusion. Means I tend to eat anything that intrudes on it."

Savitar growled again. "Acheron, since he apparently has nothing better to do with his immortality than stick his skinny little nose in where it doesn't belong, can show you where that is, then see about your ship so that you'll be gone before I finish with my siesta. Thorn will watch ye motley bunch while you're there, and make sure none of you piss on my rugs."

Thorn sputtered. "Excuse me?"

"I tried to make an excuse for you once and this is what happened. I got stuck with you being a pain in my eternity. So be a good parent and mind your children while I nap. Keep them out of my underwear drawers and off my furniture for the duration of their stay." And with that, Savitar vanished into thin air.

Thorn ground his teeth. "Is it too late to summon an angry sea deity and sink this place?"

Acheron gave him a cocky grin. "I can think of a vicious goddess of destruction who would love to help you out in that department. Especially since she's not overly fond of him. However, there is one serious downside to releasing her."

Will cocked his head. "That is?"

"End of the world," the captain answered. "Hence the whole 'goddess of destruction' moniker, lad. Goes with the territory."

"Mmm," Acheron concurred. "Much like Sallie's soul, once she comes out of her container, she's a little hard to put back in it."

"Aye, but the last time she came out, she sank Atlantis." Thorn glanced about the island. "This is considerably smaller than that. I'm thinking . . ."

A bolt of lightning flew at his head.

Thorn deflected it. "You missed me, Savitar."

A coconut hit him in the back so hard that it left him facedown in the sand.

"No, I didn't." The disembodied voice was plain and clearly Savitar's.

"I seriously hate you, Chthonian."

With no comment on that—or help, either—Acheron led the Deadmen toward Savitar's hall that stood on a hill in the center of the island.

Kalder stayed on the beach with Cameron.

"Is something wrong?"

"A bad feeling in me gut, is all. I just can't seem to shake it."

She nodded as she scanned the horizon. "I feel it, too."

It wasn't just about his brother. Or hers. There was something more. Something he couldn't name. Only sense. And that made this all the worse.

Not sure about much of anything other than the desperate need he had to keep her safe, Kalder took her hand into his and placed his mother's ring on her finger.

"What are you doing?"

"I know nothing of me real and true mother. But if what the

captain said about her and this ring was the truth, I want you to have this."

"What if *you* get into trouble?"

"I'm always in trouble." He winked at her. "There's never anything new to that, love. You know me. But I want you to have some way to protect yourself." Kalder brushed her damp hair away from her cheek and smiled at her wilted state. "Did I tell you earlier how beautiful you are?"

She snorted. "On with you, love. You're such a dashing liar with those honeyed words and sweet tongue. Think you I don't know what a mess I be right now? Look like something the cat hacked up on the floor and scattered about a bit, I do."

He kissed her lips and nuzzled his face against her soft cheek so that he could breathe in the sweet scent of her skin. "Nay, me love. You're still the prettiest thing to me eyes. Always. And I can prove it."

"How's that?"

Cameron didn't really expect him to meet her challenge. Not until he pulled back with a wicked gleam in those mismatched eyes and took her hand into his. Cupping her chin in his palm, he kissed her while he led their entwined hands down his body so he could press her fingers against the part of him that was swollen with need.

Her eyes widened at the unexpected size of him.

"Are you still in doubt?"

Nay, no one could doubt *that*. 'Twas truly something to behold—in more ways than one. But she found it incredible that a man such as he would crave her so. And especially to this extent.

Yet even so, she was terrified of what the morrow would bring for them.

"Tell me something, Kalder. You are freed now . . . will you come with me back to Williamsburg?"

She saw the hesitation in his eyes, and that made her heart sink. Perhaps he was every bit as fickle toward her as Paden claimed.

"I would love nothing better than to be with you, Cameron. But I took a vow to the captain and this ship and crew."

"And you've been freed of it."

He shook his head. "It's not so simple."

"I don't understand."

Kalder sat down on the beach and pulled her to sit in his lap so that he could hold her. He tucked her in beneath his chin and held her close and yet she sensed his anguish. "I've done far more evil in me life than good, Cameron. And every person I save is another victory against the evil that festers in this world and inside me that I fight to restrain. I will not rest until I've made good some of what I've done."

It was quite a goal her mermaid demon had set for himself. "So you will never lay down your quest? Never know marriage or family?

"Marriage." He spat the word as if it were poison on his tongue. "That unholy union between two people? For what purpose? To make them both miserable? To take two people who might have fondness for each other and lock them in hell together until they learn to hate the very sound of the other's breathing? It never gave me father a moment's peace. You saw the bitch he married. She drove him to war and ultimately his death. Which he no doubt welcomed, as it finally bought an end to her whining, bitchtress tongue."

Cameron was taken aback by his hostility. True, she'd often said similar things in anger about marriage herself, but deep down she didn't mean them. Nay, marriage could and should be a wonderful thing.

"I don't believe it has to be that way," she said, confessing her true thoughts to him. "Imagine a marriage where two people respect each other. Where they are partners and allies against the world. Like me parents were. They loved one another, Kalder. To the day they died. And Paden loves Lettice. Despite his multitudinous flaws, I've seen the way he cares for her, and she for him. Even now, when she carries his child and is terrified of what the future means for her, she's sworn that she'll take no other to husband, even though it's the shame of an unwed mother she'll be enduring. She'd rather bear the brunt of that nightmare than marry any other when there's less hope than the size of an eye of a needle that Paden will come home and make an honest woman of her. But so long as any hope whatsoever remains, she won't give up on waiting for his return."

He snorted at Cameron's optimism. "You're sober and speak more foolishness than I do whenever I'm drunk." He pulled his shirt collar away from his chest, where a vicious scar lay near his heart. "You see this?"

"Aye." Cameron traced the raised, whitened skin with her fingertip. She watched as chills spread over Kalder's flesh, but they did nothing to dull the fury in his mismatched eyes.

"Me father gave me that when I tried to keep him from killing Bron. He turned on me and said I wasn't his son for protecting the shrew." His voice was hollow, as if he told her of someone else, and yet as she stared into his eyes, she saw the torment he concealed. The agonized grief. "I can still see the hatred on his face as he denounced me for a faithless, worthless bastard for saving a bitch who turns out now wasn't even me mother and hated me for that very fact. What kind of fool am I?"

"Their sins are not on you."

He scoffed as his tortured gaze locked with hers, and it burned her with its intense sincerity. "I think a part of me always suspected the truth. That it's why me lands and title never meant anything to me. They're not really mine."

"Aye, they are. Inherited through your father. You heard what the captain said."

"But I was never really part of their family, Cam. And I think some inner part of me always felt it. You don't know what it's like to be a stranger in your own home. To know you don't belong there and wonder why you're not quite welcome. To wonder what's so wrong with you that no one can love you. Not even your own parents."

Cameron sat in silence as she realized Kalder had just entrusted her with a secret that emotionally devastated him. That this man who trusted no one and stood strong against the entire world had just bared his very soul to her.

He'd made himself vulnerable to her alone.

She reached up and placed her hand against his stubbled cheek. "I will always welcome you, Kalder Dupree. Wherever I am, you will forever have a home and all the warmth there you could ever desire. And you are more entitled to your noble status than any man I know. For you are honest. Decent. And good."

He grunted at that. "Perhaps you need to get out more."

She smiled at his teasing. "I get out quite enough to know the truth."

He dipped his head down and kissed her gently on her lips. The taste of him invaded her head and set it reeling. His kiss was fierce, demanding.

Scintillating.

Breathless from his touch, Cameron didn't protest as he laid her back against the damp sand. Her body burned at the intimate contact of his body pressing against hers. It was the most wondrous thing she'd ever experienced. His chest to her breast, his legs to hers. A deep-seated fire started inside her, making her hot and aching.

Making her want more of him.

Again.

Kalder licked and teased her mouth, wanting to taste more of her. Nay, he *needed* to have her.

Her taste and scent were all he could think of. And the feel of her beneath him was more than a mere mortal demon could take.

Kalder didn't know what it was about her, but she touched something inside him. Some alien part he'd never known before.

Right now, he needed a physical connection to her. Needed to feel her wrapped around him as he physically lost himself to the softness of her body the way he'd lost his heart and soul to her already.

Cameron moaned as he buried his lips against her throat and teased her skin with his tongue, his teeth. Overwhelming chills ran the length of her body. She was on fire from his touch.

Kalder pulled his shirt over his head.

Cameron ran her hand over his sculpted shoulders. They were

hard and filled with strength. And the way they rippled when he moved . . .

It was more than she could stand.

He laid himself down between her spread thighs. The material of her gown trapped her legs while he loosened her pantaloons.

"Are you afraid of me, *ma petite*?"

She shivered at his use of French as his breath tickled the skin of her cheek.

"I'm not afraid of you." It was herself that scared her. The intensity of these feelings that made her tender and weak toward him. Because she knew how much control he had over her when she'd vowed to never allow anyone else any form of sovereignty when it came to her well-being. Yet Kalder made it easy to rely on him and he didn't make her pay for it. Didn't make her feel weak for needing help. She was strengthened by his presence.

Made better.

No one had ever made her feel like this.

He brushed her top aside to bare her breast. Heat stung her cheeks as he dipped his head down and took her taut peak into his mouth.

Hissing in pleasure, she cupped his head to her and held him there while he tasted her. She felt every flick of his tongue deep inside her body, all the way to her stomach, which contracted with each nibble.

Kalder growled at the taste of his Cameron. Her hands were buried deep in his short hair, stroking his scalp and making him harder than he'd ever been in his life. The satin of her gown caressed his skin, but was nowhere near as soft as her pale, tender skin that he wanted to nibble on for the rest of his life.

The mere taste of her made him drunk and left him craving more.

Suddenly, he hated the gown that kept her body from him. Kissing her nipple, he quickly undressed her until she was bared to his gaze.

"You are beautiful," he whispered.

Cameron bit her lip while Kalder undid his breeches and she became aware of where they were. Just how "exposed" they were.

Suddenly nervous, she glanced about. "You don't think the others will come back, do you?"

He wrinkled his nose at her. "I'll kill them if they do. Gouge out their eyes and feed them to Strixa or Savitar."

She laughed at that. "I'm serious, Kalder."

"So am I."

Kalder returned to dip his head down to tease her breast while she explored the part of his body that was so incredibly different from hers. "I promise, I'll hear them, and give you warning."

"You better."

With a roguish grin, he sat up on his knees and cupped her face in his hands. "You've no idea of how badly I want you to ride me right now, Cameron. How much I want you to ride me."

"Ride you how?"

"In ways that would shock you." His eyes tender, he kissed the corner of her mouth. Then he moved lower. This time he barely flicked his tongue over her breast before he moved down toward her stomach.

He pushed her back on her arms while he trailed his lips lower and lower.

"Kalder?"

He didn't answer her as he nudged her legs apart, then buried his lips against her.

Cameron fell back at the incredible feeling of him there. She swore she could see stars as his tongue did the most incredible things to her body and flesh.

Kalder took his time teasing and tasting every inch of skin. He'd never known any greater peace than being by her side. Now that he had her where he wanted her most, he wanted to take his time with her. To explore every inch of her body until they were both sated and exhausted.

And when she came, he smiled, but still he didn't stop. He refused to.

Growling, he looked up to see the pleasure on her face as she writhed and moaned.

It was a beautiful sight.

Kalder waited until the last tremor shook her. He wanted to make sure that when she left him, she never forgot him for as long as she lived. That she never craved the bed or touch of anyone else.

She was his and he never wanted to share her with anyone.

For the first time in his life, he was truly possessive of something.

Possessive of someone. That part of his personality scared him, for he'd never thought of himself as a jealous creature. Never cared enough about anyone to notice who they were with or where they went off to.

Cameron was completely different.

She mattered to him. And he'd denut any who came near what was his.

More than that, her sadness was a knife in his heart. Her tears gutted him. For her happiness, he would bleed and cut his own throat. No one should have the kind of power over another person that she held over him, and yet she held it without guile. Without even trying. He'd surrendered to her with no battle or fight. She'd won him with the deadliest of all weapons.

Kindness and love.

And right then, he needed to be as close to her as possible. To feel united with her.

Kalder took her hand into his and held it tight an instant before he slid himself into her body.

She groaned in pleasure the instant he filled her, and tightened her grip on his hand. He reveled at the way she smiled at him. At the way she wrapped her legs around his waist and cradled him with her entire body.

Aye, she was right. Here, he felt at home. Welcomed. Warm. For the first time in his entire life, he had a place, and it was with her. He knew it with every part of his being.

Kalder held his breath as he fought down the demonic part of himself that didn't want to be gentle. The part that could devour her. But he refused to hurt her.

She'd given him what no other woman ever had. How strange, really, when he thought about it. He'd purposefully avoided virgins for fear of being trapped in a wedding.

Yet Cameron wasn't out to trap him as her husband. Nor was

she out to claim him as a trophy. She was sharing herself with him. Offering him comfort and warmth.

For no reason other than she loved him.

He'd never felt anything like this.

She was special to him in a way no woman had ever been. He doubted if any woman could ever mean as much to him as she did right now.

Cameron almost wept from her overwhelming love as Kalder tenderly kissed her hand that was joined with his while his mismatched gaze never wavered from hers. Gone was the pain, and in its place was a light she'd never seen there before.

Slow and easy, he started to thrust against her hips.

Licking her lips, she felt his restrained strength and knew he was being gentle so as not to harm her in any way. He was so precious to her for the care he gave when she knew it wasn't in his nature to be so thoughtful.

So kind. He could kill a demon with a single blow and yet he was more tender with her than she'd ever imagined. It was the fact that she knew what he was capable of that made his tenderness all the more touching. The fact that it wasn't really in him to be like this. He was a hard, harsh man.

Just not with her.

She listened to his breathlessness that matched hers as she arched her hips to draw him in deeper. Her heart raced as she dragged her nails over his back and she saw him protecting her again.

"I love you, Kalder." The words tore themselves from her throat at the same time her body exploded.

Kalder cried out as his own release came and he heard words

that both scared and elated him. He buried his face in her neck and inhaled her sweet scent, while a part of him wished he were dreaming. That she loved anyone else *but* him.

Please don't let me cause her death.

Because as those words echoed, he had a bad premonition. One he couldn't banish. Over and over, he saw an ending that haunted him. One that seemed to be stalking them both.

Cameron lay still as he clutched her. His heart pounded against her breastbone while his ragged breathing caressed her ear.

"Thank you, *ma petite*," he whispered.

She squeezed him tight. "Ever me pleasure, me lord demon pirate."

Kalder kissed her as he withdrew. She was amazing and he savored the way she looked up at him like a woman well sated. Pleased and welcoming.

And it was then he knew he would have to do the right thing by her. No matter his convictions on the subject.

No matter his common sense. Or what the future held. Or what premonitions haunted him.

He was honor-bound to this.

For her. And for him, too, if the truth were told.

Taking a deep breath, he forced himself to utter the very words he'd sworn to himself that he would never speak to anyone. "Will you marry me, Cameron Amelia Maire Jack?"

She looked up at him, blinked, then burst out laughing.

13

Cameron was certain Kalder had to be japing. Surely he didn't really expect her to marry him? Not now! What madness would that be?

But the offended look on his face told her his question had been quite earnest.

And that made her feel awful. Guilty, even, for laughing at his offer. She wasn't the kind of woman to ever intentionally hurt another's feelings, least of all Kalder's. "Sorry, me love. I didn't realize you *actually* meant that."

She quickly pulled her gown on, over her head.

After all, some things were best done while dressed, and confronting a demon about an unwanted marriage proposal seemed like it ought to be one of them.

Though this might be better if her gown wasn't covered in sand and grit. Now she knew how Chthamalus and his crew had felt earlier.

Kalder made no moves to dress himself. Instead he lay there in all his naked glory, completely bare and enticing. Making her mouth water and her mind consider the possibility of being with him—which she had proposed first, roundabout. "Of course I am. You said it yourself, right? That was what you meant when you asked me to return with you to Williamsburg, wasn't it?"

Honestly, she hadn't thought *that* far ahead. When she'd asked him that, it'd been for purely selfish reasons, in that she hadn't wanted to say good-bye, and had wanted him to stay near her.

"Maybe?"

"Maybe? Seriously?"

"Well . . . Why would you consent to marriage . . . with me?"

He looked as baffled by her question as she was by his. "I took your virginity."

She snorted. "How magnanimous of you," she said, allowing the full weight of her sarcasm to show. "But you didn't *take* anything, Kalder. I *gave* it to you. That doesn't require a marriage proposal."

He scowled at her. "Is that not what humans do? You're a lady, aye?"

Was he trying to be insulting? She had a sudden urge to slap him for that.

But she was trying to be understanding and so she took a deep breath and reminded herself that he wasn't from the human world. Perhaps where he came from being labeled a whore wasn't as biting. After all, she had met the woman who'd raised him as his mother. . . .

And he is a fish, at the end of the day.

Just look at his freaky, weird eyes.

Eyes that weren't as cute right now as they'd been a few moments ago, before the insulting began. Mostly because right now she had a sudden compunction to slap them out of his head.

"Last time I checked, I did possess feminine body parts. Pretty sure you noticed that as well, given what you just did and all. So what has that do to with anything?"

He brushed his hair back. "What if you're pregnant with me wee spawn?"

"What if I'm not?"

His frown deepened, as did his stern tone. "Cameron, be reasonable."

"You be reasonable." She stood up to gather the rest of her clothes and finish dressing. "I'm quite certain I'm not the first woman you've been with. In fact, I know I'm not, as that harlot at the party was quite quick to point out. And you weren't in any hurry to marry her. So why this hurry to rush me to an altar?"

"They were different. *You* are different!"

"Well, I'm glad to hear it." It was nice to know that he hadn't just tupped her without some thought to the matter. Perhaps he even held some true feelings for her underneath that male arrogance that was suddenly getting on her nerves and coming close to proving her brother right. That thought made her much warmer than it should. "But it changes naught, as I'm rather sure you've no desire to really marry me."

"But—"

She placed her hand over his lips to stop his words. "Answer me honestly, Kalder. Do you truly, deeply wish to marry me, or are you only asking because you think it's the right thing to do, and because Paden would expect it?"

He looked away and she had her answer.

"As I thought." She dropped her hand.

Were she to ever marry anyone, she could imagine no one finer than Kalder Dupree. His taste and feel would haunt her forever.

But that was no reason to rush headlong into a lifetime commitment that could destroy the fragile friendship they shared.

Not to mention the rest of her life.

And his.

Cameron desired more than obligation for marriage. She wanted real love. A burning, lasting, fiery romance.

The last thing she wanted was to come to hate the man she shared her life with. As insane a notion as it was, she wanted a man she could love for a lifetime. One who respected her and who took her wishes into account whenever he made a decision regarding her, her children, and their life together.

She would settle for nothing less than what her parents had shared.

"You're not ready for marriage, Mr. Dupree," she said gently. "And neither am I. What we shared today was wonderful. Incredible even, and I thank you for being me first, and for being so considerate with me body. But it shouldn't make either one of us do something we'll come to regret. I want to open up me tavern and settle for a quiet life on shore, and you're a creature of the sea, on a quest to save the world. What kind of marriage could we have if one of us had to give up our dream for the other? In time, we'd come to hate the other for it and we both know that."

Still lying on his back while he watched her, Kalder took her hand into his and held it over the center of his chest, where she felt his heart beat a slow and steady rhythm. His grip was firm and binding, her hand pale against the darker tone of his skin and the outline of his tattoos that marked where his fins would spring out of his body whenever he was in the sea. Aye, they were different in every way.

His hard, muscled body was taut with his masculine strength and power. Even naked, he was a force to be reckoned with. One she found impossible to deny.

But she must, for both their sakes.

"And if you carry me spawn?"

"We will deal with that when the time comes. There are plenty of women who have survived the birth of illegitimate children—such as Lettice is doing even as we speak. For now, let's not rush headlong into disaster. Besides, I can always tell them that I married during me time away and that me husband perished on the journey home."

Though her solution annoyed him, Kalder was amazed by her as he watched her honest and open stare. Never in his life had he met her equal when it came to courage and conviction.

Any other woman would have leapt at the chance to lay a marriage noose around his neck.

But not her.

Cameron was fair in everything.

He kept her hand in his and reached with his other hand to tease a lock of her dark hair. "You are truly remarkable."

Her light blue eyes teased him with warmth. "You say that only because you took one too many knocks to the head and your wits are addled."

He snorted. "Me wits are fine."

Her smile dazzled him.

And he still couldn't get over her beauty and grace. Not once in his life had he thought to meet a woman who could tempt him to marriage.

Yet he felt that temptation now.

What would it be like to have a wife this strong at his side?

Forever.

Someone who wouldn't just submit docilely, but who would question and speak her mind regardless of consequence? Unlike the others of her species, she wasn't turned by his looks or title. While other women crawled naked into his bed just to boast later that they'd been with him, he knew Cameron would never tell a soul of what they'd shared.

And it was a sharing. Unlike anything he'd ever experienced before.

He felt his body stirring again at the memory of what she'd been like under him.

Cameron's eyes widened as she noticed him growing hard again. "Seriously? Does it do that a lot?"

Kalder pulled her closer to him. "Only when I think of you."

Cameron moaned as he captured her lips. He buried his hand in her hair and drew her closer. She felt his fingers splay against her scalp as he held her tightly to him.

Oh, this was heaven. She inhaled the crisp, manly scent of him. Let the warmth of his body seep into every part of hers. She could just melt into him.

Skimming her hand down his lean, hard body, she delighted in the rugged male terrain. She loved the sensation of the thick thatch of hair that nestled his cock. He growled and deepened their kiss as she raked her fingers through that most private area until she could cup him in her hand. His shaft turned rigid once more as she explored it from the very bottom to the tip.

Sucking his breath in sharply, Kalder covered her hand with his and showed her how to stroke him a few seconds before he pulled her hand away. "You'd best stop doing that."

"Why?"

"Because if you don't, I'm going to be inside you again, and you're far too new at this to have me again so soon. It'll make you even more sore."

Cameron didn't feel sore, but then, as he said, she knew very little about this physical side of love, other than what she'd seen or overheard in passing in the taverns. "Have you taken many virgins?" she asked before she could stop herself. "You seem to know much about us."

"Nay, love. I've only had you. But I've heard other men talk enough to know."

She smiled at his confession. Though why it pleased her, she couldn't imagine. "Who was your first lover?"

He looked a bit startled by her question. "Do you truly wish to know?"

"Seems only fair since you know who mine is."

He gave an odd half laugh at that. "The Shadow herself."

Cameron choked on the last thing she'd expected to hear him say. "Scáthach?"

"Aye."

"So war wasn't the only thing she trained you for?"

"It didn't happen the way you're thinking."

"How do you mean?"

Kalder sighed and reached for his breeches. "Scáthach had come to me father's kingdom. I was in Wyñeria when I first saw her. She seduced me there and told me of Dún Scáith"—the fortress of shadows—"and said that if I was man enough, skilled enough, that I should fight me way into her fortress and that she'd train me to be an even greater warrior than me father."

"And of course you did."

He winked at her. "Of course I did. Had me reputation to live up to, don't you know?"

Cameron couldn't fault the woman for being entranced by Kalder, and she wished she had known him then. Had he been as handsome as a young man as he was now?

"Was she much older than you?"

"Aye, quite a bit, but it didn't matter. She was still beautiful beyond belief and I was stunned that a queen of her caliber was taken by a boy of me age."

"And how old were you?"

"I'd just turned ten-and-five."

Cameron was stunned by his words. "You were far too young for her."

"She thought not."

Cameron rolled her eyes at his arrogant boasting. Typical male to say such. "Have you seen her since you left your training?"

"Nay. It's not how she does things. As her name goes, she's the Lady Shadow."

That was what they said, but still . . .

"Do you miss her?"

"Nay, I barely knew her, even though I lived in her lands for a year. Again, she's a creature of mystery and likes it that way. I don't think anyone has ever really known much of anything about her. Not even her children."

Kalder helped Cameron dress while she reflected on what they'd done, and everything she'd learned about him and his family, and world.

As she smoothed her gown over her stomach, she paused her hand there. Surely she wasn't pregnant. The women in her tavern were forever carrying on with men, and seldom did they seem to come up pregnant over it. Lettice and Paden had been lovers for almost two years before she'd conceived. . . .

Even so, the prospect of having Kalder's baby wasn't quite as scary to her as it should be. Instead, a part of her that was terrified almost hoped for it.

What would it be like to have a child growing inside her? To see Kalder play father to a child of his own?

He would be a good, kind da, she was certain, like her own father had been to her and Paden. Protective and loving. Patient.

But with that thought came the bitter reminder of what had happened to her father. Of the hard, harsh life he'd lived.

Kalder had even more enemies out to end him.

He's not human. . . .

Neither are you.

And that was the most sobering thought of all. Their children would be forever hunted. For his abilities and for hers. They'd never know peace. Or safety.

Instinctively, she flinched away from him.

"Cameron?"

"Forgive me," she said, forcing those thoughts out of her mind.

She'd been right. There was no hope whatsoever of any kind of future with him. To think of one was all kinds of madness. It was cruel to even entertain a moment's thought of it.

And to put a child through that kind of nightmare would be the ultimate cruelty. Nay, having been orphaned and forced into hiding herself—to live a lie where she had to conceal something as basic as her own gender—she couldn't subject her own child to that kind of life.

How could she even think it?

"What is it, *ma petite*?"

"Nothing."

He tilted her chin until she looked up at him. "Tell me."

Cameron never got the chance. Instead, a weird, foreign buzzing started in her ears. One that drowned out Kalder's voice and left her unable to hear him.

Kalder stepped back as he saw the change come over Cameron. Her skin turned a bright orange. Blackness filled her eyes.

In an instant, he realized what they'd done to her.

"Cameron?"

She couldn't see him or hear him. She was an Iri . . . a Dark Seraphia. It was the tainted blood that Vine had used to corrupt her.

"Cameron! Listen to me! You have to focus on me voice."

But he knew she was past that. This was his nightmare. She was the very thing now that he was sworn to destroy.

Worse, he heard Gadreyal's voice. "So you've finally chosen. . . ."

"Chosen what?"

"Whose life you value most."

His heart went still. "Pardon?"

Too late, he realized the trick Bron and Muerig had played on him. That hadn't been his mother's ring Bron had returned to him.

He'd felt the cold power of it for a moment when Cameron had placed it on his finger, but their attack had distracted him, especially since he'd drawn power from everyone right after that to escape there. Not to mention, he hadn't known his mother, so he'd had no way of recognizing the fact it wasn't his mother's powers.

"She's not me offering to you!"

"Aye, but she is. You cling to your past. Wallow in it. Your fears define you, and so you've given us your future."

Disembodied laughter rang out. "A soul escaped and a soul must be returned. Yours is worthless to us. . . ."

Because it was corrupted already.

Unlike Cameron's, which was pure and untainted.

The dark clouds returned. Along with the thunder.

"Give us what we want, little fish. Death doesn't bargain with anyone. Especially not you. And not even with the mighty Thorn."

14

Thorn's head throbbed as he watched Bane and his crew of Deadmen making the most of their small hiatus. He envied them their merriment.

There had never been a time in his life when he'd been so carefree. Not even as a boy. Indeed, his stepfather had made certain that no one enjoyed their time in his court. His idea of music had been the agonized screams of those being tortured. His favorite pastime had been feeding children to wild boars.

Given that, he could almost forgive his mother for what she'd done to escape his stepfather's wrath.

Almost.

Had his childhood not been the Stygian hell it was, he might have mustered a degree of compassion for her. But as it was . . .

He'd hate her for all eternity.

Most of all, he'd hate himself. His life had never been anything more than one bad decision after another. A choice between being mauled by a lion or devoured by a dragon.

"Are you all right?"

He looked up at Valynda's question and had to force himself not to wince over the unfortunate circumstances that had made her a member of this Deadman crew. What had been done to her was the cruelest blow of all. Bringing her back in that temporary body to serve in this latest fiasco had probably been the worst bargain he'd ever made.

"You're wrong, by the way."

Thorn scowled. "Wrong? About what?"

"This is nowhere near as bad as being dead. I will never be able to thank you enough for your mercy, my lord. Even if I'm never human again, I should rather spend eternity in this body than spend it where I was."

He wondered if Valynda would always feel that way toward him. Funny thing about gratitude . . .

Like snow, it never stood up to the test of time. And people quickly forgot all the nastiness it'd swallowed the minute the warm summer of abundance came again and melted the bad memory of the cold snowstorm away. No one ever remembered being out in the frigid wind when the sun was shining bright on their face.

But worse than that, gratitude left a chill on the soul once it was gone, as the person who ought to feel it oft held it against the person who'd once done them the favor.

Aye, gratitude was a double-edged sword that was too often turned against the one who was only trying to do good in the beginning.

Thorn wasn't sure where the corruption came in. If it was the pettiness of the person who did the original favor wanting more for their sacrifice, or the guilt of the person who received the favor who knew in their heart that they didn't really give a shit about the person who'd made the original sacrifice, and were only using that person to get something from them they hadn't earned.

Either way, he had no use for gratitude. It, much like the balls of a flea, was a tiny useless thing.

But what stunned him was the guileless depth of hers. Valynda actually meant what she said and truly felt grateful to him for what he'd done. Even though that meant trapping her in such a horrible in-between state.

How peculiar.

"You're a remarkable woman, Ms. Moore."

"Not really." She handed him the cup in her hand. "But I should like to think that I'm not a stupid one."

He smiled at her logic before he tipped the cup to see that it contained wine, and not the blood Devyl was fond of feeding him whenever he wasn't paying attention to the large, hulking bastard.

"Can I ask you something?"

He swallowed his drink. "You can always ask." He just seldom ever answered.

"What made you bring me back?"

Thorn started not to answer, but there was something vulnerable about her. Something that reminded him of a girl he knew a long time ago, and it weakened him. Before he knew it, the truth came out against his will. "I owed a favor to a friend."

"Do you always take such elaborate steps for friends, my lord?"

"No. I normally kill them."

Her eyes widened at another truth he was shocked to hear leave his lips. Being around him was indeed hazardous to people's health. They hadn't once called him the Death Collector for no reason. Mercy and compassion were alien concepts for him.

Just ask his son. Cadegan's current stint in hell, where he cursed Thorn's every breath, testified to what a heartless bastard he was.

You save the world, spare all those around you, and yet leave your own flesh and blood to suffer. You are despicable.

From my first breath, to my last.

Thorn ground his teeth and did his best not to think about something he dared not change. The consequences could be too dire.

For all of them.

Valynda eyed him with way too much sagacity for his comfort. "You like to frighten people. It keeps them away from you. You have that in common with Savitar. But even nightmares have things that scare them."

"I have no nightmares, child."

He *was* the nightmare.

She cocked her head as if listening to something only she could hear. After a moment, she spoke in a whisper. "Here's to the future. . . . May it never bring to me what I deserve."

Thorn almost dropped his glass. "What was that?"

"It's your toast, is it not? One that you're fond of making?"

He tried to shrug it off. "Just something I say. It has no meaning."

She shook her head. "I don't believe you, and I know you don't yourself. You're as afraid of the past catching up to you as the rest of them. That is the true demon that relentlessly flogs your soul."

Thorn didn't speak as she wandered off. There was nothing to say about the truth.

Suddenly, he wasn't as fond of her as he'd been before. Indeed, he had a sudden urge to feed her to one of Savitar's Charonte. Too bad they didn't like rag dolls. . . .

"You're looking grim."

Thorn groaned at Acheron's bad joke. "Ever wonder why they shoot the messenger?"

He screwed his face up in pain. "So not punny."

Thorn begged to disagree. He thought it was quite a clever play on the fact that Acheron was the harbinger of death for his mother. Or at least that was the role he was supposed to have been born for.

But like Thorn, Acheron had chosen another path for himself than that which his parents had wanted. And for which they'd bred him.

"Nice coat, by the way. I particularly like the bloodstain on the lapel."

Acheron glanced down and cursed. "Thought I got all that out."

"Should I ask?"

He shrugged. "I liked the cut of it. Didn't like the cut of the man who wore it. Nasty bastard. Pirate hunter. Human trafficker. Decided the world was better off without his participation in it."

Thorn arched a brow at that uncharacteristic confession. "Thought you'd taken a vow to stay out of human affairs and to let nature run its course."

"Had a moment of weakness. Needed the target practice."

Thorn snorted. "Look at you . . . I'll make a human of you, yet."

"Don't insult me."

"And yet you head up the Dark-Hunters?"

"Only because I'm an idiot with nothing better to do. As you said, too much time on my hands."

But Thorn knew better. While Acheron wasn't altruistic, he wasn't callous, either. They were both driven by guilt and demons that warred within them. Both running from a past they wanted to forget.

And a family that wouldn't let them live in peace.

Thorn let out a long, weary sigh. "It's hard to walk in the light when the darkness is forever calling you."

"Not really." Acheron shrugged. "I stub my toes a lot less often in the light."

"True, but the dark doesn't burn your skin, and it makes hiding your flaws a lot easier."

"That's the problem, though, isn't it?"

"What?" Thorn asked.

"Sooner or later, your flaws are always seen for what they are."

"It's why I pick such good ones."

Acheron gave him an arch stare. "Do you?"

Thorn nodded, then counted them off on his fingers. "Being too good-looking, having too much money, and sleeping too late."

Acheron laughed. "You're incorrigible."

Thorn didn't comment on that. Instead, he changed the subject. "So how's that boat coming?"

"Waiting for her crew. I think Bane will be quite pl . . ." His voice trailed off as his eyes turned dark, fiery red.

The room darkened as if a typhoon was rolling in.

Thorn stood and set his cup aside. "What is this?"

Belle answered. "Evil walks on calm legs."

The windows shattered and blew glass shards through the room, sending the white curtains of the Omegrion's chambers twisting in the violent wind.

Acheron held his arm up to shield his face, and the moment he did, a shadow shot out from his sleeve to wrap itself around him. "No, Simi!"

But his demon didn't listen. She took the form of a young woman, dressed in breeches and a striped shirt. "You needs to leave, Akri! What lives in the sea can eats you, and it don't need no condiments, neither!"

"I'm not afraid."

She glared at him while Devyl and his Deadmen took positions around Paden.

Thorn summoned his burgundy battle armor. For a moment, he considered calling out to the Hell-Hunters for assistance, but he knew better. Michael and the rest of the Kalosum army hated him and his Hellchasers. No matter what they might say, they didn't trust them.

They never would.

Nothing would change that. Not even the Malachai crashing open the gates of hell and this latest test of arms where the world might be ending.

But the day would come when they'd realize that they weren't so different. That even though they were born worlds apart, their goals were the same.

That they all bled red.

And that the only way for them to have the peace they so desperately wanted, to have the world they craved, was to unite together and fight side by side as one family. Not to let their petty differences divide them.

Strong alone.

Stronger united.

So long as their suspicions kept them at each other's throats—so long as their enemies had them tearing each other apart, they would always be weak. The Mavromino would always have a way to break through.

Just like now.

That was the strength of the darkness. It was what kept it coming back even when they thought they had it defeated.

Paden cried out in pain. His eyes turned black.

As did his hair.

"What do we do?" Will asked.

Bart unsheathed his sword. "Stab him while we're able!"

Belle grabbed his hand and stopped him. "You can't do that! He's one of us."

"Was." Bart gestured at him. "Look at him now. He's turning to the Iri. He'll destroy us all."

As Bart went to make the killing blow, Paden caught his arm and wrenched it hard. "I'm not against you, you fool!"

Before they could ask what he meant, the doors splintered open to show Cameron.

Only Thorn had never seen her look like this before. . . .

She was glittering white. A pure perfection that seemed ethereal and unreal.

Unnatural.

Except for her wings, which were a vibrant red. At first glance, they appeared to be bleeding, but the illusion was caused by her motion of flight as she flew toward Devyl.

"They took Kalder!"

"They?" Mara asked.

Her lips trembled. "The Malachai. He's intending to march on Azmodea and slay his masters so that he can absorb their powers, and then take down the light gods—Verlyn, Rezar, and Cam."

Thorn felt his legs go weak at the news. That would have the Malachai with the power of all the original Source gods.

Except one.

The mother of the Malachai. But given that he was her son, he already carried a great deal of hers to begin with.

Were he to combine that with the others . . .

The Malachai would rule all worlds.

"Can they do that?" Devyl turned to face him.

Avoiding the question, Acheron cut a nervous stare toward Thorn. "Do they know where Cam and Rezar are?"

Thorn's stomach twisted with fear. "They could use Verlyn to find them. Even Seth could track Rezar, if needs be."

Mara scowled. "Seth?"

"Nothing." Thorn cleared his throat. "How did they get Kalder?"

Fury darkened her cheeks. "The ring he was given wasn't truly his mother's. It was a *subjicible krogŭ*."

Thorn growled at the ancient term used for a Simeon Mage's mastery ring. Though rare, they'd been created to bind a demon's powers and enslave the creature to whomever had bespelled it.

Total subjugation.

Once activated, the wearer had no mind or will of their own, other than what their masters gave them.

It was an insidious device that had been denounced by the wizards as unethical centuries ago. Banned by their council, who feared what the demons might do to them in retaliation for creating such a thing, the rings had been ordered gathered up and destroyed.

Apparently, they'd missed one.

Probably more.

Damn . . .

Paden took his sister's arm. "What happened to you?"

Cameron hesitated as a single crystal tear fell down her cheek and she recalled the entire event in her mind. The pain of it all was still raw and bleeding and left her ragged. "Not knowing it was a trick, Kalder gave the ring to me."

Over and over, her mind replayed Kalder rushing to her defense. She saw his love for her as he placed himself in harm's way while the Malachai's new forces surrounded them. Forever the traitor to any cause save her own, Gadreyal was no longer in league with Noir and Azura.

Kalder's jaw had dropped at the sight of her and Vine. "Do your masters know where you are?"

Vine had laughed in their faces. "We have a new master now. And the Adarian Malachai has no use for the Dark Ones. He's rising now and they will soon be nothing more than a forgotten nightmare for us all."

"Beware the gods and heroes you rip down in your quest for power. What rises up to replace them may not be the dream you think it. Rather, the hungry wolf that leads you today can oft be the same one that turns its sights to you tomorrow. For once one enemy falls, it looks for another to attack. Pray that you aren't the next in line for its venom."

Gadreyal laughed. "We're immune. He's promised us a better day."

"As do they all. Hard to get anyone to follow you when you promise them a worse one. Open your eyes before it's too late. See the path not just before your feet, but where it will ultimately lead you."

"'Tis your own arse you'd best be worried for, mate," Vine sneered. "As it's the one we're about to feed to the Malachai."

They advanced on Cameron to separate her from him.

Kalder moved to cut them off, as if he could stand alone against the entire horde that was fast coming for them. "I won't let you touch her."

"We're not asking."

"Neither am I. I'm telling you to back away from us while you can."

Gadreyal had again laughed in his face.

Her mistake.

Kalder had lifted Cameron's hand in his, and locked gazes with her. "All my life, I've seen poison in others, and I've struck out in fear against it. Since the hour of my birth, I've refused to be owned by anything or mastered by anyone. I'll be damned if I'll stand by and see these bastards pluck the only *lilium inter spinas* I've ever known."

And before she could move, he kissed her.

The moment their lips touched, she felt him drawing something out of her body. Something she couldn't name or even begin to describe. With it, all the color rapidly drained from her body and caused Kalder's to darken again to the scarred Cyphnian beast who'd first terrified her.

The fire returned to his body as he pulled the ring from her finger.

"A school of mistakes, Miss Jack, is called life. Be damned if I let you be one of mine. I've enough of them. You are and will always be my sole light in the darkness. They want a servant, then they'll have the devil to pay for it."

Before she could protest or stop him, Kalder launched himself away from her, toward the sea. "I am me father's son, Gadreyal. And me mother's. If it's a battle you want, let's swim for it."

When Cameron had gone to fight by his side, she'd been thrown away from him by some unseen force.

One moment she'd been on the beach.

The next, she'd been outside the doors of the hall where the Deadmen were gathered.

Now, she stared at her friends and wiped at the tears on her face. "We have to help him!"

Devyl shook his head. "I swear, that boy gets into more shite. I'm half tempted to let them keep him this time."

Thorn arched a brow at that.

"I'm not going to. Merely said I was tempted." Devyl glanced to Sallie. "Unleash your soul, man. There's another fight to be had."

Acheron grinned. "I'll wake Savitar from his nap. This should be fun." Sarcasm dripped from his tone. "Like being gutted in a public forum."

Thorn clapped him on the arm. "Which is why I'm glad you volunteered for it, as you're one of the few he tolerates."

Simi wrinkled her nose at them. "The Simi will wakes him. He likes me bestest. And can I eats the demons on the beach?"

"As long as they're not one of mine," Thorn said gently. "It's too hard to replace them."

She sighed as if terribly put out by his restriction. "Well, poo on that, but okies."

Cameron took Paden's sword from him.

"Hey! What are you doing?"

"They've contaminated this, brother." She felt the difference in the metal the moment her hand touched the hilt. "It's been infecting you since they released us. And it's why you've been such a jerk."

"I have not!"

She gave him an arch stare as she crossed the room to hand it over to Thorn. "Can you tell a difference?"

He hissed the moment he touched it and dropped it as if it were on fire.

They all stared at his reaction.

"What?" Thorn growled. "Not like all of you don't know my origins. 'Tis a Seraph sword. Those are lethal to one of my ilk. And while it isn't Michael's soul inside that one anymore, it still burns the shite out of me."

"What?" Paden's color drained.

Thorn jerked his chin toward the sword as Cameron retrieved it. "Your sister's correct with what she said. It's Gadreyal's medallion controlling your sword. Not Michael's. That's why you're no longer fair when she's near you and you're under attack. You have to get your medallion back. So long as Gaddy has it, she can infect and control you."

"Is there no way to cleanse it?"

Thorn gave him a look that said he was completely moronic for asking such a question. "Aye. Get your medallion back. Or you can take the sword to Michael and ask him for a favor. I wouldn't suggest the latter, as he's a testy, volatile little bastard. Likely to run you through rather than help you. But hey, you can always try that stupidity." He took his handkerchief out to wipe at his hand. "In the meantime, I wouldn't suggest using that. However, 'tis your choice of funeral. Have a nice wake."

"And we're wasting time!" Cameron headed for the doors. "Me Kalder's out there. Alone. We stand and we fight. Not for ourselves, but for what we love and value. Our friends. Our families. Our futures. Now you demon bastards better run!"

Devyl laughed at her spunk. "Aye, aye, Miss Jack. Ever at the ready."

Stretching her wings, Cameron flew back through the storm as fast as she could.

But it was one of the hardest things she'd ever done. The high winds tore at her body, and threatened to send her straight to the ground. Strixa flew by her side in her black owl form, helping her as best she could.

"Keep your head down. Don't fight the current or it'll shred your wings."

Cameron obeyed.

And when they reached the beach where she'd left Kalder, her heart stopped beating. Never in her life had she seen so much carnage. Bodies were strewn everywhere. Blood and entrails soaked the sand.

Her stomach heaved.

She landed hard on the ground and staggered to her knees, fearing that one of those twisted, unidentifiable remains was Kalder's.

An eerie silence rang out. Not even the wind made a sound.

Strixa landed next to her and took on her human form. "What happened here?"

Cameron couldn't speak. Was this what they had to look forward to? Was this what the Malachai and his army were capable of?

In this moment, she saw the future of the world, and it terrified her. No wonder Thorn had been willing to barter with the devil himself to bring the Deadmen back to fight. This was too horrifying to contemplate.

She pressed her fist to her lips as she bit back a scream. How could this have happened? She hadn't been gone that long.

Chthamalus slid in by her side and patted her back with two tentacles. "I know, my lady. I know. The sight of my prince's skills are a bit overwhelming."

Cameron froze at those unexpected words. Stunned, she turned toward him to make sure she'd heard that correctly. "P-p-pardon?"

He looked at her blankly. "This mess . . . he's not a tidy one when he gets busy in battle. You should have seen him in his younger days. He was much worse."

She blinked and blinked again. "Are you saying he's not dead?"

Now it was Chthamalus who appeared shocked. "I should think not." He blinked and glanced about. "Nay. Not over these paltry few."

Cameron forced herself to stand on shaking legs. "Kalder?" she called out.

Their answer came as a bright flash and a brilliant explosion that shook the ground under them.

Then Cameron saw a small glimmer in the water that she recognized. Chthamalus was right! It was him.

Tears filled her eyes.

But her relief was short-lived.

Something seemed to be wrong. . . .

Her heart pounding, she took flight and headed for him. Sure enough, it was Kalder, and for reasons she couldn't fathom, he was struggling to remain afloat. There was no mistaking the panic in his eyes that were once again their beautiful pewter color.

Cameron dove for him. "Kalder!" She held her hands out.

Without hesitation, he reached up for her.

She grabbed hold, and though she lacked the strength to lift him from the water, she was able to keep him afloat with her wings until they reached the shore.

There, Bart and Will, along with the captain, helped to pull him onto the beach. Cameron fell to her knees, by his side.

He was terribly wounded. But what shocked her the most was that he didn't have any fins or markings. He appeared to be human.

Confused, she rubbed at his back. "Kalder?"

Choking, he wheezed and coughed. "Never piss off a Malachai."

Devyl pounded on his back. "What happened?"

"Not sure." He stared at his hands. "But I think he sucked me powers out." Scowling, he looked up at Thorn. "Can he do that?"

"I have no idea. Honestly. I would say no, but he's the Malachai. Older than shit and with the memories of a creature a lot older than any I know. Even Savitar or Acheron." He looked up as Savitar joined them. "What do you know about him?"

Savitar didn't speak.

A bad feeling went through Cameron at the way he stood there, staring at them with eyes that said he carried a deep, dark secret.

"What is it?" Cameron asked.

"As Thorn said, the Malachai isn't like any other. Adarian is crazier, and more powerful, than all who've come before him." He sighed heavily. "To answer your question, kid, yes, he can take your powers if you get close enough to him. I didn't know he'd mastered that little skill set. But . . ."

"What?"

Acheron moved to stand beside Savitar. "While we weren't paying attention, Adarian's demons snuck around us."

Devyl froze. "Where's Mara?"

"He took her and Valynda."

Cameron gasped. "Why?"

Thorn cursed as he met Devyl's gaze. "Because she's a Deruvian and she's pregnant. And Valynda because of me."

Cameron didn't understand. "You?"

He nodded. "I shouldn't have gotten any of you into this."

Thorn started away.

"Hey!" Savitar shouted. "Where are you going?"

He appeared aghast by that question. "To deal with this."

"You can't fight him alone, Leucious. Are you insane?"

Thorn glanced around at them. "I can't endanger you. I've already asked too much."

Devyl gaped. "That's my wife and child. You don't think for one minute that I'm going to stand by and let you fight without me?"

Kalder stood and took Cameron's hand. "We're family. All together. United."

"Dysfunctional," Zumari added. "But never boring."

Sancha kissed his cheek and draped her arm around his shoulders. "Aye to that. Deadmen forever."

Devyl nodded. "Launch our colors, Mr. Death. We have another adventure before us. And we won't be stopped."

Mara blasted at the doors with her powers.

Valynda ducked as the lightning-like blast ricocheted off and narrowly missed her straw head. Her luck, the blast would have caught her on fire. "Beg pardon, mum? Could we hold our tempers a bit?"

"I'd rather hold my sister's head in a forge."

At the moment, so would she. But irrational tempers wouldn't get them far. "I'm sure the captain and the others will be coming for us."

Mara nodded. "That's what worries me."

Valynda paused as she noted the way Mara's hand lingered over her stomach. It was a unique way women touched themselves whenever they . . .

She cursed silently. "By chance, are you expecting?"

The high blush on her face answered even before she nodded bashfully.

Well, that explained why their enemies had been so eager to lay hands to the captain's wife. Valynda could only imagine how much power was flowing through the body of a pregnant Deruvian. Given Mara's powers when she didn't have the additional life inside her, it stood to reason that she'd be even more potent now.

But for them to take her . . .

You know why.

Her stomach cramped in fear and she prayed she was wrong. But a few moments later when Gadreyal appeared, the expression on the Irin's face said that Valynda had been right in her initial assumption.

"The Malachai wants a word with you."

Valynda cocked her head. "Are you sure about that?"

"Aye, and if I were you, I'd do what he says and summon the Ghede Nibo for him."

She laughed at the pompousness of that statement. "One doesn't evoke the Ghede, and especially not Nibo. You ask nicely, and if he wishes, he comes."

"I defy you to say that to the Malachai."

Valynda cut a glance to Mara. "Do you see the fear in our keeper's eyes, mum?"

"Indeed."

"Then perhaps I should invite the Nibo to our party and educate you all on what happens when you play with things best left alone."

BLACK SWAN TAVERN

EPILOGUE

Kalder sat on the docks, staring out at the dark sea while the crew took on supplies for their voyage. They had yet to find the location of where Vine and Gadreyal had vanished off to with Mara and Valynda, but they weren't daunted.

They would find them and there would be the Devyl's hell to pay for it.

"Are you missing your swim, Mr. Dupree?"

He smiled at the sweet dulcet tone that left him

harder than granite. "Aye, Miss Jack. But not as much as I be missing something else."

"And that be?"

He reached up to take her hand and pull her down to sit next to him. "Me most precious angel."

She smiled at him as she melted into his arms so that he could hold her. "The captain said he wanted us to stay behind and return to Williamsburg. Since you're no longer bound by the Deadman's mark and you've lost your powers from the Malachai, he doesn't want to risk any harm to you or to me."

"Is that what you want?"

She met his gaze in the darkness and smiled. "Me home is wherever you are, Kal. I'll follow wherever you lead."

"Even if it isn't back to your tavern?"

She bit her lip as her gaze turned dark. That expression worried him.

"Cameron? What is it?"

"Just thinking . . . a tavern's no place what to be raising a babe alone without its da. Especially when the babe might be mistaking its mum for its da."

It took him a second to realize what it was she meant. When it finally dawned on him, he felt as if his stones had been hammered. "You're pregnant?"

She nodded. "The Lady Belle confirmed what I suspected."

"Flowers? Flowers for the lady?"

Kalder froze as an old woman shoved a wilted bouquet between them. Normally, he'd have sent her on her way, but . . .

"Aye. Thank you." He pulled out his coin to pay her.

Smiling, the toothless crone handed over the bouquet. "Gardenias and violets for your boy to come. A beautiful future has he. Pull the string and see."

"Pardon?" Kalder scowled as shock and fury tangled inside him. Was she a demon or some other creature sent to wreak havoc with them?

The old woman placed a kind hand against his cheek. "No parent should be forced to live without their babe. There is no greater pain. For a child is the heart that grows and beats outside the body. Time and distance makes no never mind to a such an organ, as it has no ability to judge either. Rather it just feels and it knows." She squeezed his cheek. "It always knows."

And with that, she vanished.

Kalder cursed as his skin began to burn.

Gasping, Cameron leaned back. "Your fins . . ."

His jaw went slack as he glanced down to see that his marks had returned.

Cameron crossed herself. "Kalder . . . methinks that was your mother, love. Your *real,* true mother. Melusine."

Unable to believe it, he pulled the string that was wrapped around the delicate lace that held the bouquet. The moment he did, he realized not one, but three rings were tied and knotted to it.

A man's ring that was a silver signet ring with a skull and crossbones. A tiny woman's ring of delicate scrollwork and a large sea green stone. And another ring that held the crest of the great sea goddess herself.

Cameron was right.

"It was me mother." He breathed the words, still unable to believe that he'd actually met her.

Wishing he'd known it while she'd stood before them, he stared out at the water with an inexplicable ache that he'd come so close to seeing her and yet he'd failed to realize it until it was too late. How could he have been so blind?

"What's that?"

He glanced down to see that Cameron was fingering something else from the flowers. A leather envelope had been tucked inside the wrapping.

Kalder pulled it out and opened it.

Even more stunned, he handed it over to Cameron to see. "It's the deed to your Black Swan." For the briefest moment he'd wondered how his mother had known about it, but then she was a goddess.

Cameron gasped as tears filled her eyes. "Thank you, me dearest sweet Melusine!" she shouted out at the sea. "Thank you! I promise you I'll take good care of your boys. Always."

Kalder kissed her. "And I'll take care of you."

Pulling back, she fingered the markings on his forearm and wrinkled her nose. "But not before we finish this mission?"

His eyes twinkled in the darkness. "First we attend to the evil so that the evil doesn't attend to us."

"Then let hell know we're coming. And we're going to get our ladies back even if we have to track them down to death's door and beyond."

Do you love fiction with a supernatural twist?

Want the chance to hear news about your favourite
authors (and the chance to win free books)?

Keri Arthur
Kristen Callihan
P.C. Cast
Christine Feehan
Jacquelyn Frank
Larissa Ione
Darynda Jones
Sherrilyn Kenyon
Jayne Ann Krentz and Jayne Castle
Lucy March
Martin Millar
Tim O'Rourke
Lindsey Piper
Christopher Rice
J.R. Ward
Laura Wright

Then visit the Piatkus website
www.piatkus.co.uk

And follow us on Facebook and Twitter
www.facebook.com/piatkusfiction | @piatkusbooks

piatkus